CAPTAIN JENNY &
THE SEA OF
WONDERS

CAPTAIN JENNY &
THE SEA OF
WONDERS

DUNCAN THORNTON

COTEAU BOOKS
WWW.COTEAUBOOKS.COM

This is a work of fiction. Names, characters, places, and incidents either are the product of
the author's imagination or are used fictitiously. Any resemblance to actual persons, living
or dead, is coincidental.

Edited by Geoffrey Ursell.
Cover image and interior illustrations by Yves Noblet.
Cover and book design by Duncan Campbell.

Printed and bound in Canada.

National Library of Canada Cataloguing in Publication Data

Thornton, Duncan, 1962-
Captain Jenny and the sea of wonders

ISBN 1-55050-194-1

I. Title.
PS8589.H556C36 2001   JC813'.54   C2001-911227-0
PZ7.T567CA 2001

10 9 8 7 6 5 4 3 2 1

401-2206 Dewdney Ave.
Regina, Saskatchewan
Canada   S4R 1H3

AVAILABLE IN THE US FROM
General Distribution Services
4500 Witmer Industrial Estates
Niagara Falls, NY, 14305-1386

The publisher gratefully acknowledges the financial assistance of the Saskatchewan Arts
Board, the Canada Council for the Arts, the Government of Canada through the Book
Publishing Industry Development Program (BPIDP), and the City of Regina Arts
Commission, for its publishing program.

 The Canada Council for the Arts
Le Conseil des Arts du Canada

SASKATCHEWAN
ARTS BOARD

Canadä

CITY OF REGINA

For my nieces:
Petra, Jaime, and Evana
(in order, and so far)

Table of Contents

THE VOYAGE OF THE OTTER

THE VOYAGE OF THE RUGGLES

THE VOYAGE OF THE NONESUCH

List of Illustrations

JENNY, HER BOOK

B EING A TRUE ACCOUNT OF THE
Explorations, Battles, Encounters with
Great and Strange Personages, and Sundry
Surprising Discoveries of Jenny, a Fisher-Girl
– Captain variously of the *Otter*, *Ruggles*, and
Nonesuch – along with Sparky, her friend
Tom's dog, and her brave though occasion-
ally fractious and peevish Crew (particularly,
though not exclusively, the First Mate, Cook,
Carpenter, and Ship's Boy), based on her
own authentic and modest report.

THE VOYAGE
OF THE OTTER

The King Beneath the Sea sent an otter

CHAPTER ONE:
THE KING BENEATH
THE SEA SENT AN OTTER

O NE EVENING IN THE WARM SPRING, AS THE LIGHT shone soft and the waves grew gentle, the King Beneath the Sea sent an otter to speak to Jenny.

"Many sailors wait their whole lives and never hear a Call to Adventure," the Otter told Jenny, after he appeared out of the foam in the little cove where she tied up her fishing dory.

"Nevertheless," said Jenny, "I am not surprised to hear you. Except that I had expected a flounder would speak to me rather than a sea otter such as yourself."

"Will you quibble, or will you hear your Call?" asked the Otter.

Jenny had several things to say then, but she remembered her manners and reached into the bottom of her little flat boat to throw the Otter a small fish. Jenny had spent the whole day catching those fish, for though she was still a young girl, she lived by herself and had to earn her own keep. And because she lived on her own and read so many books, and worked with all manner of crusty old fishers and sailors besides, she had many odd turns of phrase.

"Thank you," the Otter said, and pulled at his whiskers. "Do you know the Old Sea?"

"If you mean the Sea of Heroes, all sailors know it," said Jenny, scornfully. "Or again it is called the Sea of Wonders Found and Forgotten. There great stones clash together, Corsairs sail to torment decent folk, forgotten temples stand, conquering fleets set out only to vanish without a trace, and all manner of giants, monsters, mermaids, mazes, treasure, and shipwrecks crowd the depths and shores.

"And there," Jenny continued, for she was both a proud and wordy young girl, "there an age ago, the Lost City sank beneath the waves, which no Explorer yet has found – not even the great Maxim Tortuca, or my friend Tom, who was able to circumnavigate the globe last year with the crew of the *Volantix* because I looked after his dog for him."

"The Old Sea," the Otter said. "The Sea of Heroes, the Sea of Wonders Found and Forgotten. Indeed, that is where your adventure shall be found."

"What adventure shall I find?" asked Jenny. "For I have heard –"

But the Otter interrupted her. "I shall tell you," he began, before Jenny interrupted *him*.

"I believe otters rarely speak," Jenny said, "which lack of practice may excuse your rudeness in not letting me finish telling you about one of the several wonders that –"

But the Otter was already talking again: "I may interrupt you because, firstly, I am a magical beast, and Chief Pet to the Maid of Saltwaters, who is a great-great-granddaughter of the King Beneath the Sea, which can be seen by this fine golden collar I wear, whereas you are only a girl," the Otter pointed out.

The Voyage of the Otter

"And because, secondly," he continued, "otters cannot be expected to pay attention for long to anyone who is not busy throwing them more small tasty fish of the sort you have caught today and which I can smell lying in the bottom of your boat."

Jenny took the hint and threw him another fish. "These fish are *sprats,*" she said, helpfully. "A sort of lesser cousin to the herring which school abundantly in these waters."

The Otter swallowed the little fish. "You needn't tell me what a sprat is, as the knowledge of fish is within my nature," he told Jenny.

"Yet there are otters upriver who live on field mice and duck eggs," Jenny said. "And I doubt they would know a pilchard from a flounder, or indeed a tuna from a sardine."

3

"I believe you may consider me a sea otter of a rather higher order than these river-dwelling egg thieves of which you speak," the Otter said, preening himself. "Which an intelligent young girl might have deduced from my well-polished speech or, again, my fine golden collar. And in any case I was about to mention another reason I may interrupt you, which is, thirdly –"

"Thirdly," Jenny interrupted for she couldn't contain herself, "thirdly, because you shall grant me my great wish and give me a ship, and a crew of sailors, and I shall be captain!"

"No," said the Otter. "No, because, thirdly, you asked what adventure you shall find, but *finding* shall be your adventure. For it is time that the Lost City that sank beneath the waves was found again."

Jenny looked at the Otter, and then out at the steep wet

rock around the cove, and to the sea beyond that was rolling gold under the sunset. "And how shall I find the Lost City?" she asked at last, merely out of curiosity, and not from any lack of spirit. "For I have only my little fishing dory, which would not survive the rigours of the Old Sea, the Sea of Heroes, the Sea of Wonders Found and Forgotten."

"Well, as for that," said the Otter, offhandedly, "I shall give you a ship and crew, and you shall be captain."

Jenny was quiet for a moment, for that had always been the dream of her heart.

Then the Otter stared at her curiously. "Are you surprised that a young girl such as yourself shall be captain, rather than a grizzled sailor of vast experience?" he asked.

Jenny threw the Otter another sprat. *"No,"* she said.

The Otter chewed on the fish for a moment. "Well, I certainly am," he said.

Now, AS YOU'VE HEARD, even though Jenny was a young girl, she lived by herself, in a cottage above the little cove, just in sight of the harbour town where her friend Tom and his father had a house. But Jenny's Godmother kept an eye on her, and that night, after the Otter's visit, Jenny took a lantern and walked by herself under the full moon, past the town, and down the lane along the fields that ran into the trees, and through the dark woods to the little stone hut in the forest where her Godmother lived.

For other people called Jenny's Godmother the Wise

Woman of the Woods Nearby, and they listened to what she said, and were a little afraid.

WHEN JENNY ARRIVED, her Godmother had an extra bowl and cup set out, ready for the two of them. "For I always know when you are coming," her Godmother said. "And of course, it's High Midnight Tea tonight."

Jenny only said, "Yes," for her Godmother was the only person who made her feel shy of talking. And she didn't say anything about the Otter or his sleek and preening ways.

Then Jenny sat by the fire while her Godmother finished getting everything ready, just so, and then they waited until the clock struck twelve, the cat Pawlikins asked to be let out, and the kettle began to whistle, all at once. Jenny's Godmother looked at her significantly and blew out all the lanterns and candles but one. Jenny opened the door for Pawlikins, and now they could hear the wind rise outside, and the cats begin to howl, and the wolves, farther away.

The Wise Woman of the Woods Nearby dropped her voice down low. "It's time for the High Midnight Tea," she said.

ACCORDING TO JENNY'S GODMOTHER, midnight tea was properly the last meal of the day, following breakfast, morning coffee, dinner, afternoon pie, supper, and cookies.

But on nights like this one, nights with a full moon, Wise Women called it *High* Midnight Tea, which meant not only tea and bread and honey, but butter tarts, a round of cards (with round cards), and then last of all a *divination*. And when it was time for the divination, Jenny's Godmother would cast the dregs of tea against a tall stone in her garden and peer into the drops and dribbles shining in the moonlight and tell Jenny's future, or anything else she saw.

But first there was strong tea, and good bread and honey, and butter tarts that were better. And the card game went on for a long time before Jenny's Godmother – who never lost – had gathered all five jacks under the Queen of Swords and called "Full Court!" to win the game.

And then they went outside under the moon, where they found Pawlikins, a wise cat the colour of night (except for its paws, which were white), waiting for them in the garden. They threw the last of their tea onto the tall blue stone, and Jenny's Godmother looked close at the wet shapes. Jenny felt her heart beat faster.

For sometimes the tea showed things that came strangely true, like the time the Wise Woman had said, "You may have a swelling of the eye," only two weeks before Jenny had won her prize expanding telescope.

And other times the tea held advice, as when Jenny's Godmother had looked up from the dregs and said, "No one wants to see your tonsils, so cover your mouth when you yawn."

And then other times still, like when her Godmother had examined the Casting Stone for a long time before announcing with great portent, "Hopscotch is a fine way to pass the time,"

6

Jenny wondered if Wise Women just made things up.

But now the night wind rose again as her Godmother bent over the weathered rock; old leaves scattered along the forest floor; three owls perched on the roof of the hut hooted once each, in order of size; and Jenny shivered, wondering what her Godmother would see in the wet marks shining in the moonlight.

"You are going on a long trip," the Wise Woman of the Woods Nearby said.

"Yes," Jenny said.

"You will cross the water," the Wise Woman said after she looked up again.

"Yes," said Jenny, "and I shall have a crew and a ship and I shall be captain."

"Captain Jenny," her Godmother said, and Jenny smiled, for that was the first time she had ever heard those words outside of her own heart.

"Captain Jenny," Jenny repeated. "And my ship shall be named the *Nonesuch*."

Jenny's Godmother examined the stone more closely. "Perhaps," she said. "But here I have seen your rede." Now, a *rede* was less than a prophecy, but more than a piece of advice, and Jenny knew that even though Wise Women could be strange, willful, eccentric, or silly, if one of them pronounced a rede, it was something to remember.

"Mark these words," her Godmother said. *"Before you come home, you will need friends more than a ship or a sword."*

Jenny nodded, even though she didn't understand. "An

The Voyage of the Otter

Otter visited me today," she said at last.

"Of course he did," her Godmother said. "Did he wear a golden collar?"

"Yes," said Jenny. "He gave me a Call to Adventure, but he was arrogant and officious, as well as sleek and preening."

"A messenger from the King Beneath the Sea, no doubt. Did you give him some fish?"

"Yes," said Jenny, "three sprats in all. But I would rather have caught him in my nets, or a magical flounder perhaps, so that I could have made him grant me my wish without tedious conditions." Then Jenny told her Godmother all that the Otter had said, including the rather sketchy directions for the voyage: "Through the Great Pillars of the Sea, and East to the Lighthouse of the Ancients, and so to the Navel of the World and on to Babbylantium, and then doubtless you can figure the rest out on your own, if you are half, or even one-quarter, as clever as you seem to believe yourself to be," he had said.

"I'm glad you fed him nonetheless," her Godmother said. "For it is always wise to be polite, especially to magical beasts that speak and wear golden collars. And you can't disobey them; it's the Law of the Sea, as you know very well."

"Perhaps I can find my own golden collar in the treasure of the Lost City that sank beneath the waves," Jenny said.

"Perhaps you can," the Wise Woman said. "But I have another rede for you."

"But you have never pronounced more than one rede at a time," Jenny said, and then quailed as her Godmother gave her a look of the sort that made some people afraid of the Wise Woman of the Woods Nearby.

"Indeed, and you have never been visited by an Otter wearing a golden collar before, and I have never felt my bad knee ache like this unless a storm approached, and you have never been content to do as you were told, not since you were a wee tad who was always trying to crawl into the cupboards where I keep the awful secrets of my craft. So perhaps I should keep this rede unpronounced and you can sail away to the Navel of the World and then discuss your voyage with the dreadful Oracle of Babbylantium without further benefit of my conversation."

Jenny blushed and was quiet for a moment. "I'm sorry," she said. "Please tell me this second rede."

"The second rede is: *'Pride goes before the waterfall.'*"

"I shall remember that," Jenny said, "although I can't quite smoke out its meaning."

"Not yet," said her Godmother. "But you're a clever girl and may understand before it's too late."

And Jenny would have asked, *too late for what?* except that she knew a rede never came with an explanation, so she only said, "Thank you."

Then suddenly – she never knew quite why – Jenny began to wonder if she would see her Godmother again. "And thank you for your advice," Jenny added, "and for your butter tarts and the games of cards, and for watching after me my whole long life, and –"

Jenny would have gone on like that for some time, but

her Godmother said, "And thank you, for being the most amusing goddaughter I've ever had."

Jenny stopped. "How many goddaughters have you had?" she asked.

"One hundred and twenty-seven," the Wise Woman said. "So far."

Then Jenny almost asked how old her Godmother was, but decided that was rude, and besides, just then Pawlikins rubbed against her leg and she began to feel how tired she was.

"WELL, GODDAUGHTER, it is well after midnight tea, and time to be home in bed," the Wise Woman said. "But the wolves are out tonight. Will you feel safe going home?"

"Yes," Jenny said, for she was never afraid to go anywhere. But as if they'd been listening, it was then that the wolves began to howl again, from one hilltop to another, across the woods, the fields, and all the countryside around between the stone hut and Jenny's cottage.

"Lately, I think I hear a tapping late at night too," her Godmother said. "As if the wee men who sleep in the mines deep in the hills have begun to wake and hammer again."

"But you have said the wee knocking men are friendly to those who treat them fairly," Jenny said.

"Yes, and Wise Women like myself are friendly too, but nonetheless many people would rather not meet them by accident in the deep of the night. So perhaps you would like the cat Pawlikins to follow behind you?"

The Voyage of the Otter

"Yes," said Jenny. "For on nights like this cats grow restive and appreciate long walks."

"I may not see you for a while," the Wise Woman said.

"No," Jenny said, and she wondered again if this was the last time she would see her Godmother. "And so I will have no source of advice or counsel."

Her Godmother smiled. "I think you will receive advice all along," she said. "But since you are going that way in any case, you should not forget to ask the advice of the Oracle of Babbylantium."

"I won't," Jenny said. "Thank you."

"And I'll give you this blessing," her Godmother said. *"May everything lost below rise above."*

"Like my prize expanding telescope that sank beneath the waves but which my friend Tom returned to me from the Eaves of the World?" Jenny asked.

The Wise Woman of the Woods Nearby looked at her. "Yes," she said, and her voice dropped low again. "I meant something like that."

Then Jenny walked back through the woods and fields with Pawlikins creeping beside her to scare off the wolves. They still howled in the distance, and far off, Jenny and Pawlikins could hear the little hammers of the wee men striking deep in the old mines and echoing across the hills. And Jenny's head was full besides from everything the Otter had said, and from the divination, and from the blessing. But she knew what she would dream about.

For tomorrow she would see her ship.

The Voyage of the Otter

II

CHAPTER TWO:
EYES PAINTED ON ITS
PROW TO FIND ITS WAY

W HEN SHE WOKE EARLY THE NEXT MORNING, JENNY made herself some coffee and thought a bit.

Then she packed her duffel bag for a long trip. She closed up her cottage tight. She put on her peacoat and tricorne hat. And then she tucked her prize expanding telescope under her arm and she rowed her dory out of the cove and towards the harbour, looking for her *Nonesuch*.

IT WAS A FINE BRIGHT DAY in the harbour, and the sea air blew light and cool. Other fishers hailed Jenny as their boats set off, and farther out where the tall ships were moored, their masts cast long morning shadows over the sea.

Jenny rowed about, looking for her ship. She knew most of the vessels in the harbour already: ketches with normal names like the *Stoutling* and the *Sea-Maid,* and one big three-master with an elf name, the *Maerial Farilex II,* named in honour of the original *Maerial Farilex,* the ship that had sunk with all hands in a light June breeze a long time ago, with Jenny's mother and father aboard.

In the village, some people said that disaster only hap-

pened because someone had forgot to paint eyes on the figurehead. In any case, the figurehead on the *Maerial Farilex II*
had very large eyes, eyes that were wide, wide awake.

But then Jenny turned away from the big ships as a dark
cormorant came swooping down over her dory. The bird
grunted once, then skimmed along the water towards a
strange blue galley, a galley that sat almost as low in the
water as her own little boat.

Jenny had never seen such a ship before.

As Jenny rowed nearer, she heard the voices of the
galley's crew carried over the water, voices that seemed
familiar.

"A flounder appeared from the water," a sailor with a
timid voice was saying. "Then it told us to come," another
timid voice finished. "So we had no choice!" they cried
together.

"Yes, and it was a flounder what told me to come too,"
a grumpy voice declared.

"You can't refuse a flounder what speaks!" a voice cried.

"Or an otter, you can't; it's the Law of the Sea!" cried
another.

"Well, it's better if you catches them first so they grants
you a wish rather than gives you orders," said an unhappy
voice.

"We got mighty cold sailing North through the Eaves of
the World," said the grumpy voice, "and strange things befell

us, but we never took orders from fish, and only ate them."

Now Jenny was right next to the blue ship, a strange thing indeed. It had one square mast, eight oars on either side, a tall sternpost that curved up from the rear, and in the front, a long prow that ran forward into the water like a dart. And if it was much larger than her fishing dory, it was still small compared to the tall ships in the harbour. Jenny peered over the low gunnel and saw the sailors on benches by the oars, but they didn't see her, for they were deep in discussion.

"But as the flounder caught you, rather than vicey-versey, it's befitting you accommodates yourself to the fates of the sea and doesn't complain," the oldest sailor was saying. "For the Captain of the *Volantix* has retired to a tower on the Northern coast to write an account of our circumnavigation, and has borrowed my parrot to help with the strange words. Leaving us to wait for this Jenny to be our new captain."

So Jenny found out her ship, and learned that the sailors who had been with her friend Tom aboard the *Volantix* were to be her crew. When Tom had sailed with them, they had gone North, through the icy Eaves of the World, and so circumnavigated the globe, which no one yet had done. (And had survived facing fearsome cold, snow-goblins, and Boogey Pirates – twice – along the way.) So Jenny was relieved, as she knew them already, knew

The Voyage of the Otter

them to be seafarers of great resource, if somewhat prone to complaint.

Jenny stood up so they could see her. "Yes," she announced, straightening her tricorne hat. "I am to be your captain, commissioned by the Otter with a Golden Collar, Chief Pet to the Maid of Saltwaters, who is a great-great-granddaughter of the King Beneath the Sea. Pipe me aboard, for I am your captain. It's the Law of the Sea."

THE SAILORS LOOKED AT JENNY, astonished, for after all, she was only a young girl. Then they looked at each other.

"It's Jenny, Tom's friend!" one of them said in surprise. And, "It's Jenny the Fisher-Girl!" another said.

"What an irregular start to a voyage!" cried the two sailors with timid voices, who sat on the benches amidships.

And then the Cook – the sailor who had the grumpy voice – spoke very slowly. "Well, that's just fine," he said, "and more or less what we deserve for taking orders from some flat fish."

Jenny stood as tall as she could. "Avast such talk!" she cried. "For I am captain, and the *Nonesuch* is my ship, which name I shall give it because –"

"Begging your pardon, Captain Jenny, sir," said the First Mate, the oldest sailor, as he touched his knuckle to his cap in respect. "But this here ship already has a name. It's the *Otter* you're captain of, not the *Nonesuch*."

The Voyage of the Otter

15

"The *Otter,*" Jenny said.

"The *Otter,* sir, doubtless named after himself by the Otter what gave you your orders."

"Doubtless," Jenny said, trying not to show she was disappointed. She looked her crew over. "The *Otter.* Well, that's a fine name for my first command all the same," she said. "Now pipe me aboard."

"Who brought the pipe?" one of the sailors asked.

"I'll just whistle!" whispered the First Mate.

And so the sailors all stood, and the First Mate whistled the little tune to welcome a captain aboard, while Jenny climbed over the side of the dory and into her *Otter.*

16

JENNY LOOKED AROUND the little ship with satisfaction, and prepared to make a speech. It would be a fine speech, she thought, a speech that would inspirit the crew while emphasizing the dignity of her position.

"But girlie –" the Cook said before she could open her mouth.

"Captain Jenny," Jenny reminded him.

"But missy Jenny," the Cook said. "Where are we going, for this is an odd ship, and an odd voyage even for us who's found our way through the icy narrows of the North and so circumnavigated the globe."

"There's only one cabin, and it hardly has room to stand," one of the sailors pointed out. And, "There's no wheel," another said. And, "There's no figurehead to see where we're going, or place to put one, which can only be bad luck!" cried the two sailors amidships.

"And there's no proper captain neither," muttered the Cook. "Just a girl with a hat."

But Jenny heard that, and she put her hands on her hips and made a face. "There'll be no cook soon either, if there's any more of that talk," she said. "And as for your questions, we're going to sail the Old Sea, the Sea of Heroes."

"Also called, 'the Sea of Wonders Found and Forgotten,'" the First Mate put in, to be helpful.

"Yes," said Jenny, "and there we'll find a wonder forgotten: the Lost City that sank beneath the waves, of which you have all doubtless heard. And then we'll come home rich in treasure and covered in glory. Or if you prefer, you can break the Law of the Sea and jump over the side and see what happens to you.

"As for the ship," Jenny went on, before anyone could interrupt, "The *Otter* is light and without a wheel or full decks or cabin because we'll sail close to shore, and in and out of islands and archipelagoes, just as the old heroes did." The crew was quiet now, though the two sailors amidships scratched their heads over 'archipelago' while the First Mate rubbed his rough hands together in anticipation of a properly salty voyage.

"And finally," Jenny said, thinking almost as quickly as she talked. "Finally, as to having no figurehead, a ship like this one only needs eyes painted on its prow to find its way, as anyone familiar with the exploits of the heroic sailors of

17

The Voyage of the Otter

old would know at once. In fact, I'm surprised you even asked."

The sailors nodded, most of them. But the Cook said, "And who'll do that wet, miserable work?"

Now Jenny was properly angry, for all good captains she'd ever read of had run a tight ship, and been loyally obeyed by their crews, and here the voyage hadn't even started and already a sailor needed to be told his place. She pointed her head up to look the Cook in the eye. "Why, you'll do that wet, miserable work," she told him.

As the rest of the sailors laughed, the Cook stomped his peg leg in frustration. But his friend the First Mate (who also had a peg leg) put a hand on his shoulder. "Now, she's our captain, and you had that coming," the First Mate told him. "Besides, it's a careful job that needs a skillful hand."

"That's true, it does," Jenny said, to be diplomatic.

"Now," she told all the sailors, "I'm going ashore to consult with my advisors, and I expect you'll be ready to sail, with the eyes painted on the prow, and 'Otter' sewn onto the ribbons of all your caps, in time to leave with the ebb tide, when I shall have returned."

"Aye aye," the sailors said. A few of them even remembered to add, "captain."

WHEN JENNY TOLD HER CREW that she would consult her advisors, she was trying to sound masterful and important, for all she had in mind was to talk with Tom and his Dad

The Voyage of the Otter

before she set out. Of course, all the crew knew Tom, who had sailed with them aboard the *Volantix* on its long voyage through the cold Eaves of the World. But since Tom had borne no proper rank, though he had kept lookout from the crow's nest, Jenny thought it might impair her dignity as captain to let it be known she was seeking his advice.

But as soon as Jenny had rowed her dory out of earshot, the crew of the *Otter* began talking. Some of them were still unhappy.

"What business did the Otter have picking such a captain?" the Cook asked.

"Captain Jenny is Tom's friend," one of the sailors pointed out.

"Well, Tom was a good lad, to be sure," said the Cook. "But after all, he was only our lookout on the *Volantix*, without proper rank, and this Jenny wasn't even there, but is only his acquaintance."

"Stop all this conjobbling," said the First Mate (who had a weakness for fine language). "For Tom wasn't just our lookout; he was our luck, who was always spotting danger. And at the end, when the rest of us had settled down to sleep forever in the cold, Tom was the one who went and found help."

"That he did," one of the sailors agreed. "But what was the help he found? I'm forgetting already."

"You're a fool," another sailor told him. "It was – it was – it was the Herders of the Reindeer."

19

The Voyage of the Otter

"No, it was the Snow People!" cried a third sailor.

"It was Grandfather Frost!" the two sailors amidships cried in frustration, "and at his lodge beneath the great mountain that reaches to the Roof of the World he had the Herders of the Reindeer and some of the Snow People as guests."

"Oh, so it was," said the sailor who had forgotten. "I thought I dreamed that."

"That's the way of Grandfather Frost, that's what the captain of the *Volantix* said," announced the First Mate. "But you can bet Grandfather Frost will be in his account of our circumnavigation."

"Well, perhaps it was Grandfather Frost," said the Cook. "For I think I've dreamt that too. Or maybe it was the Snow People or the Herders of the Reindeer, for who can remember clearly what happened after we woke from the cold? But it certainly wasn't this girl Jenny."

"Quiet again – or are you talking mutiny?" asked the First Mate. "For you and I are grizzled old sailors of vast experience, and have even completed the great circumnavigation about the seas. But never yet have we sailed deep into the Old Sea at the Middle of the World, which would be the thundering clincher to our nautical careers."

"But I did sail it once," declared the Cook.

And, *"What did you find?"* asked all of the sailors together.

"A waterspout," said the Cook.

"A waterspout!" cried one of the sailors amidships. "A

The Voyage of the Otter

whirling devil of the sea!" cried the other. Then, *"Did you survive it?"* they asked together.

"Only barely," said the Cook. "It wrecked our ship against an unknown shore, and we was forced to walk North through a great dark forest for two months before we found another coast where a tramp ketch that smelled of turnips brought us home."

"Well, since you was merely wrecked at once last time, our current voyage can hardly help but be somewhat more prosperous," said the First Mate, "– if you're willing to lend a hand."

"Well, of course I know the Law of the Sea as well as any of you," said the Cook. "And you all know I won't talk mutiny. I'll obey this girl Jenny, as long as our ship don't wreck. I might grumble, but I'm a good sailor."

"True enough," said the First Mate. "And may we all profit by your experience."

Then they set to work, according to Jenny's orders.

21

Tom and his Dad lived in a house with one tall turret, and any number of dusty books, and at least seven writing desks full of notebooks and scraps of paper.

For Tom's father spent his life composing a Great Work, a book he hoped to call *The Universal Encyclopædia Comprising All Things Worth Knowing: Practical, Historical, and Mythological, As Well As Useful, Useless, Interesting, and Quaint.* ("It will be a large volume," he had told Jenny once. "But I hope to issue an edition in reduced type accompanied by a magnifying glass, so that people might edify themselves at any passing moment.")

So when Tom's father answered the door, Jenny greeted him by saying, "Good morning, sir. I hope the Great Work is going well."

"Very well, thank you," said Tom's Dad. "For I have invented a new principle of organization, far superior to the normal historical or alphabetical, or even to my previous system of beginning with the long entries and proceeding to short. Now items concerning the stars will be at the front, those about the land and sea in the middle, and those discussing the deeps of the Earth at the end."

"The reorganization will be done within five years, my Dad says," Tom said.

Jenny nodded thoughtfully. "Where will *Explorers* go?" she asked. "For some of them explore mountaintops, the deeps of the Earth, and land and sky alike. Maxim Tortuca, for example, drifted so high while tied to a kite that he saw half the world at once, but when the kite fell, he woke up in a series of caverns which led to the hot centre of the Earth, where –"

"Maxim Tortuca!" Tom's Dad cried. "Tom, I told you I had forgotten something, and without Tortuca the *Encyclopædia* won't be universal."

Jenny didn't say anything, for Tom's father was a learned man, but she couldn't imagine anyone forgetting the Explorations of Maxim Tortuca.

22

The Voyage of the Otter

"Perhaps Tortuca's story could run in a ribbon along the bottom of each page," Tom suggested. "That way, he would pass through all the layers of the *Encyclopædia*, from the sky through to the deeps of the Earth."

"Yes, excellent!" cried Tom's father. "Although that suggests a new and even better system of organization, which –"

"Should we invite Jenny to breakfast?" asked Tom.

"Oh, yes – I'm forgetting my manners," said Tom's Dad. "It was the problem of Maxim Tortuca, which – well, never mind. Young Jenny, please join us for breakfast."

OVER BREAKFAST (cereal, kippers, and hot chocolate), Tom's father made conversation. "Do you like the cereal?" he asked Jenny. "It is formulated according to a new and comprehensive formula of my own devising, consisting of dried raisins, rolled oats, puffed wheat, cracked rye, and ground barley sugar."

"It tastes comprehensively, sir," Jenny said, catching Tom's eye. Then Tom had to try so hard not to laugh that he ended up by coughing and emitting a dried raisin from his nose instead.

But as they drank their hot chocolate, Jenny told them about what had happened since the Otter with a Golden Collar had appeared in her cove.

"So you'll be sailing with the old crew of the *Volantix!*" cried Tom.

"Could you come, too?" asked Jenny. "For though they

23

are seafarers of great resource, they are somewhat prone to complaint and querulousness, and they hardly know me. You would be lieutenant, and entitled to at least one-quarter share of all glory, treasure, and renown."

Tom looked at his Dad. "I've had my adventure already," Tom said. "And it wouldn't be fair to leave my father alone for so long again when there are all these slips of paper to sort."

Then Tom's father looked up, for he had been distracted from sorting through all those slips of paper, arranging subjects according to how adventurous they were, from stones (hardly at all) to birds (very much).

"Tom come with you?" he said. "It's true that since Tom has seen the Eaves of the World, sailing the Old Sea and seeing perhaps the Navel of the World would complement his knowledge nicely, but it might not be wise. For the Otter issued the Call to Adventure to you, while various magical flounders told these sailors to be your crew, and no unusual creature has asked Tom, except yourself. And many authorities hold that such instructions are to be obeyed without addition."

Jenny was downcast, but she admitted that was true. "For example," she said, "the famous Privateer of the North, Ola Olagovna, who was about to eat a potato when it opened its eyes and told her that if she would only let him alone, he would let her know where she could trade other potatoes for golden eggs. This alone would have given her fortune enough to retire, but when she told her

24

consort, Prince Rasketinius, to come along and also bring his own potato, disaster ensued in the form –"

"Exactly," said Tom's Dad. "Disaster." Then he began scribbling on a new slip of paper. "Yes," he said. "Prince Rasketinius, we mustn't forget him again, eh, Tom?"

"But still," Jenny said, "happy as I am to have become captain of the *Otter*, it will be a lonely post, from the necessity of remaining aloof and superior to the crew, and so having no one to talk to."

Tom and his father looked at one another. "You could take my dog with you, for company," Tom said. "For you are friends already."

"Sparky?" Jenny said, and her eyes almost welled up. "But –"

Tom's Dad nodded. "I don't believe any authorities have said that bringing a dog would violate the rules," he said.

Sparky, a timid but faithful dog, came running up then, for he had heard his name. "He couldn't come North with me," Tom said, scratching his dog behind the ears. "For it was too cold for his paws, and besides, I was only the lookout. But the Old Sea is warm waters, and you are captain of the *Otter* and may do as you please."

Jenny crossed her arms. "Sparky is your dog," she said, stubbornly. "And you would miss him."

"I'll miss both of you," said Tom. "But I can't come, so I'd rather you had Sparky at least, for it's true that a captain is often lonely in command."

"Thank you," Jenny said, almost overcome. Then she

saw a faraway look in Tom's eyes, the look that means a sea-longing. "When you were on your Exploration, I often dreamt of you wreathed in cold mist, wandering in the dark Northern wastes," she said.

"That was true!" Tom said. "And I saw you once dreaming, with Sparky beside you."

"And you will dream of my voyage now, and Sparky's," said Jenny. "Though this will not be so perilous. And those dreams will also be true."

Then Tom's Dad interrupted, producing several slips of paper and a small leather-bound book. "And," he said, "along with Sparky we must send the following Necessities for the Voyage along with you. First, a copy of the digest form of my life's work, called the *Representative Encyclopædia Comprising Many Things Worth Knowing*.

"I wish I'd finished it in time for Tom's voyage through the Eaves of the World, as it would have provided many hours of amusement and edification. But I was in the middle of reorganizing the material so that items with the shortest names came first, and those with the longest names last." Tom's Dad shook his head at his own foolishness.

"And second, coffee," Tom said, looking at one of the slips. "And then a speaking-trumpet for bellowing orders on the open deck despite the worst weather, and a pair of glasses with special lenses, dark blue ones so your eyes won't squint shut in the sun."

There were several more items on the list, but Jenny

began to protest, pointing out that: first, she could look after herself; and, second, she had already packed her duffel bag of Necessities for the Voyage; and, third, as a fisher of long standing – and now captain of the *Otter* – it wasn't seemly to be babied.

But Tom was already packing the supplies into a sea-chest, while Sparky danced around, worried that, whatever this trip was, they would probably leave him behind.

"It's true that you are a captain, and have received a Call to Adventure from an emissary of the King Beneath the Sea," Tom's father told Jenny. "Still, it's hard for a child your age to be comprehensive in her preparations."

"Besides," Tom said, "you gave me a tinderbox for my voyage North."

"All right," said Jenny, while Sparky wriggled in her arms. "But I want to leave with the ebb tide."

"Entirely correct," said Tom's father, looking into a large book of maritime calculations and then checking his pocket watch. "You have only three hours and seven minutes."

"Three hours and seven minutes," repeated Jenny. "And then my adventure will begin."

Tom's father looked at his pocket watch again. "Three hours and six minutes now," he said.

27

THE FOUR OF THEM made their way down to the wharf with several minutes to spare. Tom carried Jenny's sea-chest, Jenny carried her duffel bag, Tom's Dad carried a pocket notebook, and Sparky simply carried his tail high in the air, for pride of being in a parade, which none of the other dogs were. "The *Otter* looks fine, don't you think," Jenny said to Tom and his father. "It looks crack and sharp and seaworthy."

Tom nodded. The galley was looking fine; its sides were blue and its hull was black with new pitch, and its new eyes were sharp and straight.

But Tom's Dad said, "The long projection from the prow, is that a ram to sink other ships?"

Jenny was hardly listening, for she was looking at her ship, but she shook her head. "It is a blunt snout, not a beak, and offers a useful handhold," she said.

28

And now her crew had seen them, and they were wearing new ribbons in their caps, and they cheered at the sight of Tom.

"Tom, our lookout and our luck, come aboard!" they cried. "Tom, it'll be a warmer trip, with less time shivering," they cried. And "Tom, we need your good humour!" they cried, for they knew that, left to themselves, they were somewhat prone to complaint.

But the First Mate took off his cap to Tom; and the Cook, he only said: "Don't be coming with us again, Tom, for you were lucky to get home once."

Tom laughed to see his friends, but he couldn't trust himself to speak, and only bent down to talk to his dog: "Be a good dog," he whispered to Sparky. "And help them all come home safe."

"Tom's dog!" some of the sailors whispered. "Why, that's almost as lucky as having Tom aboard."

Then Jenny set her tricorne hat straighter on her head and nodded at Tom and his father.

"Accurate charts and helpful strangers," Tom said, by way of wishing her goodbye.

"The tide is going, if you mean to go with it," said Tom's Dad.

Jenny looked at them, for she had considered at length the proper goodbye for the occasion. "Good books and absorbing plans," she said. Then suddenly she put her prize telescope in Tom's hands. "Watch for our return," she added.

Then the crew shifted Jenny's things aboard, and she led Sparky onto her ship.

Tom cast loose the mooring rope, and the *Otter* pushed off, under Jenny's direction. The crew raised their oars straight in the air by way of salute, and then they dug them into the sea and the little blue galley began to pull away.

"It's a small ship for the open sea," Tom said to his father.

"But it rides the waves lightly, like a dolphin," his Dad said.

At last, the Otter *was at sea*

CHAPTER THREE:
EVERYONE BUT THREE GOATS AND A DOG

A T LAST, THE *Otter* WAS AT SEA. AND AS THEY LEFT THE shelter of the headlands, the crew pulled in their long oars and loosed the sail. The sail was painted with a rising – or setting – sun, and the fresh North wind stretched it tight and pulled the ship along.

Jenny stood on the foredeck beside the small cannon, the bow-chaser they called it. She gripped the rail and looked ahead over the sea through her strange blue glasses. Behind her, the crew took their ease, except for the First Mate, who was at the helm, and stood on the stern deck and managed the *Otter*'s steering oar.

It was fine weather for a shallow vessel like the *Otter*. And if the sailors weren't accustomed to meeting the sea in such a small ship, to Jenny, who was used to her little fishing dory, the *Otter* felt not small and frail, but large and substantial. Substantial, but quick in the water – lively as a mermaid, lively as a dolphin, even lively as an otter.

Jenny could feel the pull of wind, the rise over a wave and the quick plunge down the other side. Spray leapt up from the waves, spray from the wind, spray from the galley's long snout as it cut through the water. And at the end of the snout there was a handhold where the rushing water bubbled up, so the galley seemed to snort, like a horse beginning to run.

"This is fine work!" Jenny cried.

"It's wet work, and we'll end up swamped," said the Cook, but he had his teeth showing in a sort of a grin as he said it. "The water burbling through the hole in the snout is an odd sound, and certainly forebodes –" But for once even the Cook couldn't think of anything actually gloomy to say, and fell silent.

And, "Fine work!" the First Mate cried as the bows met a wave. "There's a sort of satisfying palpability to the wee barky!" The junior sailors looked at him, for the First Mate's language often exceeded their understanding. "I mean you can feel the sea," the First Mate added. "It's wet-like, I mean."

"No worry of falling from the rigging, anyway," shouted the two sailors amidships, who were handling the sail. "Only over the side," added one. "Or –"

"Avast all such gloom!" cried Jenny. "It's a glorious day for sailors, and should be enjoyed as such." Then she took off her hat and felt the sun on her face. For a moment, she enjoyed feeling her hair blow freely in the wind, and then she put her hat back on, for she felt a captain should retain a certain dignity.

As for Sparky, he stood beside Jenny on the foredeck and looked ahead. He barked at each wave as it came close, and barked again for pleasure as they splashed through it and down the other side. He was all wet, but he thought it was fine work, too.

SO THEY RAN SOUTH, in fine spirits, except once or twice Jenny was mystified when she used her speaking-trumpet to hail a fishing boat and got no response, except that the fishers cut their nets loose and immediately began bearing away, fleeing East down the channel.

"Perhaps the noise of your voice through the speaking-trumpet frightened them," said one of the sailors amidships. "It frightened me," said the other.

"Well, it was an awful noise," said the Cook, "but perhaps they was really frightened by Tom's dog."

That didn't seem likely, and Jenny looked at the Cook sideways, to see if he was making fun of Sparky. But it was then the First Mate checked the angle of the sun with a sextant and nodded to Jenny.

33

"Cook," she said, "what's for lunch?"

"That'd be what the *Otter* had stowed aboard when we arrived," said the Cook. "Lemonade. Crackers."

"That's not bad," said Jenny.

"Dried fish," added the Cook. All the sailors groaned. "Crackers and lemonade are all fine and well," the Cook added. "But it'll be fish for breakfast, lunch, and dinner. Indefinite, like."

It's a curious thing, but most sailors, who spend their lives in the sea and surrounded by fish, would rather not eat them. "I guess fish is to be expected when a ship is pro-visioned by an otter, even one with a golden collar," the First Mate said. "But it'll remind us tediously of work."

"Well, I can fix it different," pointed out the Cook. "Fish stew, fish soup, fish paté, fish on crackers, crackers with fish. But it'll still be fish."

"And how is it you'll be fixing it today?" asked Jenny.

"I can't do much preparing, for it's the middle of the day and we're in the middle of the sea," the Cook said.

"I know," said Jenny. "But I'd rather have rough and ready now than something fancy and delayed later. For the work and the sunshine and the fresh breeze has put us all in the way of being hungry."

"Very hungry," said the two sailors amidships.

"And I'd say the same," said the First Mate, "except that a more sailorly term would be 'rapacious.'"

"Fine, then," said the Cook, who was touchy about his proper job along with everything else. "You'll all be having lemonade and crackers and cold fish jerky. For which I expect my usual few thanks."

"Fish jerky," repeated Jenny sadly, for fish jerky is tough and chewy and a sailor's least favourite dish.

"Crackers!" the two sailors amidships cried in excitement.

So THEY HAULED UP THEIR SAIL, and dropped their sleeping stone – a large rock with a hole in it that served as a sea anchor. And then they all stretched out and ate their poor lunch as the ship rocked in the sea.

"A pleasant excursion, and I hope you're all mollified to the situation," the First Mate said. "For while it's true we don't have young Tom here for luck, at least we have his dog." And all the others nodded.

The crew did seem mollified, Jenny thought, now that they were properly underway, and had a bit of food in their stomachs. She strode up and down the gangway between the oar benches, with her hands behind her back, inspecting.

Her duffel bag and sea-chest had been stowed in the one small cabin below the quarterdeck (where there wasn't even room to stand). The Cook kept his tiny kitchen on the foredeck, and underneath that there was another low space where the ship's stores were kept. Otherwise, there was neither deck nor hold; everything was open to the wind and the rain. It was lucky, Jenny thought, they were sailing to the warm Old Sea.

The crew had been busy, she knew, while she had been consulting with Tom and his Dad. Everything was ship-shape and just as she'd ordered, from the ribbons in their caps to the eyes on the prow.

"Those are fine eyes," said Jenny to the Cook. "Well done." She hoped with that she and the Cook could be friends.

"Thank-ee, girlie," the Cook growled.

He had called her "girlie" again! Jenny looked at him fiercely.

The Voyage of the Otter

"All right," the Cook said, looking away for a moment. "Thank-ee missy Jenny, captain, girlie, sir."

Jenny tried again. "Cook," she said, "what sort of a ship would you call this?"

And the *Otter* was an odd vessel, to be sure; a little open galley with eight long oars to each of its blue sides and only a pint-size cabin under the quarterdeck. Which isn't to mention the high, curved sternpost or the long black snout that ran ahead like a dart in the water.

"Well," said the Cook, considering, "it's a kind of small, single-masted, square-rigged, carvel-built, curve-stemmed war galley."

"Of course to that," said Jenny. "But have you ever seen its like before?"

"Aye," said the Cook, slowly. "Twice. When I was a boy."

"And when I was a boy," said the First Mate. "I saw them too. But they was bigger, those ones, and all black, with black sails."

Now all the crew was quiet, leaning forward on their benches to hear. "Black like Corsairs?" asked one of the sailors.

"Like Corsairs, the pirate ships of the Old Sea?" asked another.

"Corsairs!" wailed the two sailors amidships. "When we were bad our mum said the Corsairs would come and take us away! Corsairs!"

"Aye, like Corsairs," said the Cook. "And when the

Mate here and me was boys, they sailed from the South and up the rivers, and *did* take children away. And they brought them up to be slaves what worked the Corsair ships bound in chains – or perhaps was just sold to do kitchen chores for the idle rich."

"Or so we heard," said the First Mate. "For none of them that was abducted in those dark days – mothers, fathers, children, or dogs – ever came back to report."

"Indeed," said Jenny. "Perhaps that is why all the fishers we've met so far have fled before we could hail them. They think we're Corsairs."

BY THE MIDDLE OF THE AFTERNOON they could see the Western corner of the Continent to the South – and seeing land is a great comfort to sailors in a small, open ship.

"The navigation from here will be easy enough," said Jenny to the First Mate, as he stood at the steering oar, solid as a greybeard statue. "We round the corner and keep land in sight to port" – by which sailors mean the left side of a ship – "until, many days from now, we turn East and find the Great Pillars that stand at the entrance to the Old Sea, the Sea of Heroes, the Sea of Wonders Found and Forgotten."

"Terrible weather at the Pillars," observed the Cook.

"Is there?" said Jenny.

At once the sailors began to call out what they knew: "Gales and such!" "Heavy swells!" "Waterspouts that wrecks your ship!" and so on.

"Where did you hear such things? – which I'm not, however, saying aren't true," asked Jenny.

But the Cook, who had told them these things, only said, "Less jibber-jabber, lads, and get to the oars, for the seas are growing rougher now."

The sea *was* growing rougher; the waves were heavy and disordered here where the sea rolled eastward through the channel before the Great Continent to the South. Now they had to angle to the West, and that meant they had to row hard.

Jenny stood on the quarterdeck by the First Mate (he wedged his peg leg into the timbers of quarterdeck for better leverage as he steered) while the Cook stayed on the foredeck and beat a drum to help the sailors keep time. *Bom* – and all the crew pushed the oars forward; *bom* – and all the sailors dug them into the water; and *bom* – they put a foot against the bench in front of them and pulled back, hard, very hard. And then over again and over again. *Bom – Bom – Bom.*

It was rough water for the little *Otter*, but the crew all knew what they were doing. "The present duties of my office merely include worrying!" Jenny shouted to the First Mate as he leaned on the steering oar. "I am more ballast than captain!"

He laughed then. "And what is it you think a captain is for?" he asked. "For the crew can only worry in their spare time, but who's to do it when there's work to be done?"

"But I should shout encouragement to the crew!" Jenny declared.

"Yes," said the First Mate. "And lend your weight to the steering."

Which is what Jenny did, leaving only Sparky without employment, other than barking at the waves and the spray. But for all their hard work, if it hadn't been for the North wind, the *Otter* might not have rounded the corner.

And when they had rounded the point, and could raise their oars and merely let their sail pull them South again, they were nearly blind from exhaustion.

"Well done," said Jenny, hoarse from her encouraging. "Well rowed, well sailed, well steered." Then she took the steering oar on her own, and let the crew lie back while she and the North wind shared the work.

"That was only a test, Captain Jenny," said the First Mate, as he mopped his face dry with a bandanna. "By the time we're home, we'll call that a holiday."

"Only worse from here," the Cook said, with a gloomy satisfaction.

"Nonetheless," said Jenny, who had indeed worried hard, "well done."

39

SO THE WIND AT THEIR BACKS blew them South over the rolling salt water, with the Great Continent to the East always green, the wide outer sea stretching out West beyond the sun.

The Voyage of the Otter

The sailors' work was easy now, and Jenny went into her little cabin below the quarterdeck and dried Sparky off. "A proper way to start such a voyage," she told the dog as she rubbed him down with a towel. "For the ship and the sailors got used to the oars, and then our seaworthiness was tested in rough water, and now we coast along until we put in for the night."

Though her cabin didn't have room to stand, it had been fitted out cunningly with drawers and cupboards so that all of Jenny's things and Necessities for the Voyage were put away snugly, just as they were at home. The cabin's door was marked with a wave and a tear, as the sign of the Maid of Saltwaters, who is a great-great-grand-daughter of the King Beneath the Sea; and the ceiling had two small skylights, one on either side of an elaborate painting.

40

Jenny lay on her bunk and studied the picture, which was of the Otter with a Golden Collar, who was Chief Pet to the Maid of Saltwaters. He looked rather regal and self-important, she thought, which was probably in the nature of talking animals. He looked supercilious, and surprised to find that she was captain of his ship, but that was fine with Jenny. She would just prove him wrong, she thought. Then she stuck out her tongue at the painting.

Jenny could feel the sea just beneath her, could hear every creak of the steering oar, every flap of the sail; could listen to the sailors' easy talk, for they were satisfied too.

Jenny was nearly dozing, but she smiled and stroked

Sparky's soft ears. "Our cabin is after smelling of wet dog," she told Sparky. "I hold you responsible, though I am not reprimanding you, for that's probably in your nature as a dog on a sea voyage."

So the *Otter* sailed on, as the sun dipped towards the Western sea and the light began to change to gold.

Now, ON A TALL SHIP, the kind that Tom had sailed through the Eaves of the World, the crew slept in shifts belowdecks, and so kept sailing through the night. But the *Otter* was a shallow galley, so as evening came on, Jenny and the First Mate were happy to reach a bay where a river emptied into the sea.

"Haul down the mast and break out the oars," the First Mate told the crew. "For we'll row upriver and find a place to beach for the night."

Then the Cook (who was worrying what would go wrong when he fixed supper that night) spoke up. "When I was a lad this was called the Duchy of the Corner by the Sea, and ruled by the friendly young Duke," he said. "But since the Assembly of Rational Deputies took charge, it's gone to pot. Like everything else."

"What's it called now?" asked the two sailors amidships.

"It's called District Seventeen (formerly the Duchy of the Corner by the Sea)," said Jenny, who had been reading up in the *Representative Encyclopædia* that Tom's Dad had given her. "And instead of the Duke, it's administered by

The Voyage of the Otter

the Duly Elected Deputy for Reason Seventeen."

"What's Reason Seventeen?" asked one of the sailors.

"You mistook the sense of it," explained Jenny, "for seventeen is the number of the Deputy, not the reason." The junior sailors scratched their heads.

"Reason for what?" asked another sailor.

"Again, the sense of it is lost when you ask in that way," said Jenny. "It is not a reason *for* something, but a Deputy *for* Reason, as you're a sailor *for* an Exploration."

"I'm a sailor *for* a flounder told me to come," a third sailor pointed out.

"That don't signify," said the Cook. "For you're a numbskull."

"For you're a barnacle-backed, brine-blooded, peg-legged grizzle-pot," replied the sailor.

"I'm sure you meant that in the way of a compliment," the First Mate suggested, rather significantly.

"Yes," said the sailor, quailing a little, for he knew he had forgotten his place in the heat of the debate. "As the Cook, like yourself, is a sailor of vast experience."

"Well, thank you," said the Cook. "That's most generous."

"Is the Deputy nice?" asked one of the sailors, to change the subject. "Will it be dangerous?" asked another. And, "Does 'reason' mean Good or Bad?" a third one asked.

"Quiet," growled the First Mate. "For we're only camping for the night, which is as reasonable as could be."

The Voyage of the Otter

So they rowed the *Otter* up through the bay, where ruined towers stood watch on either side, and into the river's mouth. The river was wide and slow here by the sea, so they went upstream easily enough, through a gentle country much like their home. "There are animals in the fields," said Jenny. "And farm houses – but no people."

"It's suppertime, ain't it?" said the Cook.

At last the First Mate guided the small ship to a muddy little beach at the edge of a rough meadow. Sparky jumped over the side at once and splashed through the water to the grass. While the dog ran about, barking for pleasure to be on land again, the sailors leapt out and pulled the *Otter* up the riverbank and onto the meadow.

There were tended fields beyond the meadow, but the land around was still oddly quiet. To the Southwest was a tangled wood, and beyond it they could just see the edge of a village rising up on a hill. The Cook nodded at it. "Why don't you send someone up to buy fresh provisions for supper?" he said.

Jenny stared at him, for she was vexed that she hadn't thought of it first. The First Mate nudged his friend. "I only meant it as a suggestion, missy," the Cook said. "Captain-missy, I mean."

"It's a good suggestion," Jenny said, still determined to be friends. "Who'd like to go?"

"We're not afraid to go," said the two sailors from amidships, who were struggling to rig up the sail as a sort of awning. "But we don't know the language."

43

The Voyage of the Otter

"I'll go, Captain Jenny," said the First Mate. "For they understands our talk around here, though they decorate their words by adding 'ooh' and 'eh' to the end sometimes." And this was true, and in fact, Jenny's crew soon stopped paying attention to any of the strange accents they heard. It turned out that no matter where they went, the people there always thought it was the sailors from the Exploration who spoke strangely, and believed it was their own manner of speech that was normal.

Jenny straightened her hat. "I'll come too," she said. "For Tom's dog is after wanting the exercise." Then, to exercise her authority, she told the others, "Have the camp made by the time we return."

44

THE LAND GREW QUIETER STILL as they entered the wood, so quiet that even Sparky began to walk more solemnly among the budding oak and hawthorn trees. Not far along the path began to lead down, and soon they were too low to see either the camp behind or the village ahead.

At the bottom of the dell, they found a pair of tall grey stones, one on either side of the path. The stones loomed white and huge and ominous in the dusky evening wood, but Jenny stepped forward nonetheless. She would have gone on, but then Sparky did a strange thing – instead of marking the rocks, like he did almost anything that rose out of the ground, he cowered back and began to whimper.

"Excuse the dog, Captain Jenny," the First Mate said.

"For he probably knows it's bad luck to pass between them. Or so sailors believe – though I've seen 'em more dire-looking myself."

Jenny picked Sparky up. "Never mind," she told him, "we'll go around through the trees and so circumvent the problem." And the First Mate nodded, for he approved of both the plan and Jenny's fine language.

On the other side of the stones, they rejoined the path. Soon it climbed up again, and soon after that they emerged from the wood to find themselves at the edge of a village.

But it was deathly quiet.

Wrecked, roofless houses stared out from empty shutters. Even the chimneys had fallen, and sat as blackened stumps. Jenny and the First Mate gazed at the ruins until Sparky began to whimper.

"It's after being empty," Jenny said at last. She spoke quietly, for in that place it didn't seem right to speak up.

"Aye," said the First Mate. "It's after being sacked."

BACK AT THE CAMP by the ship, the Cook was making a fish casserole on the fire.

"But where have Captain Jenny and Tom's dog and the First Mate got to?" asked one of the sailors. "What has delayed them?"

"Ghosts?" suggested one of the sailors. "Spirits?" put in another. "Wood-goblins!" a third one shouted.

"It'll be the ruin of my casserole, anyway," said the Cook. He straightened up and took off his apron. "But I'd better go find out if they've been done in by something. Hand me a sword, though I expect I'll just get done in too."

Just then they heard a rustle from the path. "Wood-goblins which sneak in the dark and takes you away!" cried the two sailors from amidships. "We'll have to face a mighty battle in which many of us will perish!"

Then there was a terrible clamour, and Sparky emerged from the trees, barking. "Ah!" cried the two sailors before they recognized him. "Swords! Swords!"

But Jenny was right on Sparky's heels, and the First Mate after her. "Don't be sparrow-hearted," he told the sailors. "For it's us."

The Cook put away his sword. He was relieved, though he only said, "It's scorched fish casserole for dinner then – unless you brought fresh provisions from the village, which I fail to see."

"There's no provisions from the village having no villagers, only a monument in the middle," said Jenny.

"I wonder what the monument was for," said one of the sailors. The First Mate looked at Jenny then, and she nodded.

"You're forgetting that some of us is literate," the First Mate said. "Although the monument told a grim tale."

"Is it what I think?" asked the Cook, who wasn't slow on the uptake.

46

The Voyage of the Otter

"If you're thinking gloomy, which you habitually are, it is," said the First Mate.

"It read like this," Jenny said:

Here lies the village of Noan-mlee-gone-ger, quiet as an empty grave. For it was sacked by Corsairs, who abducted everyone but three goats and a dog, never to be seen again.

"Corsairs!" cried the sailors.

"Corsairs," said the First Mate. And, "Damn their hides," he and the Cook said together.

47

THAT NIGHT they set a watch to keep guard. Jenny had her own little tent, which she had found stowed in the cabin, while all the others only wrapped themselves up and made their beds on the soft meadow grass around her. Still, Jenny couldn't sleep.

Every hour, she heard the watch change: the grumbling of the sailors woken up; the small noises of their pipes; the soft South wind in the trees; the scurrying of small animals in the grass; the rippling water of the river below the camp. Sparky couldn't sleep either, for he'd been restless and nervous since they had come to the standing stones, and he squirmed and twisted around by her side.

Finally Jenny got up and put on her hat and cloak and walked out to the fire, where the ship's carpenter was smoking a pipe as he stood his watch.

You might be surprised to hear there was a carpenter aboard the *Otter*, but of course a ship requires all manner of skilled crafters among its crew to keep it in good repair: a rope-and-sailmaker; a blacksmith; a cooper for making and mending barrels, and so on; so many, in fact, that there's not room to talk about them all. But on a wooden ship, a carpenter is especially important. The Carpenter was nicknamed "Chips," from the mess his work made, and Chips was a steady old hand, who could tell his captain was agitated.

"Captain Jenny," the Carpenter said with a nod.

"Chips," Jenny replied, nodding back. Now Jenny felt less like sleeping than ever, for the firelight only reached to the edge of the trees, and beyond that was only blackness and moon-shadow.

But Chips tried to make conversation to pass the time. He gestured at the full moon, hanging low in the Southern sky. "This year," he said, "Her" – by which he meant the moon – "Her will just miss being full for Spring-Day, which won't arrive until three days after tomorrow."

Jenny looked at him, for of course she knew the day that spring began. But Chips had a bent for mathematics and astronomy, and it was all he knew to talk about, besides carpentry. He swallowed and went on: "Last year – that was the year we was stuck in the ice – Her had a thin crescent, just starting to grow, on Spring-Day, though you'd have hardly know it was spring, what from how cold

48

and dark it was. Now, at Spring-Day next year, Her won't show at all, and, well, it will be darker I suppose...." And he trailed off, for his store of conversation was already more or less exhausted.

So they sat for a while as the Carpenter puffed at his pipe, and Jenny did look at the moon. It had only been the night before that her Godmother had read her future by its light!

Now the wind brought dark clouds drifting up from the South. They covered the moon, but some of its light still came through, pearl-like and obscure. Everything was quiet. The world was dark and slow.

And then two owls hooted from the big willows by the river, and Jenny felt Sparky rise up. Then another owl hooted from the woods to the Southwest, and Jenny felt Sparky tense as though he was about to bark.

49

But Jenny tightened her hand on his collar and spoke softly to the dog. "Quiet, Sparky," she said. And then, still softly, she spoke to Chips: "I'm thinking there's trouble about," she said, trembling. "Go quietly among the crew and wake them, and tell them to have their swords to hand."

The Carpenter just nodded, for he was a steady old hand, and set down his pipe and began to creep away. He was barely gone before the First Mate and the Cook stole up around the other side of the fire. They each carried one of the ship's muskets, and had a knife in their teeth. They looked like Corsairs themselves.

The Voyage of the Otter

The First Mate took the knife out from between his teeth. "You heard it too," he murmured to Jenny, who nodded. He handed her a pistol. "We're scuppered," he added, "For they could be coming from anywhere."

Jenny's heart was pounding. *Corsairs!* Corsairs were in the woods. Then she saw the Carpenter signal to her from across the camp. The crew was all awake.

"Well, missy?" said the Cook. "Of course, we're doomed to be slaughtered, but it might be more seemly to put up a fight before the end. If you had any orders."

Jenny glared at him. "Stand up!" she shouted. "Backs to the fire! Draw your swords! And, and –" And no one, including Jenny, ever knew what she would have said next, for just then a musket flashed among the trees, and Jenny heard it – *crack!* – as the shot passed close by.

Then Jenny had no words left. They had fired at her! Sparky raced back to the *Otter*, howling. They had fired at her!

The First Mate and the Cook aimed their muskets blindly into the trees and fired in turn – *crack! crack!* – while Jenny only held her pistol by her side, not sure what to do.

"They fired at you because you're the leader," the First Mate explained.

"It was the hat what gave it away," the Cook added. "And they'll be reloading now."

If she hadn't been Captain, Jenny would have begun sobbing then. For what was she to do, what could she do, when she was only a young girl, and all she knew of battles was what she had read in books? And then all the battles she had ever heard about came tumbling into Jenny's head, and she knew there was only one thing to do – caught out in the open, and silhouetted against the fire.

She raised her pistol. "Charge the woods!" she shouted. "It's Corsairs!"

And as the crew of the *Otter*, who'd been in their share of tight spots, began to run for the enemy hidden in the woods, they screamed, "Woe! Woe from the *Otter*!"

And as they ran, voices answered from the woods: "Corsairs! Revenge! Revenge!"

It was all wrong, Jenny knew. Their first night, her first day as captain, and her crew was running into battle against unknown foes hiding in the woods. And she was only a girl, and already falling behind the charging sailors.

In a moment her crew would be among the trees and the killing would begin.

JUST THEN there was a pistol shot, and the sound of hooves. A horseman was racing in from the fields to the South, his gun held high, and Jenny swallowed hard, cocked her pistol, and aimed it at him.

But he was already shouting: "Stop, all of you! Put up your arms!"

The Voyage of the Otter

CHAPTER FOUR:
THE DOLPHINS CALLED BACK IN STRANGE VOICES

T HE HORSEMAN HAD PULLED UP BETWEEN THE TREES and the crew of the *Otter*. He raised his arms, his empty pistol in hand, and he looked right at Jenny.

Jenny had only an instant to decide what to do; for while her crew had been thrown into confusion, if this was some trick, whoever was hiding in the trees would be reloading in the woods – and if it wasn't, it would only take one sailor to cry "Charge!" before the fighting would start again. But in that instant, the man on the horse, middle-aged and pot-bellied, winked at Jenny. "Please," he said.

"Stop!" Jenny shouted at her crew. "Stop!"

"Thank you," the stranger said. "And if the gentleman with one leg and a dagger in his teeth who is even now crawling around to attack me from behind, if he could stop too –"

"Mate!" Jenny called.

"All right, Captain," the First Mate said, as he stood up. "Only a precaution. He don't look like a Corsair, I'll admit."

"No," said the horseman, "for my friends believed you to be Corsairs."

"Then let's see 'em," said Jenny, who still held her pistol by her side.

"Of course," said the stranger. "Come out, all of you, there's no danger, come out!"

Three young men with clubs, two old men with pitch-forks, and one old woman carrying a giant, antique musket slowly emerged from the trees. All of them were dressed like farmers, not Corsairs.

"All of you!" repeated the stranger.

A skinny young boy, smaller than Jenny, came out from behind the willows on the riverbank with a slingshot in his hand.

"Now," the horseman said, with a bow towards Jenny. "If you would do me the courtesy of explaining who you are, and what you and your friends are planning here –"

53

The stranger was very polite, but still presumptuous, Jenny thought. "We are here passing through," she said. "And we plan to use the privilege of strangers to make our beds, and then wash up in the morning. As for who we are, I think first we should know who was firing muskets at me, which is not the sort of welcome all tales say should be accorded strangers."

"Quite true!" one of her sailors said, and "Not cour-teous at all, I calls it," another added. The others threw in their opinions too: "Boorish! Wouldn't be done at home! Goblins would have shown us more welcome!"

"Indeed," said the stranger. "And I can show you where the wood-goblins dwell, and you can ask for their hospitality if you wish. As for these people, they live in this land, and were defending it as I asked; and if you sail in a Corsairs' ship, you should not be so disconcerted that the sentries at my towers imagined you Corsairs. For we have suffered much from their depredations in the Corner by the Sea. In my father's time, not a hundred years ago, Corsairs landed in this very spot, and do you know what they took from the village that lies to the south?"

"Everyone but three goats and a dog," Jenny said, remembering the monument they had found. "And now the village of Noan-mlee-gone-ger lies quiet as a grave."

The stranger bowed again. "Just so," he said. "And of late there have been storms and rumours of approaching smoke and strife from the East, and so you will forgive my people for their caution. As for me, I am the Duly Elected Deputy for Reason Seventeen, and it is my task to look after these peaceable folk."

Jenny bowed in turn. "I am Captain Jenny of the *Otter*," she said, "and this is my brave crew, who sailed the ship *Volantix* through the Eaves of the World in the course of a unprecedented circumnavigation, of which you have no doubt heard."

The crew of the *Otter* puffed up, pleased to hear Jenny speak of them so.

But now the skinny young boy was standing right behind Jenny, and poked up at her hat. She swatted him with it. "Be not irksome to your elders," she said. Then, "How did you come to stop these hostilities?" she asked the Duly Elected Deputy.

"When I heard the captain of the ship was a little girl, I knew it couldn't be Corsairs, and I rode as fast as I could," the Deputy said, with an apologetic smile.

"I'm sorry I fired at the girl," said the old woman. "Now we can see she is not an ugly dwarf with magic powers, but only a harmless child."

"Grandmother once shot her blunderbuss at a kite she mistook for a dragon," one of the farmers said.

"Quiet," said the Grandmother. Then she added to Jenny, "I'm sure you would be lovely if you were cleaned up and properly looked after."

Then the skinny boy spoke up. "A *captain,*" he said. "Wearing a hat doesn't make you a captain. If I had a hat, it wouldn't make me Deputy for Reason."

55

"I told you it was the hat they was shooting at," the Cook murmured to Jenny.

"I am not Captain because I wear the hat!" shouted Jenny. "I'm captain because I was commissioned so by an Otter with a Golden Collar, who gave me three things: a ship, a crew, and a Call to Adventure."

"A talking otter!" said the skinny boy scornfully. "She said it was a talking otter!"

Jenny whirled on him. "On my ship if you spoke that way about me or the Otter – who is Chief Pet to the Maid of Saltwaters – I would have you confined to the dark brig for a week while you scraped rust off the cannonballs," she hissed.

The Voyage of the Otter

"A cannon?" the boy said. "Would I get to fire it?"

"No," said Jenny.

Then the Deputy spoke again. "A commission from a talking animal must be obeyed," he said, seriously. "That is the Law of the Sea. Let us all return to our beds. Captain Jenny, I would be honoured if you and your crew would stay over, so that I may return tomorrow and see how we can help you with this Adventure."

Jenny bowed again.

"One more thing, Mr. Deputy," the Cook said. "What became of the friendly young Duke who ruled these parts when I was a boy?"

"Ah," said the Deputy. "Times changed, and the friendly young boy who was no longer a Duke grew older until he became suspicious, middle-aged, and duly elected. And now, good night!"

"Good night!" called all the sailors, and "Good night!" called the farmers with a friendly wave. And Sparky came out from the ship at last and began barking.

"Is that your dog?" the young boy asked Jenny. "My dog is much bigger."

"Good night," Jenny said.

THE DEPUTY – or the Duke, as the Cook still called him – was as good as his word. The next morning he rode up with a small troupe of servants, and there a festival began in the meadow where they'd made camp. Pavilions were put up; their friends from the night before – and many others – came by.

They roasted pigs; they made pies. The farmers and the sailors had tugs-of-war and ball games and foot races and wrestling matches. The sailors did only poorly at the foot races, for not spending much time on land, but the biggest and fattest sailor wrestled the village blacksmith to a draw. There was music (fiddles and bagpipes) and dancing, and Tom's dog raced about from one group of people to the next.

Three of the girls had a jump rope, and were playing a skipping game. And as they lived in the Corner by the Sea, their rhyme had a nautical flavour:

> *One wave, two waves, three waves rising*
> *Big water, sea water, oceans tall!*
> *Each wave's bigger, till it's surprising*
> *Anyone's left to count at all!*

57

Jenny watched them for a while, considering the words of the song. Then she cleared her throat. "I believe your song speaks of ancient things," she said. "I believe it speaks of the passing of the Lost City, which catastrophe occurred long before you were born, and far beyond the memory of anyone still alive. How did such young girls as you come to learn this rhyme?"

The girls paused in their skipping and stared at her, for Jenny was hardly any older than they were, even if she spoke in such an odd and formal way. And of course, it was strange that she was dressed like a captain.

"My cousin taught me," the oldest girl said, "but now that she's grown and married, she's forgot."

"And this cousin," said Jenny, "was it that she was taught this rhyme by some grandmother, or elderly Wise Woman, who perhaps lives nearby?"

The middle girl stared at her strangely. "You don't learn skipping songs from grandmothers or elderly Wise Women," she said. "You learn them from other girls."

"And who taught them?" Jenny wanted to know.

"*Other* other girls, or boys," the youngest girl said. "Grown-ups always forget them. Don't you know that?" Then they all stared at Jenny until finally the oldest girl held out the rope. "Do you want to take a turn?" she asked.

Jenny paused, and then she remembered that the sight of her skipping with the girls might impair her dignity in the eyes of the *Otter*'s crew. "No, thank you," she told them. "But that's fine skipping," she added. "Well done."

And while the girls stared, not sure what to make of her, Jenny wondered how long a rhyme could be remembered among girls and boys, when even grown-ups forgot them. Could they remember things that were older than Wise Women, older than books?

AFTER A WHILE, Jenny joined a group of her sailors watching a game of horseshoes. "This is the sort of celebration we usually have before we leave," said the sailors.

The Voyage of the Otter

"Not just sneaking out of harbour without so much as a kiss goodbye. That was unseemly."

"Yes," said Jenny, impatiently, while she watched the Carpenter, who was playing against one of the farmers. "But we usually aren't after getting orders from a school of flounders and an Otter with a Golden Collar either."

"Well," said the Cook, "if we sailed out of our own harbour so directly on Otter-orders, why are we stopping now?"

"For this is part of the Adventure already," Jenny said. "Don't you have provisions to see to?"

"The Duke has fitted us out with meat both fresh and salted, and dried peas, and portable soup," the Cook said. "Which will vary our diet tremendous."

"Well done, then," Jenny said, up on her dignity again. "Carry on."

59

The skinny boy from the night before had been watching the horseshoes too. "What's portable soup?" he asked.

"Soup boiled down to jelly," replied the Cook. "Then you puts it in water and boils it back up to soup."

"That sounds awful," the boy said.

"You won't be eating it," the Cook said, "so it's rude to say so."

"Can I come with you?" the boy asked.

"*No,*" Jenny and the Cook said together.

"I could be a better captain than her," the boy said, dancing around them. "My dog is bigger."

After a moment, the Cook said, "There's more to it than having a dog."

The Voyage of the Otter

"Go away, boy," Jenny said.

"I could get a hat, too," the boy said. "And don't call me 'boy,' it's rude. My name is Gimlet."

"Go away, Gimlet," Jenny and the Cook said together.

The Carpenter had just pitched a horseshoe that clanked as it landed against the iron spike. "A leaner, well thrown!" Jenny called, and "Good job, Chips, one point!" the Cook called.

But the boy Gimlet stuck his thumbs in his ears, waggled his hands, and made a raspberry noise. "Heroes get ringers but losers get leaners!" he called, and then ran away before the Cook could swat him.

"What an annoying and self-important child," Jenny said. The Cook stared at her for a moment, for he had often considered using similar words about Jenny, but for once he kept quiet.

"A 'gimlet,'" said the Carpenter, "is also a small tool used for drilling holes."

So the festival wore into evening and then night. The moon rose, and fires were lit, and the Cook served out hot *skillygally* (which was a kind of porridge, like most of his dishes that weren't a kind of stew). Then the Duke, or the Deputy as he was now called, came with some maps and charts and sat in the torchlight with Jenny and the First Mate to discuss the journey ahead.

"I shall give you this pennant, to signal that you are not

The Voyage of the Otter

Corsairs, and so ease your passage South," he said. "The great bay that lies South of the headlands of my country can probably be crossed on the open sea, saving you time and many alarms such as you raised among my people. After that, unless you wish to face the great Ocean to the West, you must stay close to shore, until you come to the Great Pillars. And if your little craft can make its way through the Pillars, you will have entered the Old Sea."

"The Sea of Wonders Found and Forgotten, the Sea of Heroes," Jenny said.

"Here we call it also the Sea of Corsairs," said the Deputy.

"And once in the Old Sea," Jenny said, "we are to make East for the Burning Mountain that is the lighthouse for the strait of Doom on the One Hand, or on the Other Hand, Doom."

61

The Duke looked at her. "You intend to sail this strait of manifold disaster?" he said. "For I am no mariner, but I know how sailors dread that passage."

Jenny nodded. "We must," she said. "And then make our way to the Navel of the World itself, and so find our bearings for the great market city of Babbylantium. There – well, perhaps there the Oracle will guide us."

Now the Duke looked at the First Mate, who nodded at him. "Even if we was to get no farther than the Navel of the World, we could dine on the tale for the rest of our lives," said the First Mate.

"But you mean to sail still farther East in your little

boat? East where storms and rumours of troubles and strife arise, East to the market of Babbylantium – and *then* the Oracle will guide you farther still, to the Lost City that no one yet has found?" asked the Deputy. "Indeed, you must be sailors of both great resource and immense courage." For the Deputy saw trouble on the charts spread before them, and he was worried for these strange, foolhardy visitors.

Jenny said: "This was the crew that sailed with my friend Tom aboard the *Volantix* and steered through the Eaves of the World, which no one else has done. Their courage and resource is in fact proverbial."

"But you were not their captain then," the Deputy said softly.

Jenny flushed, for she knew the Deputy spoke from concern rather than scorn, and that made his words harder to bear.

"An Otter with a Golden Collar has picked her to be our captain now," the First Mate said. "And it is the Law of the Sea that we go."

"Just so," said the Deputy. "An unexpected thing. But perhaps that is fitting, as finding the Lost City that sank beneath the waves will be the most unexpected thing of all."

Jenny looked down at the Duke's pennant, which was green and white. "Do you know anything about the Lost City?" she asked.

"Once I had a dream," their host replied. "I had a dream after I had lost being a Duke, and before I found being a

Deputy. In that dream the dolphins swam along streets that shone green in the light of lamps that burned below the sea. I swam after them, for you can swim very well in dreams."

"I can't," said the First Mate, "but always returns to the waking world before I drowns."

"Nevertheless, so it is for me," the Deputy replied. "And in my dream I asked where we swam, for I could speak in the water too. And the dolphins called back in strange voices that hung and echoed in the mazy water, 'We are in the city that sank beneath the waves and so was found.'"

The First Mate laughed. "For it's all in how you see it, you mean," he said. "Fair enough."

But Jenny was quiet for a moment, thinking of what her Godmother would say. "A dream of swimming or flying is of the highest order," she said. "Thank you for telling us of the place you found."

63

"You must all take care of each other, once you leave my company, to sail East, where troubles grow," the Deputy replied. "For although you are absurd, I have grown fond of you."

The next morning the *Otter* set out again, and was carried downstream to the sea. And when they reached the mouth of the river, they heard cannons fire a salute from the ruined towers, where the Deputy must have had sentries all along. And then they stepped the mast and set out to cross the Great Bay by the open sea, according to the Deputy's advice.

Jenny remembered that strange night of peace at the start of their Adventure for the rest of her life.

The Voyage of the Otter

IT WAS SOME TIME LATER that Jenny wrote an important letter, sealed it carefully in a bottle, and consigned it to the sea.

Jenny had written her message after the fashion of proper exploring captains, with many abbreviations to save space, and the free use of capital letters for emphasis:

By the hand of Jenny, Captain of the *Otter (commissioned by the Chief Pet to the Maid of Saltwaters)* –

Salutations to Reader of this Msg.:

All Tales confirm that in Dire Circumstances such as being Marooned, Shipwrecked, Captured by Pirates, & so forth, a Captain of Foresight will enclose an Account of how this came to be in bottle. Said bottle being consigned to Sea, it Invariably is carried through desire of King Beneath Sea to appropriate Person, which I believe in this case would be my friend Tom.

So, After leaving continental land of District 17 (formerly Duchy of Corner by Sea) w. Advice & good Wishes of Deputy (formerly good Duke), we effected a Crossing of Great Bay. Sailors hands growing used to oars, & Wind being at best crosswise to our intended course (S.S.W.), we stepped down mast and made our way Rowing in shifts through Days & Nights. Sailing mostly uneventful, & other Ships friendly as a result of Deputy (or Duke's) Pennant of Passage.

The Voyage of the Otter

Except 2nd night, when Rowing stopped for Commotion in forward hold, revealed to be result of Stowaway: one Gimlet, a tedious, implike Child who boarded *Otter* while we enjoyed Hospitality of Deputy.

Great palaver followed among crew, many solutions to problem of stowaway being proposed, such:

A – throwing him Overboard for being Impertinent, or
B – throwing him Overboard for being Unnecessary, then (both A & B being rejected as Cruel, though Satisfying)
C – wasting several Days in returning him Home (which tedious Imp himself protested as being pointless, for he would merely Stow away again, & besides he Hated his brothers for calling him Names, & was Mad at his Grandmother for making him go to Bed early, & Large Dog he had spoken of was only a Dog he wisht he had & not a Dog in Fact which required his Care), or
D – letting him Remain until there was convenient way to Dispose of him (though making tedious precaution that this not amount to Selling him to Corsairs), or again
E – throwing him Overboard for Wasting Our Time in so much Palaver.

Imp Gimlet then Sobbing & Running about Ship

The Voyage of the Otter

so as to make it nearly Capsize, I decided upon D, pro-visionally, & rated him Ship's Boy, in charge of all tedious lubber-work that might keep him out of our way. Other Nautical Terms were suggested for his Rating, particularly by Cook, such as Ship's Snotter, Fid-Brain, & Jackanapes, which led to General exchange of Opprobrium between Cook & Imp, such: *Peg leg! – Larrikin! – Barnacle-Back! – Lubber-Lad! – Brine-Breath!* – & so forth, ending w. Ship's Boy Gimlet falling Overboard from trying to evade Cook's Fist & having to be Fished w. much attendant Grumbling from crew, some saying plans A, B, or E had been effected by Fate & to Leave Well Enough Alone, before Charity Prevailed.

This being related, it remains only to add: after 4 Days & Nights at Sea, & several times in danger of being Swamped by Waves falling over her low sides, *Otter* made Land on other side of Great Bay. Which Coast we followed w. greater Security, running *Otter* in at Night again, for 1 wk. & 2 d.s. Various Farmers & fishers friendly but cautious, as rumours of desola-tion & calamity precede us. Rumours are rumours, but now our Charts suggest Pillars of Sea & their Real and Well-Known attendant Dangers await us Tomorrow.

Crew is in harmony, w. exception of tedious Imp, now Ship's Boy, Gimlet, & Cook, who must Now & Then be reminded Who is Captain & Who is Not.

The Voyage of the Otter

Please convey this to Tom, once of ship *Volantix* & to my Godmother, who is Wise Woman of Woods Nearby.

— Jenny, Captain of *Otter*, & so forth

P.S. *Otter* not yet in Dire Circumstances, but I had never put msg. in bottle before.

NOW THEY WERE come to the Southwest Corner of the Great Continent. It was a warm land, and the small beach where they had run up the *Otter* was still hot from the sun.

Around the beach were bluffs where scrub and broom bush grew, and white wild roses bloomed. North beyond the bluffs rose rocky hills dotted with cork oaks and what the Cook called *gummy trees*.

67

Jenny had thrown her bottle into the waves just as the sun set, and now they built a bonfire and ate the last of the provisions the Duke, as the Cook insisted on calling him, had given them.

It was as fine a moment as the Adventure ever had. For they had full stomachs and the warm sand beneath them. The breeze carried the pleasant scent of the gummy trees down to mix with the meaty smells of dinner. The fire was crackling, and small waves were breaking in the sea to the South, and the foam shone violet in the evening light.

Tom's dog dug frantically in the sand — in twelve different spots — until his nose was scraped pink.

The Voyage of the Otter

"Why does your dog dig so?" Gimlet asked Jenny. "He can't have anything buried, for he hasn't been here before."

"How do you know where this dog has been?" asked Jenny. "And as to the digging, it's in his nature."

The boy did three somersaults on the sand. "It's in my nature to do somersaults," he told Jenny.

"It's in your nature to bother others," said Jenny.

"It's in your nature to be grouchy and full of yourself," said Gimlet, and ran away before Jenny could kick him.

As Jenny had suggested in her message, the crew had grown used to the work of rowing the *Otter*, and their rough sailors' hands were more calloused than ever. In the last few days, as the land had begun to curve in towards the East, and the prevailing winds had matched their course, they'd often been able to use the sail again, but still the solid work had got the grumbles out of their system.

"For a crew sweats out both salt and discontent," the First Mate had said to Jenny. "And the boy makes you seem more tolerable-like by comparison. Begging your pardon for saying so."

And indeed as Sparky dug and Gimlet turned somersaults, the crew slowly got to their feet and set to dancing jigs and reels and hornpipes and singing all the songs they knew, both proper and rude. But Jenny sat with the First Mate and the Cook, for they were both old sailors of vast experience, and they smoked their pipes and discussed the passage though the Pillars, the passage into the Old Sea.

"You know what I say," announced the Cook. "I tried

it once before and we was wrecked by waterspouts. So let's just go far enough we can see the Pillars, and turn around and head for home and say we done what we could do."

"You didn't want to sail North in the *Volantix*, either, but we circumnavigated the world in the end," the First Mate pointed out.

"And got cold in the process," the Cook said, and he moved closer to the fire as he said it. "Almost froze solid, if you'll recall. But fine, let's go and be shipwrecked. Pay no attention to my reservations. I'm only the Cook, not a flounder or an otter or anything important of that nature."

"I don't want us shipwrecked either, but nonetheless we must make the passage," Jenny said. "We'll have a West wind, I'm thinking."

"True enough," said the First Mate. "So West wind and West water, and it'll all be running through the narrow Pillars."

"The whole Western sea," the Cook agreed. "Rising up as it squeezes through, and us sailing a small open galley."

Jenny pulled her cloak around her, for now she felt the breeze from the cliffs blowing down upon them. "Are you saying the Corsairs are better sailors than we?" Jenny asked. The two old sailors stared at her, and she went on. "For tales, history, the *Representative Encyclopædia*, the people of the Corner by the Sea, and your own testimony suggest Corsairs have made the crossing in open galleys like ours countless times, often burdened by slaves and plunder."

"We'll make the passage," the First Mate said. "We was

only discussing the contingent difficulties."

"Of course we will," said Jenny. "And the King Beneath the Sea looks favourably upon our Adventure, and we have Tom's dog along for luck."

"We'll make the passage, missy – captain-missy – Jenny," the Cook agreed. "But then it's the Corsairs for sure."

As it got darker yet, some of the junior sailors began to repeat awful stories they'd heard about the passage of the Pillars.

"There the seas are mixed and terrible!" one cried, "There shipwrecks crowded the floor of the sea!" cried another, while a third added, "And there among the wrecks crabs make their homes in the skulls of drowned sailors!"

The two sailors from amidships shuddered at that. "We almost died in the North," they said, "but at least the cold would have spared our dead skulls the indignities of the crab!"

"Now, look," said the Carpenter, for he was a steady old hand. "The stars themselves are a good omen for our trip."

And the crew all stopped their moaning, for sailors are a superstitious lot, and they were keen to have the stars read for them. "Her," by which the Carpenter meant the moon, "Her isn't showing tonight, so the tides will be high. But there in the South, there's a bright planet, like a little moon itself, come to light us in her place."

The Voyage of the Otter

70

"And to the West, Chips?" asked the First Mate, though he knew the answer well enough.

"To the West," Chips said, "to the West, see the Hunter almost gone from sight, for he chases after the land of stories, which is always disappearing."

"And to the East?" the Cook asked, "the East where trouble is born?" For he knew that's where they headed, East towards the Pillars, and the Old Sea, and somewhere farther still the Lost City.

"To the East," the Carpenter said, "now, to the East, see the Champion of Heaven rise, to mark the Pillars which we seek."

"And to the North?" Jenny asked. "For the Queen of the Hall of the Stars is unseen. Are we too far from her home?"

71

"But the Queen does watch tonight," said the Carpenter. "Her throne is only hidden by the hills. Climb those cliffs and you will see it, low in the North, close by the Great Bear and the North Star."

Then the sailors fell quiet, for they were remembering how they had sailed aboard the *Volantix*, and been lost in the North – and how young Tom had dared to climb greater cliffs than these, had climbed a mountain of ice, hoping to find help in the Hall of the Stars.

And that had all turned out fine, which encouraged the sailors.

It encouraged Jenny too, for she was proud of her friend Tom. And a little jealous.

The tallest structure Jenny had seen

CHAPTER FIVE:
THEY WERE SAILORS,
AND THIS WAS THE SEA

THE NEXT DAY, THE *Otter* ATTEMPTED THE PASSAGE INTO the Old Sea.

Jenny and the First Mate and the Cook had all been right; as the seas narrowed before the Pillars of the Sea, the whole rush of wind and wave that had been gathering across the Ocean to the West grew high.

The weather of half the world was shouldering together, racing the *Otter* to the Pillars.

THE *Otter's* MAST had been stepped down, lest the gusting, unsettled wind toss them off their course. Somewhere above, the sun shone, but the towering waves and the foam and spray about them hid the sky.

Jenny and the First Mate stood together at the helm, as they had before, while the Cook beat out a quick time to keep the crew rowing in short, hard strokes. The wind and waves were carrying the *Otter* swiftly, but they needed to row, to row like mad, to keep steerage way. For if they let the waves overtake the *Otter*, there'd be no way to keep it heading forward and the galley would soon turn its side to the wind, and then the waves would crash over it, and then they would join the wrecks at the bottom of the sea.

When the *Otter* rose up on a wave, Gimlet would run down along the gangway to the stern, screaming with pleasure, while the crew dug their oars into the water to keep from falling back, to keep from being swallowed by the next wave. The Cook would curse at him, using language that was foul even for a sailor, but in the tumult of the sea no one could hear.

Then for a moment the ship would ride the crest of the wave, and when it finally began to tip down the other side, Gimlet would turn around and run screaming to the dipping bow. This went on until Jenny caught him by the collar and lashed him to a thwart with a half-hitch knot. "Scream at that if you want," Jenny yelled over the thunder of the sea (he did, too), "but we won't be hearing you."

"Well done," the First Mate told Jenny when she came back to help brace the steering oar. But Jenny said nothing, only stared ahead as they crested a wave. And she would have screamed too, if she hadn't remembered her dignity.

For ahead of them was the tallest structure that Jenny had seen. The sea was rushing ahead through two great cliffs, and each had been carved into a pillar, great pillars that seemed to touch the sky. And the waves that pushed through seemed at least half that tall.

It was good that the crew was busy at their oars, and so faced backwards, Jenny thought. Only she and the First Mate looked ahead, and the First Mate would keep steady,

Jenny told herself. And she would keep steady, she told herself. Jenny looked at the Cook, who faced them from where he sat in the bow beating out the time.

This was what the Cook had seen when he had crossed into the Old Sea before, and he knew from Jenny's face that now she was seeing it too. He didn't bother to turn and look himself, but for once he thought Jenny deserved a nod. At least a nod, for having looked ahead and seen those waves, waves that towered halfway to the sky, and yet to keep on.

"I am not speechless!" Jenny shouted at the First Mate, for she wouldn't admit to being humbled, not yet.

"Humbling, I calls it," the First Mate shouted back. And the Cook gave him a nod too. For even a grizzled sailor of vast experience might have quailed to be in an open galley, and see the Pillars and the tall seas that ran them, but the First Mate never let the steering oar quiver.

Jenny shook her head. "Staggering!" she said, having found at least one word. "Staggering!" Her heart was thumping, and her thoughts were racing wildly, and the salt spray all around made her face wet with cold tears. She saw the First Mate glancing at her. "If these tears are mine, I give them back to the Maid of Saltwaters!" she cried in frustration.

He nodded. "An appropriate libation for such as She," he called. "An offering, like!" And his face too was wet, of course.

Then as they rose again on a wave, Jenny saw that as the strait came to its most narrow, there was a confusion in the sea before the Pillars. The waves roiled about, not sure of pushing on. Nothing could be more dangerous than such a spot, but as the sea paused, so must they.

Down they went into the trough of a wave, Gimlet still screaming with his idiot delight, poor Sparky barking in Jenny's little cabin below the quarterdeck, where he had gone to keep safe. And then they were in the midst of it, pitching and tossing wildly, back and forth, right and left, as great and little waves assailed them in a pattern only an astrologer could have understood.

"Ease off!" Jenny called to the Cook, for there was no racing now, only keeping the little blue ship from being broached, or pooped, or otherwise swamped, and the crew needed to rest before the last push.

And a good rest seemed to come, for despite how hard Jenny and the First Mate leaned against the rudder, the *Otter* slipped towards the cliffs at the Southern end of the passage. Then it took all of their skill, and a great deal of luck, not to smash against the high rock wall. Instead they found entrance to a shelter, a stony cove set in the cliff. The cove was high with foam; the cove had unlikely creatures with too many legs and too many eyes looking down from wet ledges, surprised to have been pulled up from the depths of the sea.

From that shelter, Jenny and her crew could at least watch the troubled sea, and if it terrified Gimlet and some of the junior sailors, Jenny began to make sense of it. After much confusion, the sea would gather into an enormous wave, and then rise up toward the Pillars, and fall back.

And then another wave, just as large, would form, rise up towards the Pillars, and then fall back, and so on. But on the seventh wave, the sea seemed to pause before the trial, sucking the water from their little cove as it formed a great rolling crest, a crest that shook the mountains as it surged through the Pillars at last.

"That's the one," called the Carpenter, who had been working out the pattern too. And it was. For if they attempted the Pillars on the smaller waves, they would fall back and be pitched end-over-end.

But just as they understood how the seventh, mighty wave was their hope, the water rushed back into their shelter. The *Otter* rose up with the sea, and suddenly struck hard against the side of the cove.

"We're half stove-in!" cried the two sailors amidships. "Half stove-in!" And now Gimlet had given up screaming but was only sobbing, and as the *Otter* began taking in water, Jenny heard Sparky howling with horror in the little cabin beneath her.

"Row!" cried Jenny through her speaking-trumpet. "Pull hard, all hands! Out into the tumult, row!" Everyone saw this was their one chance, and as the water in the cove began to drain away again, they pulled into the tossing sea.

Normally two of them were always taking a turn to rest idle in the bow, but now even the idlers sat beside the two sailors amidships to share their oars. Jenny even untied Gimlet so he could help one of the smaller sailors, and sat down beside another herself.

The Voyage of the Otter

"I hate you!" Gimlet yelled at Jenny, and then more generally, "I hate you all!" But he tried to row anyway, and the others ignored him.

Now a wave was gathering under them, and they backed oars like mad, for they needed to let it pass, and then they were in the dark trough of the sea and beginning to slew again, and they had to row forward to keep their way. Another wave was forming, higher still, but they needed to let it pass too.

And when the seventh wave, the mighty wave, began to rise up, they could feel the change in the sea, and in the air; and in the East the Pillars themselves seemed to hum with the force of it. Jenny was yelling to row hard, but no one paid her any attention, for they were all yelling now, yelling from fear and excitement, and the strangest kind of pleasure. For they were sailors, and this was the sea.

Now they were racing the wave as it built, and trying to stay near its crest, rowing until they stretched flat on their backs with each pull. For if they fell back into the trough, that would be the end of them; the *Otter* would turn its flank, the sea would come over its low sides, and they would be swallowed.

And suddenly they were riding the wave, almost at its top, looking down at the great drop below. The Northern Pillar was far off to port, but just for a moment, a long moment as the *Otter* hung in the sky, Jenny saw the Southern Pillar very near indeed. She saw that the fluted sides were almost worn smooth; she noticed that someone – how? – had written a message there, halfway to the sky. But she had no time to read it, or even see what language it was in.

Then time began to move on again. They started to fall forward with the wave. And the water crashed over their heads as they rowed desperately to keep ahead. But they swept through the Pillars. Through the Pillars and on and on at a tremendous clip, until the wave spread out through the widening sea, and grew gentle at last.

They were drenched and near drowned, and the side of the *Otter* was half stove-in. They were up to their knees in water. But it was warm water, for they were under a sunny blue sky, and in the Old Sea at last, the Sea of Heroes, the Sea of Wonders Found and Forgotten.

Jenny cried aloud with joy and relief, and then she rushed to get Sparky out of her little cabin. She hugged him while he licked her face, and told him what a brave dog he was.

79

The sailors gasped and groaned, but it was the First Mate who spoke first, "The Sea of Heroes is a fitting name," he said.

ALL THE REST OF THAT DAY and into the night, they kept East (East by Northeast, to be precise), for they had raised their mast and sail again to carry them along while they bailed water.

"No waterspouts," the Cook said, to pass the time. "Yet."

"Nevertheless, that was a mighty passage, and I am

proud of this ship and crew," said Jenny.

"Who made the Pillars?" asked the two sailors amidships.

"Some say it was always so, since the world was born," said the First Mate.

"And some say it was the Champion of Heaven, who is so strong he can bend the truth," said the Cook.

To her delight, Jenny had found that while everything she had – including Sparky – had been thoroughly soaked in the crossing of the Pillars, her pocket-sized *Representative Encyclopædia* had been made in some strange, waterproof way and so survived intact.

"Here's what Tom's Dad wrote on the matter," she said, "'It is in the nature of some rock to form like crystal into pillars. But whether the Pillars that guard the Old Sea have been revealed by the action of the waves, or whether the Champion of Heaven found them when he cracked the mountain open with his fist is a subject which deserves more extended treatment.'"

"He means he doesn't know!" said one sailor. The others cried out in surprise: "Imagine Tom's Dad not knowing!" "A deep matter indeed!" "A mystery for the ages!" and so on.

"The ship isn't rocking and twisting now," Gimlet told Jenny, who tried to ignore him. "Why couldn't you sail it this way in the Pillars?"

"That is not the way for the Ship's Boy to address his captain," said the First Mate, sternly. "Now mind your bailing, like the rest of us."

The Voyage of the Otter

EVENTUALLY, they had bailed enough that the water only came up to their ankles, rather than their knees – but of course, all the time more was pouring in where the *Otter's* side had struck the wall of the cove. Now the Carpenter took charge.

"If you'd all crowd along to port, I'd be obliged," he said.

So the rest of them moved, and their weight kept the left side of the ship low in the water – dangerously low – while the right side, the damaged starboard side, rose up. The Carpenter worked on the broken planking as quickly as he could, using shims and brackets and clamps and plugs. And then when he was done with his tools he organized the others to pull a wide patch of sailcloth under the galley and fasten it so it was tight across the bottom of the hull.

"You put a bandage on the ship!" Gimlet exclaimed.

"A proper sailor would know it is not a bandage, but a *fother,*" said the First Mate.

"What's a fother?" asked Gimlet.

"Like a bandage," the Cook explained. "For a ship."

And it did work like a bandage, so that now the water oozed only slowly into the *Otter.* "That'll see us into harbour, if we keep up the bailing," said the Carpenter. "If we find a harbour soon."

"Likely we won't, but will drown instead," said the Cook, taking the chance to be miserable when he could. "Now who's for fish jerky?"

But as they drifted East into the night, East where the stars of the Champion of Heaven rose, few of them

81

The Voyage of the Otter

doubted they'd see a harbour soon. For they had made the Pillars, and the wind was warm and gentle, and their oars lifted sparks from the water to match the constellations.

Just then something leapt over the bow of the *Otter*, trailing water that glowed in the evening air. "A dolphin!" the sailors cried happily, for dolphins are friends to all sea-farers, who consider them good luck. Two more dolphins followed, chattering in the air. Sparky barked after them as though they were squirrels.

And after Jenny and Sparky retired to her little cabin again, the two sailors amidships dared to whisper what all the crew were thinking: "Jenny might be a fine captain after all."

Jenny was already drifting off to sleep, with Sparky curled beside her. But she thought she might be a fine captain, too.

82

IN THE MIDDLE OF THE NIGHT, with her little cabin dark but for the light of the Great Way amidst the stars, Jenny woke, or dreamt she woke, and looked up at the portrait of the Otter with a Golden Collar. The Otter still looked regal and self-important, and he leaned down out of the painting and pulled a watch from his waistcoat.

"Here the time is running out for you to find the Lost City, and you lie asleep in my ship with a dog on your stomach," the Otter said. "Although I am not really sur-prised, since I never expected a young girl could possibly succeed in this Adventure." At that Sparky looked up at the Otter and made a noise Jenny had never heard before.

"Here it is hardly two weeks since you spoke to me and already we sail in the Old Sea," Jenny said. "The Sea of Heroes, the Sea of Wonders Found and Forgotten. I count that good time."

"Yes," said the Otter. "I imagine a young girl would." Then he looked around the cabin as Jenny glared at him. "I smell fish jerky," he pointed out.

Jenny might have lost her temper, but she tried to think of how calm and reasonable Tom would be. "And would you like some?" she asked.

"No, for I am a picture in a frame," the Otter pointed out, as if Jenny hadn't noticed. "Nonetheless, it is polite to ask."

"Have you woken me only to carp?" Jenny asked, forgetting about Tom already. "Or do you have a rede, warning, or other manner of advice?"

83

"Do you *have* a carp?" asked the Otter. "For, perhaps you are too young to understand that it is rude to mention such things without offering.

"'Carp' in the sense of complain, not fish," Jenny said. "And I believe it is also accounted rude to wake a sailor for no good purpose."

Then the Otter smiled and leaned out of the picture frame almost close enough to touch. Tom's dog crept backwards, but did not take his eyes off the creature. "And *are* you awake?" the Otter asked.

Now this might have baffled most sailors, and most captains, even if they weren't still girls, but Jenny was acquainted with this sort of quibbling from knowing her

Godmother all her life. "Are *you* awake?" she asked the Otter back. "And how would you know?"

The Otter frowned for a moment and decided to ignore the question. "In the Passage of the Pillars, you offered your tears to the Maid of Saltwaters," he said. "And so she has become inexplicably fond of you and *has* sent me to provide advice: Your ship is being borne to an island of goats ruled by a Mad Philosopher," he said. "For it needs repair and you need fresh water. From there you may sight the Burning Mountain, the Lighthouse of the Ancients which marks the strait of Doom on the One Hand, or On the Other Hand, Doom."

"Felicitations to the Maid of Saltwaters," Jenny said, by which she meant, she sent her best wishes. "And my thanks for the aid and advice of her Chief Pet," by which she meant to keep on the good side of the Otter, unlikely as that seemed.

The Otter bowed politely. "But that was only information," he said. "This is the advice: Do not antagonize this Mad Philosopher, for he has command of the seas about his island, and do not trouble his animals, for in his loneliness they have become his friends."

"My thanks again," said Jenny. "And we shall leave his animals in peace, and keep this Mad Philosopher complaisant. What is the name of this island?"

"The Island of Philosophy," said the Otter, lighting a pipe. "Also, the Island of Fools."

The little cabin soon grew hazy from smoke, but Jenny knew there was something else she needed to know. "And the Lost City, how shall we find it?" she asked.

"I thought you were a great Explorer already at your tender age," said the Otter, "who would hardly need the help of a humble Otter. But I don't know how you imagine to find the Lost City when it is sunk beneath the waves."

"Perhaps you entertain the Maid of Saltwaters with such fooling," said Jenny. "But I am not a fool to be put off by your quibbles."

The Otter gazed at her steadily. "*If* you survive the Strait of Dooms, and *if* you find your way to the Navel of the World and so to the Oracle of Babbylantium, you must sail for the Clashing Rocks at the narrows of the Old Sea. Beyond that there is little reason for me to bother giving you guidance."

"For the way is so clear?" asked Jenny.

"For the Rocks are almost always fatal," said the Otter. And then he blew a smoke ring at Jenny.

The smoke made Jenny's eyes water, and so she blinked, and when she opened them again, she saw the bright face of dawn through the skylights. Sparky was fast asleep on her stomach, and her nose told her that somehow the Cook had managed to brew some of the coffee that Tom's Dad had sent along.

But the Otter in the portrait was now holding a pipe.

"LAND!" cried Gimlet from the top of the mast, where the Cook had suggested he go in order to better smell the breakfast. "I see land!"

The Voyage of the Otter

"Well enough," said the First Mate. "But a proper sailor would cry, *'Land, ho!'*"

"Gimlet's Land, ho!" cried Gimlet, sliding down the rigging to the prow of the ship. "I saw it first, it is mine, and it will be called after me. I found Gimlet's Land! Hooray!"

The sailors ignored him, of course, except to rise up and look themselves. And off the starboard bow, they saw a small island, shining bright under the morning sun. "It is bare and rocky," said the Cook, and, "A ribbon of smoke rises from its peak," said the First Mate.

"I shall plant a flag on that peak!" said Gimlet. "I have my own island! None of my brothers has an island, just me!"

"It is named 'The Island of Philosophy,' for it is a Philosopher who rules over it already, not you," said Jenny. "Although it is also called 'The Island of Fools,' so you may yet have title. There are goats and fresh water, and there we will mend our ship."

The sailors stared at her, impressed. "How do you know what it is called," and "How did you know what we will find?" asked the two sailors amidships.

Jenny swallowed the last of her coffee, stood up, and straightened her hat. "It's a captain's business to know such things," she said.

AFTER THEY REACHED the Island of Philosophy, the sailors ran the *Otter* up onto the beach. Then Jenny repeated her orders: "He is a mad philosopher," she said, "and will curse and otherwise bane our voyage if we antagonize him, or trouble the goats and animals, who are his friends. So leave him be atop the hill, and if you meet him be polite, or" – and here she stared at the Ship's Boy, who was walking backwards on his hands – "or keep quiet if you don't know how."

The crew all nodded and promised to be sensible, or at least quiet, and not to trouble either the Philosopher or his animals.

"Why is he called the *Mad* Philosopher?" asked Gimlet, still upside down. "Has he lost his wits after being alone so long on my island?"

Just then they heard footsteps on the rocky ledge that overhung the beach. A man with dark, shaggy hair and an unkempt beard stood above them, leaning on a shepherd's crook. His blue cloak had a deep hood, and beneath it his brow was furrowed.

87

"I am mad, for fools on my island make me angry," the strange man declared. "I am mad, for having been exiled here with nothing to read but books I write myself. And I am mad, for having only my own philosophies and the inarticulate disputations of my animals filling my head for years and years." And as he spoke, they saw clouds begin to gather in the sky.

"And since you arrive and seek the privilege of strangers *now,* just as the very waves of the Old Sea carry rumours of turmoil and strife, and plague and desolation – now I am mad at you," the Philosopher said.

CHAPTER SIX:
"I HAVE EMPLOYED TOO MUCH TACT"

After the stern and ominous words from the Philosopher, it was Jenny who recovered her wits first. For again, if you were the Goddaughter of Wise Woman of the Woods Nearby, you would be accustomed to speaking with disputatious authorities, too.

"All that you mention –" Jenny called up to the Mad Philosopher, who still looked down upon them while the skies grew troubled above his head, "the worrying of your animals, the lack of intelligent converse, and the presence of visiting fools – must be a terrible vexation to the heart and soul of a Great and Wise Personage such as yourself."

Now the Philosopher might have been Mad, but he knew flattery when he heard it, and he liked to hear it.

"It is," he said.

"You have a very hairy face!" yelled Gimlet, who, if he had ever cared about Jenny's orders to keep quiet, had forgotten them already. The Philosopher looked at Gimlet balefully, and pointed the end of the shepherd's crook at him.

The rest of the crew began to cower. "Not the crook!" whimpered the two sailors from amidships. "Not the crook! We'll be transmogrified!" they told each other.

Then the First Mate, who was always brave without making a fuss over it, stepped up in front of Gimlet. "Technically," he told the Philosopher, "the boy Gimlet is not a fool, but only a *lubber*, just beginning to understand the ways of the sea, and so has not yet learned how to speak to a Great and Wise Personage. The defect in his instruction is mine, most likely."

"See that the omission is mended," said the Philosopher. He was still gruff, but the sun had appeared from the clouds again. "One of you must follow me as Embassy and justify your continued existence."

Obviously, that would have to be Jenny. "Don't worry," she told the others. "I shall mollify him with tact."

JENNY AND SPARKY went up the winding path after the Philosopher. It was hard keeping up with him, for he was a large man with long legs. And when he had to stop now and then to wait for them, he frowned at Jenny as if it was her fault she hadn't grown faster.

The path was made of small white rocks set into the rough ground. It was poor soil, Jenny thought, but from the warmth and the damp, enough grew that the small goats seemed to find plenty to eat. Dozens of them grazed over the heights of the island, poking into ledges where shrubs grew, bounding down to small meadows of patchy grass.

Finally, they neared the peak of the island, where a rude house had been made from stones set together so cunningly that the walls stood without board or mortar. Up here, where they saw the blue seas stretching out far around them, the wind tossed their hair, and swirled the Philosopher's cloak. And the wind was cold, and Jenny understood why the Philosopher kept a fire burning.

He adjusted the hood on his cloak, and knocked on the driftwood door with his staff. The door swung open by itself, and they went inside. Then Jenny began trying to account for their existence, which is harder than it sounds.

BACK ON THE BEACH, the sailors were making the best of their time. All the long, warm day most of them laboured under the directions of the Carpenter, trying to mend the *Otter* properly.

But they also needed more fresh water, for most of their casks had been tainted by the salt sea in the crossing of the Pillars. So the two sailors from amidships went looking for a spring, and then they spent the hot afternoon rolling empty casks up the path to fill them, and then slowly bringing full ones back to shore.

Amidst all this sweating work, Gimlet couldn't settle on whether it was more fun to stand on the small water barrels as they were rolled along, or better to try to use the Carpenter's tools to modify the design of the *Otter*. Finally, the Cook told him it would be most fun of all to run up the hillside and pretend he was one of the goats.

And all the long day, the First Mate would look up at

the peak of the island and wonder about Jenny. He saw the wind about the peak pull the tail of smoke to the East, and he saw a raven sporting in the air.

"Ravens are ominous birds, which are usually only waiting for something bad to happen," he observed to the Cook.

"They're wise birds," said the Cook. "For then they eats what's left over."

So they worked, and sweated, until the Carpenter declared the sides of the *Otter* were as good as new, until there was a new coat of black pitch sealing the bottom and a new layer of blue paint on the side, until they had all the fresh water they would need.

And then at last the First Mate saw Jenny coming back down the hill, looking more weary than any of them. She held Gimlet by the collar, and Sparky trotted along behind her.

She drank some fresh water and looked at the blue ship.

"Did he grant us the privilege of strangers?" asked the Carpenter.

"Was he mollified by your tact?" asked the Cook.

"Did he feel our existence was justified?" asked the First Mate.

But Jenny only asked, "Are we ready to sail in the morning?"

AND THE *Otter* would have been ready to sail, but during the night the kind West wind fell away.

The Voyage of the Otter

91

Of course, Jenny woke when the wind changed, for her tent read the air as well as any sail, and she crawled out in the moonless darkness. "We must be quiet," she whispered to Sparky. "Like a good dog, quiet." Then they tiptoed out through the snoring sailors, and they crept up the hill, all the way to the Philosopher's house.

There on the peak of the island, with the wind blowing about her, Jenny first looked North to find the Great Bear, and the Throne of the Queen. Right overhead, the stars of the Champion of Heaven shone, while to the South all was dark, and not even the bright planets showed. But in the East the Great Way stretched across the sky. And beneath it, set on the black rim of the sea, something glowed red and smoking.

92

"Look, Sparky," she whispered, "the Lighthouse of the Ancients, the Burning Mountain that marks the way to the Navel of the World. We are on the right way, and only need to sail East."

And it was then that she heard the Philosopher begin to snore, and felt the wind begin to shift. Soon there was a steady blow from Southeast, hot and damp. It was not the wind that would carry them to the Burning Mountain.

BACK AT THE CAMP, Jenny found the Cook was already starting to make breakfast, while the First Mate sat beside him by the fire.

"We heard the wind change in the night," the Cook

said. "Your tent flaps like a canvas sail, and we heard it. It's hot and steady and damp."

"It's a foul wind, captain," the First Mate said. "Dusty and sticky, both at once."

Jenny looked at the canvas of her tent quivering, and out in the grey sea the waves breaking as they rolled Northwest. "We can't make headway sailing into that," she agreed.

"And we can't row against it neither, no one could," said the First Mate.

"We could take it as an omen," put in the Cook. "And sail back the way we came."

"We shall be stout and patient and wait out this mindless wind," said Jenny. And when all the rest had woken to feel the changed air and look out at the grey waves, "We shall be stout and patient," Jenny repeated again.

But after breakfast, when the sun was high and warm and the sailors feeling the itchy heat of the wind that held them, the Philosopher appeared once more on the ledge above their camp.

"You are still here," he rumbled, "and trespass once more on my hospitality. This requires further justification."

Jenny got up slowly.

"I want to pretend I'm a goat again!" Gimlet cried.

"Don't let him," Jenny told the others. "For if goats find him as galling as sailors do, he will put us all in peril."

And then Jenny and Sparky followed the Philosopher

The Voyage of the Otter

back up the hills to his hut. It was a long climb, and the hot, itchy wind followed them all the way.

THE FOUL WIND KEPT ON, day after day, and for Jenny and the sailors, each day was much like the last, tedious and uncomfortable. The sailors took the *Otter*'s sail and raised it on the ends of the oars to make an awning, and sat in its shade.

But even in the shade the air was bad, and the sailors grew bored, of course, and hot and itchy and irritable, and argued interminably amongst themselves.

One day, some began to claim it was even worse being marooned here on the Island of Philosophy than it had been when they sailed aboard the *Volantix* and were stuck in the ice. "For there we were cold, but could warm up by the fire now and then, but here even the seas are hot, and there is no relief."

"No," said others, "for though we are hot all day, still at night it grows cool, and we can dip in the sea."

"Well, the company here is much the worse, all the same," some said.

"The company is much the same, for we were all there, and now we're all here," the Carpenter pointed out.

"But now instead of the stout Captain of the *Volantix*, we have this girl Jenny instead." said the Cook. "And rather than brave young Tom, we have *him*." And he pointed his head at the Ship's Boy, who was sitting in a

throne he had made of sand, pretending to issue procla-
mations.

"I sit in this throne, for I am your King, Gimlet, Ruler
of Gimlet's Land!" the Ship's Boy told his imaginary audience. "Tremble when I speak!" But of course everyone just
tried to ignore him.

"The Ship's Boy is a lubber yet, it's true," the First Mate
told the Cook. "But Jenny's a fine Captain, who took us
through the Pillars, which few would dare. And if you're
comparing the warm Old Sea to the icy Eaves of the
World, don't forget that when we sailed North we was not
just, just – "

"Cold?" one of the sailors from amidships said, trying
to help out. "Freezing?" suggested the other.

The First Mate stared at them, for he was proud of his
fine language. "Those are hardly sufficient terms for the
chilly terror we was facing," he said. "The word I was
framing was – *horripilated*. And not just horripilated, but
nearly starved."

"Well, we might starve here, too," said the Cook. "For
the food the good Duke gave us is gone, even the portable
soup, and now the *Otter*'s fish runs low as well."

The sailors began to moan then, but several of them
pointed out that whereas they had found no game to hunt
in the North, here on the Island of Philosophy, or Fools,
there were goats in plenty.

"Hush, now!" said the First Mate. "For you know we
are ordered to leave the goats alone."

The Voyage of the Otter

"True," said the Cook. "Which is a pity. For goats make fine eating." Then he sighed, and all the crew began to consider the matter. They smiled wistfully, for good as the Cook was, fish jerky was still fish jerky, and a sailor's least-favourite dish.

"Roast leg of goat," one said, and their mouths began to water. "Goat stew," another said, and the sailors moaned with yearning. "Skewered goat!" they called. "Goat pie!" "Fricasseed goat!" "Northern goat-guts pudding!" and so on. They described ways of preparing goat that no cook had yet imagined, and then described some more.

Gimlet's mouth watered more than anyone's, and now he rose up and pointed at the Cook. "Goat pie! Yes, Lord Gimlet commands his Cook to make goat pie!"

"Fun's fun," the First Mate warned the boy, "but it's not for the Ship's Boy to speak to his betters in such a way."

But Gimlet had become too cranky to care. "Quiet, mould-beard," he told the First Mate. "King Gimlet speaks!"

And that was too much for the Cook. He got out from the shade of the awning, grabbed a stick of driftwood, and started towards Gimlet. "No more fun and games!" he cried. "Your disrespect has earned a thrashing!"

Gimlet scrambled off his throne, and up the path to the top of the ledge. "You can't catch me, old peg leg!" he cried. And from on top of the ledge he stared at them all, put his thumbs in his ears and waggled his fingers. Then he ran off.

Now the Cook's face was red from heat and anger and

dripping sweat. "It would be a pity," he said slowly to the rest of the crew, "if some accident befell that child."

"When will the wind change?" asked one of the sailors from amidships, to change the subject. "When will we leave this island?" asked the other.

AND *When will we leave this island?* was the question Jenny had asked herself every day, of course. For every day they were on the island, she led Tom's dog up the winding path after the Philosopher.

And if the long days of questions were gruelling for Jenny, who felt that a wrong answer might doom them all, they were boring for Sparky. For the stone house at the top of the island was not very interesting to explore; it had only one large room, with a big, rough table, and a huge fireplace.

The room also smelled of the Philosopher's orange cat, which might have caused trouble. But since the cat stayed safely out of reach up on the mantle, and since Sparky was a faithful but timid dog, the animals developed a sort of truce. Sparky could loll by fire on the floor; the cat could sleep on the mantle above, and they would ignore one another, and wait for something to happen.

"Why are you here?" the Mad Philosopher would demand some days, and whatever Jenny answered he would follow with a hundred harder questions.

Or, "Why do you wear those absurd blue glasses?" the

97

The Voyage of the Otter

Philosopher would ask on other days. Or, "Why does anything exist?" Or, "Which came first, the Chicken or the Egg?" And if Jenny didn't answer to his satisfaction – which was almost impossible – he would become dangerously agitated.

That day, he had begun by asking what the purpose of the whole Exploration was, which had led Jenny to talk about, first, Maxim Tortuca, and then, the Otter with a Golden Collar who had appeared to her out of the foam, and finally, about the Lost City that sank beneath the waves. None of it seemed to satisfy the Philosopher.

"The foolishness of the whole endeavour – of Exploration itself – is breathtaking!" he said. He gestured at the dozens of books (bound in goatskin) that were piled about his table. "For you can't find things without first knowing the words for them."

"What do you mean?" asked Jenny, with what she imagined was appropriate humility.

"Well, what would you report if you found something at this Lost City which you couldn't describe?" the Philosopher demanded.

"That I had found a mystery," Jenny said.

"Only a mystery because you didn't know the word for it," he told her. "And if you did know the word, it wouldn't be a mystery, and so wouldn't need finding in the first place."

"But where do the words come from?" Jenny asked.

The Philosopher thumped the end of his crook on the

stone floor. "*That's* my employment on the Island of Philosophy," he shouted at her. "That's what I fill my books with. I labour in solitude to construct words so that things can be understood without having first to be found." With that he stomped out, and walked around his stone house to recover his composure.

Day after day of this, Jenny thought. *I shall go as mad as the Philosopher.* She contemplated the future, and for a moment, it seemed too grim to bear: an endless span of lonely debate.

Then suddenly she understood. "Sparky!" she whispered. "He *is* mad! This daily wrangling – he likes it. The foul wind that keeps us here is by his direction. We are company to him." Sparky got to his feet then, and walked over to Jenny.

99

"I am sorry and amazed," Jenny whispered to the dog. "For I have never before employed too much tact." Then they waited for the Philosopher's return.

The Voyage of the Otter

The Philosopher, waving his crook in fury

CHAPTER SEVEN:
DAWN FOUND THEM WAKING ON A STRANGE SHORE

W HEN THE PHILOSOPHER CAME BACK IN, HE WAS huffing from his walk, but he looked calmer. And if Jenny wasn't calmer, at least she had a plan.

"I have been considering your talk of constructing words," Jenny said.

"So you now understand your foolishness?" said the Philosopher.

"No," said Jenny. "For on reflection, your speech seemed mere flummery and balderdash."

The Philosopher opened his mouth in astonishment, and Jenny wondered if she had gone too far. "Or perhaps an example of your work would speed my comprehension," she said.

"An example," the Philosopher said, beginning to sweat around his brow. "An example. Very well. Before my thoughts were disturbed by the arrival of your ship, I was contemplating the circle and its qualities. Roundness, for example. Now, what would the opposite of a circle be? Well?" He looked at Jenny first, and then Sparky.

Jenny thought hard, not just about circles, but about how to annoy the Philosopher enough to become unwelcome, without being so rude as to actually provoke his wrath. "Well?" demanded the Philosopher, as he struck his crook against the floor.

"A circle is a continuous line, which at all points is at equal distance from a centre," said Jenny quickly (and any captain who knew how to use maps would have said the same). "Its opposite would be...a disconnected line...which at all points, is at unequal distance from...." And there she stopped and looked out the window, for she had lost her way.

"No!" shouted the Philosopher. And as he shouted, the skies grew dull, and thunder rolled over the hilltop. "You prove yourself a fool again. This whole island, they're all fools, goats, kids, sailors and all –"

By coincidence, it was just as the Philosopher said "fools," that Jenny saw Gimlet outside. After he fled from Cook's fury, he had wandered up the hill, and now, against all orders, he was chasing goats again. "But what *is* the opposite of a circle?" she asked quickly, to keep the Philosopher distracted.

"A circle is a perfect round, enclosing a space," said the Philosopher, as if he were talking to an idiot. "Therefore its opposite is a space, enclosed by a perfect round. It is this I have given a name: the *circumlates.* And I have made this discovery merely by thought, and without ever having to see such a thing."

"So a circumlates is merely a kind of doughnut hole?" said Jenny. Now, it is rude to tease someone about their life's work, but Jenny wanted to keep the Philosopher from noticing Gimlet troubling his goats. Still, that's when every-thing began to go wrong.

For sweat popped from the Philosopher's brow, and when he wiped it back, Jenny saw he had two small horns hidden in the shaggy hair beneath his hood. And just then, Gimlet's voice came singing through the window:

> *Goat pie, goat stew, goats fricasseed and on a skewer;*
> *They're all good meat, and will soon be fewer!*

At the same moment, Sparky barked in alarm at the Philosopher's horns. And that frightened the orange cat, who leapt quickly onto its master's lap, where it hung on by its claws.

103

Now the Philosopher picked the cat up by the scruff of its neck, and then drew himself up to his full height. Sparky stopped barking at once and hid behind Jenny. Darkness gathered in the skies. "Cursed be your dog and doughnut holes!" the Philosopher called. He thumped his crook against the stone floor and the skies rumbled. "Cursed be your ship and all who sail on her!" he called, thumping again. And this time there was a crack of thunder.

Then the Philosopher raised the end of his crook, and Jenny jumped from her seat. "Run, Sparky!" she yelled. "For he's after being mad in both senses!"

And as they ran out the door into the pouring rain and down the rough path of white stones, Sparky howling all

The Voyage of the Otter

the way, the Philosopher's voice followed them. It was louder than ever, and it echoed over the whole island: *"And cursed be that monstrous, goat-eating child!"* Then lightning struck the hillside.

In that brilliant flash, bits of rock exploded around them. Jenny felt as if her head had been pounded by a hammer from the skies. And in the blindness that followed, they almost tripped over Gimlet.

For the Ship's Boy lay senseless where he had fallen, struck by lightning.

BACK ON THE BEACH, the sailors looked doubtfully at the clouds gathering over the little island. The damp air had grown heavy, and they could smell rain coming. "It's a storm for sure," the Cook said.

The skies rumbled around them, and then there was a proper roll of thunder, and the rain started coming down. Fat hot drops splatted on the sailcloth, whipped against their faces, darkened the sandy beach. In the rising wind, the bushes on the hillside rustled, the leaves on the scrubby trees hissed. Jenny's tent, and the awning where the sailors sheltered began to flap and shudder.

"Take these down!" the First Mate ordered. "And step the mast and rig the barky for the sea."

Now, in a storm the sea is not the place for a small open ship. Already, the water was frothing from the rain, and the grey waves were breaking as they rolled past the island. But the First Mate had a premonition, and the crew scrambled to do as he said.

Now rumblings and crashes from the hillside joined the thunder and lightning. "Our doom is coming!" cried the two sailors from amidships. And indeed, a boulder crashed down from the ledge and landed where the sailors had been sitting only a moment before.

The crew of the *Otter* worked quickly to stow and rig the ship amidst the driving rain, and as they worked they asked one another, "But where's Jenny? And where's the Ship's Boy?"

"Doubtless they've been busy," the Cook said. "Mollifying the Philosopher with tact."

"Keep the crew at it," the First Mate told the Cook and Carpenter. "I'll find the girl."

But just then they heard Tom's dog barking from the ledge above. Beside him was Jenny, panting with exhaustion, and Gimlet leaning drunkenly on her shoulder.

"Help me get the Ship's Boy down!" Jenny ordered. "For his legs have turned to rubber and his hair is crispt by lightning."

That made the two sailors from amidships quiver, but they ran up at once and began bearing Gimlet down the path while Jenny caught her breath.

"What happened to the Mad Philosopher?" asked the First Mate.

"He has been antagonized," Jenny said. "He did not feel I justified our continued existence." Another boulder bounced down the hillside just then; it narrowly missed Jenny and tumbled on to splash into the rising sea. "He is Mad," she added.

The Voyage of the Otter

"Is the Philosopher more dangerous than the rough grey sea?" asked the Cook.

Jenny nodded, still breathing hard from bringing Gimlet down the hill. Then she called out to the whole crew: "Make ready! We sail at once!"

More boulders were tumbling down at them, and Sparky howled at the wind and rain, but the sailors worked fast, and in a few moments they were running the *Otter* into the waves.

As they leapt into the boat and struck their oars against the sea, the sailors looked back at the Island of Philosophy. Lightning was crashing down onto its peak, and there, under the strange purple clouds, they could just see the Philosopher, waving his crook in fury.

The *Otter* had to escape, and the crew knew their work, and they said little as they dug their oars hard and looked back at the chasing storm. They kept rowing till they were out of the lee of the island, and then they let down the sail to ride the wind, but the sea pitched like a wild, dark horse, and the black clouds followed them.

Only Gimlet spoke, for he suddenly sat up in the bilge where they had lain him among the empty casks. "Are we on the boat?" he said, scratching his head. "Are we safe on the bo-oat?"

THE WIND BLEW THEM NORTH, away from the Island of Fools, but the waves had no one direction, and crashed against the little *Otter* from all sides. The pursuing clouds closed thickly over the blue-sided ship, and their shadow darkened the sea.

It was the worst sort of sailing for an open galley; in the deep sea, in an erratic storm. The *Otter* was half-swamped again already.

"That Philosopher has cursed us!" called the First Mate. And, "Cursed, baned, doomed!" the sailors echoed. Jenny looked to the Cook at the prow of the ship, but for once he kept quiet, and only looked back at the island, and then stared hard at Jenny.

And Jenny, she felt doomed too. She had done this. Sparky and Gimlet had done their share too, but it was her fault it had gone so wrong, and now the black cloud at the centre of the squall was closing in. They would never escape it.

"It is all well and good to speak to the Great and Important without quailing," Jenny said to the First Mate. "But Tom would have known better to mind his tongue; he would have been more restrained. The Philosopher would have liked him."

"Everyone liked Tom," the First Mate agreed. "But Tom didn't have to be captain."

Jenny looked at him as the wind began to blow the rain against them, frothing the sea. "Even the Cook liked Tom!" she cried, miserably.

"Here it comes!" called the Cook, who was looking straight back at the closing storm. "Take in the sail!"

And that was the right thing to do, for in the middle of

The Voyage of the Otter

a storm, a full sail will pull a ship about to its destruction. With the wind blowing against him, few could hear the Cook, but it hardly mattered; Jenny knew what needed to be done, as any sailor would. "Brail up!" she called, and her high voice carried well in the wind, and the two sailors amidships ran to the rigging.

But it was too late. For the centre of the storm had caught them. And now the wind was become as freakish as the waves, and no longer blew only from the South, but veered without pattern, buffeting them now from the West, now from the East, and now from every direction at once.

The *Otter* tossed and turned, trying to gain its feet in the sea, and the island behind them disappeared in the black, slashing rain. As the lightning struck loud around them, the sailors grew deaf and blind. Even the compass had gone mad, and spun wildly about the dial. Jenny looked at the First Mate in terror, but there was nothing to be done. It was all too late.

For just as the two sailors had begun to haul on the halyard to raise the sail, the squall grew twice as hard. Then suddenly it shifted to become a sailor's worst nightmare. All at once a blast of wind struck from ahead of the ship: from dead ahead.

The wind caught the sail and knocked it back. The ship rose on its beam end like a rearing horse. "Barrels!" screamed Jenny through her speaking-trumpet, and "Barrels!" called the First Mate, and "Barrels!" called the Cook and Carpenter. "Fix yourselves to the barrels!" For they knew what was happening, knew that would be the sailors' only hope. But there was hardly time. For as the wind pushed back against the mast, the forestay pulled apart.

Then the mast crashed backwards, down onto the little ship. It missed Gimlet, and only just missed Jenny. But it struck down the First Mate who stood beside her at the steering oar, and it crushed her little cabin.

"Sparky!" Jenny cried, for that was where Tom's dog was waiting out the storm.

With the mast gone, and with the sailors half-smothered by the fallen sail, the sea turned the *Otter* freely, until its low sides were broad to the waves. Which is as perilous a place as a ship can be.

Then a tall wave fell over the little galley, tossing the sailors about like spillikins. The next wave was bigger still, and the brave *Otter* turned upside down, and began to break apart in the storm.

109

THE WATER SWALLOWED JENNY, and for a moment she was calm.

You might be surprised at that, especially since most sailors cannot swim (for, as the Cook often said, swimming just means more trouble and effort before you drown). But Jenny knew that the most resourceful Explorers never gave up, and had often saved themselves by swimming. So she and Tom had spent hours and hours swimming under and around her dory, even capsizing it just for the practice of turning it right in the water again.

Now, beneath the broken ship, once she was properly under water, the sea was less disturbed. Jenny saw the shapes of the sailors, grabbing for the bobbing casks or other bits of wreckage. But Jenny swam at once into her broken, upside-down cabin, and found a pocket of air at its top – which had been its bottom. As she gasped in the dark space, with the water sloshing all about her, she saw Sparky's eyes. The poor dog was paddling frantically to keep his head above water, and he looked at her beseechingly. Jenny quickly tied a line to his collar, all the while saying, "Never fear, never fear, little Sparky." Then she hugged him close, took three quick gasps, and ducked back into the water before the sea pulled the broken ship any deeper.

When Jenny came out of the wreckage, she was still deep under water, and blowing out all the air from her lungs. The water tugged at the girl and the squirming dog, but at least it was warm. Right by Jenny, a small barrel had come loose from the ship, and was rising up. She would have grabbed it, and ridden it to the surface, but then she saw the First Mate drift by. He was at an odd angle in the water from the buoyancy of his wooden leg, but whether he was alive or dead, Jenny didn't know. She let Sparky go, for she knew the dog would swim up towards the air.

Then with the last of her breath, Jenny lashed the barrel to the First Mate.

There was so much else a proper captain in a book would have done, for Jenny didn't know what had become of Gimlet, or if Sparky or the First Mate would really reach the air, or whether the rest of her crew was already drowned. But she was only a young girl, and had no breath left. She didn't even have the strength to swim, but only put her head back, expanded her chest, and kicked once towards the air above. Then she held her breath until her eyes bulged, until she saw black.

And when she couldn't keep from gasping any longer, she breathed in air at last. Tom's dog was barking, and Jenny ducked under again as a wave tossed something at her. And when she bobbed back up, coughing and choking, she saw it was the mast that had nearly cracked her skull. She swam to it in the tossing sea, and saw Sparky doing the same.

Jenny tied them both to the mast, senseless of anything else, and then she knew no more.

III

THE STORM ROARED ON through the night, carrying the wreckage of the *Otter* North and East away from the Island of Fools. Some of the sailors clung to casks, some tied themselves to bits of wreckage, and some clung to those who knew how to swim.

But all the sailors were scattered by the storm, and none knew who might have been drowned, or who still struggled in the sea. None knew where Jenny was, or who was in command. All they knew was that the *Otter* had been lost. And the storm blew on, until the wind and the wrath of the Philosopher were exhausted.

And so dawn found them waking on a strange shore.

The Voyage of the Otter

CHAPTER EIGHT:
THE TWO NUMBSKULLS
HAD NOT FALLEN
DOWN A WELL

THE COOK WAS THE FIRST TO OPEN HIS EYES ON THAT strange shore. He got to his knees, coughing sea water, and for a moment, after he stood up, he could only look about, amazed. For where the Island of Fools had been a dry and barren place, even in the grey half-gloom of early morning, he could see he had come to a lush and pleasant land.

Huge olive trees were near the shore, and stands of lush cypress, and beyond them were meadows of wildflowers instead of rock and scrub. The skies above had blown clear, and the wind was fresh and light.

But there on the beach, flotsam from the *Otter* lay scattered about, and rising from it were the two sailors from amidships. "We dreamt we drowned!" one of them said. "We dreamt we were gathered to the bosom of the sea!" said the other.

"Maybe you did drown, and this is your dream of heaven," the Cook said. "For it's the pleasantest country we've seen since we left the harbour of home."

The three of them poked around the beach then, looking for other sailors – drowned or alive, though they found neither – and gathering anything they could find from the wreckage that might be useful: ropes and planks and what few provisions hadn't been offered to the deep.

"What happened?" one of the sailors asked the Cook at last. "What happened after we got to the Island of Philosophy?"

"The Island of Fools is the better name," said the Cook, looking South, back across the grey sea. "For we was fools to be there, and fools to be led by Jenny, and fools to let her be our Embassy to the Philosopher." Then he glared at them. "And we was all fools to be talking of cooking the Philosopher's goats as well. For he was antagonized, and hurled us across the waters in a tempest, and who knows where we are. And I was a fool to come at all, orders from otters and flounders notwithstanding," the Cook finished. "For this is twice I've been to the Old Sea, and twice I've been shipwrecked."

"Don't you know where we are?" asked the two sailors in dismay.

"We're North of the Island of Fools, that's clear enough from how the sun hangs in the sky, as you ought to know," the Cook said. "But whether we're on an island, or on the South coast of the Great Continent, I can't say." He was still poking around as he talked, and had found a compass. The needle on the compass pointed straight down, which was not where he believed North to be.

"If it is an island, we may be marooned," the Cook went on, and now he found a broken biscuit barrel, the very one he had stuffed the Ship's Boy in for safekeeping. "Those of us who survived," he added.

The two sailors sat back down on the beach as the enormity

The Voyage of the Otter

of their plight struck home. "What if it's the coast?" they asked.

"If it's the coast," said the Cook, "if it's the coast, why then it's only a thousand miles or so of walking North, and we'll see the channel between us and home. I've done it before, and it's tedious even with two legs." And then the Cook stopped, for he saw the First Mate, half-hidden in a tangle of rigging and seaweed.

He knelt down by his friend while the two sailors came close. "He breathes," the Cook said at last. "The hip on his good leg is broke from the mast falling on him, and his head is thumped and bruised, but he breathes. Look, he lashed himself to a cask for buoyancy. Do you see that?" he said, looking at the two sailors from amidships.

"That's a sailor's work, to manage that in a tempest! And with a broken hip and a rattled head! Remember how bravely that was done, if you ever wish to be mate or master on a ship. He lashed himself to the cask, and so he didn't drown, but will wake and heal again."

The two sailors bent closer, for they remembered all the First Mate's bravery, both on the *Otter* and on the old *Volantix*, during their circumnavigation. "But that's Jenny's knot!" one cried. "That's the crow-hitch Captain Jenny uses to be quick and sure!"

The Cook looked at them bleakly. "If it is, that was the least she could do for him," he said, and there were tears in his eyes. "For he'd never have been in such a plight if not for a child calling herself captain, and leading us all on such a terrible Exploration."

The Voyage of the Otter

THEN UNDER THE COOK'S DIRECTION they made a little camp on the beach, and lit a driftwood fire as a signal to any other sailors who had survived. And they laid the First Mate carefully under a shelter made of cypress boughs.

"Now go and explore," the Cook told the two sailors. "For we'll need water, and perhaps some of the others might be found, or help of some kind. I'll watch after him."

And so the two sailors did, without much complaint, which, compared to how very timid they were when Tom sailed with them aboard the *Volantix*, was a great change. For while they were still given to lamentation, when needed, they were rarely lily-livered, or at least not very much.

While they were gone, and once the sun had risen higher, the First Mate opened his eyes for a moment and looked at his friend. "Well, you're alive," the Cook said. "Surprisingly."

The First Mate smiled faintly and then grimaced from the pain. He was just closing his eyes again when he said, "But where's our Jenny?"

"Taken care of," said the Cook, patting his friend on the shoulder. Then the First Mate drifted off again, and the Cook wondered himself what, exactly, he had meant by that. But when he looked down he saw the First Mate grimace with pain, even as he slept.

And so they stayed for a long while, under the rough shelter they had made, the Cook holding his friend's hand. And gradually some of the other sailors did mark the smoke rising from the beach, and staggered in to the camp. Each had

115

The Voyage of the Otter

their own story of surviving the wreck, but none knew what had happened to Jenny or Sparky after the mast had fallen.

IT WAS INDEED AN ISLAND, and not the North coast of the Old Sea that the two sailors from amidships were wandering, though they didn't know it yet. It was the most pleasant of islands, in fact, and in the full face of spring. The leaf and grass were both bright green, and wildflowers bloomed in plenty: purple heather and blue iris and wild, white roses.

They had found a spring soon enough, for this was the most pleasant of islands, and there they drank their fill, for they had tasted no fresh water since the day before. And then they found trails where horses had been ridden, and tended meadows, but no sign of the people who had made these things.

"If we keep climbing, we are bound to find some vantage to look about, or perhaps a castle and people who may help," one of them said.

"But if we go over there, where there is an orchard, we may find fruit to eat, and bring back to our friends," the other said.

And while the prospect of finding a vantage to scout the island seemed noble, but long and difficult, the notion of apples and oranges made their mouths water and their stomachs grumble.

"Perhaps we could gather fruit, and *then* find a vantage

or dwelling," the first one said, and so they were agreed.

But in the orchard, no sooner had one sailor climbed up on the other's shoulders to gather fruit than he was hit on the nose by an apple core. "Thief!" a strange voice cried out from behind a tree. "Thie-eef!"

The two sailors fell in a heap, of course, but as soon as they stood up again and brushed each other off, the other sailor got hit in the nose by an apple core too. "Thie-ee-eef!" the voice called again, but it wasn't a very frightening voice, and so the two sailors ran through the trees after it.

In most orchards, the trees are laid in neat rows, but here the trees ran in twisting lines, spreading apple, and twisting orange and lemon, all jumbled together, which made it hard to find the voice. Most orchards don't bear fruit in spring, either, but the two sailors were too hungry to think about that. "Who are you?" one called after the unseen voice. "Don't eat all the apples!" the other added. But in reply they only had another apple core thrown at their heads.

"You can't ca-atch me!" the voice called. "Ca-an't!"

And then they saw it, darting out from the trees. A small figure, like a little man with hairy legs and cloven hooves. And a hairy face, a little beard, and two small horns coming out from between a golden circlet set on its head. "Slowpokes!" it yelled. "Slo-ow!"

"A *faun!*" cried one of the sailors, for they had heard of such things. "We are in the Sea of Wonders Found and Forgotten indeed," cried the other. But catching the faun wasn't easy, for it bounded about on its goat legs, quick and

The Voyage of the Otter

agile, and led them through strange paths in the trees, and in among hedges, until they were entirely lost.

BACK ON THE BEACH, most of the sailors had found one another and told their stories. Some had bobbed through the tempest clutching an empty cask, some tied to bits of wreckage. The biggest and fattest sailor, who could swim very well, had towed three of the smaller ones all through the storm. And everyone had lost their cap with "*Otter*" sewn on the ribbon.

But by noon, there was still no sign of the two sailors the Cook had sent exploring, so the others went and found the same fresh spring easily enough, and brought back water for the parched crew.

Towards evening, the Carpenter too had arrived from the sea, and in fine style. For that steady old hand had made himself a small raft out of the forward hold, and so ridden out the storm. And when he woke within sight of the island, he saw the line of smoke stretching up from the little camp, and used a broken oar to paddle towards the beach.

It was well that the Carpenter arrived when he did, for with his help they made a shelter for the night that was more ship-shape, as the First Mate called it in a brief moment of lucidity.

But the First Mate was not doing well, and could make no movement without pain and difficulty. The Cook said as much to the others while he toasted the bits of ship's biscuit they had found. Of course, none of the sailors had escaped the

118

wreck of the *Otter* without a bump or a scrape, or maybe a cracked bone here and there, but the ones at the camp had survived it at least. For they began to count the Ship's Boy as lost, and even regretted it, though he had only been a gall and annoyance. And no one had seen Jenny since the ship capsized.

As night began to fall, there was another worry too. "For the two numbskulls I sent exploring have probably fallen down a well," said the Cook. "And have brought no help for the First Mate and his broken hip and his poor cracked pate."

THE TWO NUMBSKULLS had *not* fallen down a well. In fact, as they could see by the bright full moon, they had gotten themselves lost in a winding maze instead – which could happen, they reasoned, to anyone.

From time to time they still heard the taunting bleats of the faun, but it was hopeless to try and follow the sound now. One of the sailors had suggested instead an infallible system by which to find their way through the maze: if they would always follow one side of the hedge, however it turned, eventually they would get to the outside again. And if you are ever lost in a maze, that is a good plan, as long as you are better than the two sailors at remembering which side it was you are trying to follow, your port or your starboard. And whether you are heading fore or aft.

So the sailors only drew themselves deeper into the maze, the dark hedge maze; and night fell, and they had nothing to eat. Except sometimes the faun would pitch an apple core over the wall of the hedge, and whoever got hit on the nose would nibble at that.

But in the middle of that night, they found the centre of the maze at last. There a tall woman robed in white stood by a pool of water. The woman and water both shone in the moonlight, but the woman had black hair coiled above her head, and by her stood the faun, and she scratched behind its ears absently.

"See what my new pet has brought me," she said.

THE TWO SAILORS fell at her feet, begging for mercy, and asking that they not be eaten.

"Well," the Lady of the Island said, "you don't look good to eat, so I don't think so. What are you?"

"Shipwrecked sailors!" one of them cried. "Sailors who've been shipwrecked!" the other explained.

"Are there more?" asked the Lady.

"Some," one of the sailors said. "On the beach," the other added. "Those who weren't drowned. Hurt and waterlogged and famished! Oh, help us, please!" they cried.

"You didn't tell me," the Lady reproached the faun. She clapped her hands twice, and the sailors heard a kind of processional music, heard pipes and humming horns start from beyond the maze.

The Lady smiled at them. "Those are my people, setting out," she said. "They will bring your friends here."

"Here?" the sailors asked. "Here in the maze? Won't they get lost?"

"To my gardens," the Lady said, "which surround the maze." And then she grabbed the faun by the hands, and they danced in wide spirals that led the sailors out of the hedge-maze, and along a curving path, until they entered a wide circle of stone columns that held up a dome painted like the stars of the sky. There were tables set there, with baskets of bread and fruit, and there were couches and canopied beds, and torches burned among them.

As the two sailors gaped, twelve maidens dressed like the Lady herself came dancing in a curving line. They played pipes and horns, and behind them their friends from the *Otter* trooped slowly, as if they were still asleep. Last of all came the Cook leading two donkeys with a litter between them, and lying on it was the First Mate.

The Lady ran to him at once. "You should have come to me much sooner," she reproached the sailors.

The Cook had a mind to say something then, but he saw how skilfully the Lady and her companions began to tend to the First Mate. And then he saw the tables set with food, and then he saw the beds prepared, and then, like all the other sailors, he ate and drank, and then slept until the new morning was well along.

IN THAT FAIR MORNING, the First Mate sat up at last. "Where are we?" he asked. "For I am reminded of our voyage North when we lodged with – was it the Herders of the Reindeer we lodged with?"

The Voyage of the Otter

"They was there," said the Cook, rising up from the softest bed a sailor had ever slept on. "But it was someone else, I think, that was host." He lowered his voice. "I think it was Grandfather Frost."

"Yes," said the First Mate with a smile. "So it was. And isn't this like it?"

"Well, for all the free vittles that appears like magic, and the cozy beds where none was expected, yes," the Cook said. "How do you feel?"

"Well, somewhat improved," said the First Mate. "My bones are set in order now, though they still must mend, and I doubt I'll ever be the man I was. For I was struck hard by the mast, and believed myself dead. Now, where's Captain Jenny?"

"The girlie's missing," said the Cook. "And Tom's dog, too. And the Ship's Boy. Lost, we think," the Cook said. "Lost at sea."

"It should have been us," the First Mate said, "for we've had our time."

"It was all foolishness, from the start," the Cook said, shaking his head. "Which we should have known from when we was signed on by flounders. But a sad way to end our careers nonetheless. I'm glad you're talking, but it's a sad end."

The other sailors were rising now, safe and refreshed, and there was a breakfast set for them already, which they fell to at once, eating gluttonously, like pigs.

And when they had poured their coffee, and stood among the pillars looking out at the lush land around them, the Lady of the Island appeared again, with her com-

122

panions in train and the faun beside her. They all began to dance in a circle, weaving through the columns, singing something none of the sailors could understand.

But in the bright morning light, the Cook and the First Mate had a good look at the faun at last. "Gimlet!" growled the First Mate. "Have you traded your wits for those horns?"

For it *was* Gimlet, despite the horns, and the hairy face, and the goat-legs.

"Faun!" called the Lady of the Island disapprovingly. "You told me you were born from a wooden egg."

"True enough," the Cook said. "For it was an empty barrel I had stuffed him in that broke on the beach."

Then the two sailors from amidships caught on at last: "He antagonized the Philosopher and so was cursed!" they cried.

"It's not a curse!" Gimlet said. "I li-ike it! Fid-brains!"

"Sh!" the Lady told him at once.

"Can you turn him back?" asked the First Mate. "For it impinges his dignity."

"And he needed what little he had," the Cook added.

"I have power over this island, but not over the Philosopher," the Lady replied. "There is nothing I can do, and the spell must take its course. The Philosopher is not a bad man," she added, "unless you are rude, foolish, or disputatious."

"Between Jenny and the boy, I'm sure all three were covered," the Cook said. But Gimlet only began to chew on the First Mate's bandanna.

"Faun Gimlet," the Lady said fondly, scratching the boy behind his hairy ears. "It's a pleasant name for a pet."

The Voyage of the Otter

123

"Begging your pardon, Lady," said the First Mate. "But he's been rated Ship's Boy, and will have to leave with the crew."

Some of the sailors groaned at that, for it seemed the Lady was offering a way to be done with Gimlet without resorting to cruel measures such as Jenny had vetoed, like throwing him overboard, or selling him to the Corsairs.

The Lady knitted her brows. "No," she said. "He can't leave. None of you can."

The First Mate rose up on his couch then. "My Lady," he said, "I'll always be in your debt, for having saved my life. But is it that we are your prisoners?"

She laughed. "No," she said. "You are my guests."

The two sailors from amidships sighed with relief. "For how long?" they asked.

The Lady turned. "For how long?" she asked, and now she drew herself up. "Why, for your whole long lives."

"What is this place?" cried the Cook.

"Don't you know even now where you are?" the Lady asked, and now she seemed very tall. "You have come to the Isle of No Return."

THE COOK spat out the coffee he was drinking and glared at her, for he saw at last the kind of doom they were come to. And the First Mate said nothing, but only wished Jenny had not been lost at sea, for though she was a young girl, at least she knew how to talk to the Great and Important without quailing.

Which was lucky for her.

The Voyage of the Otter

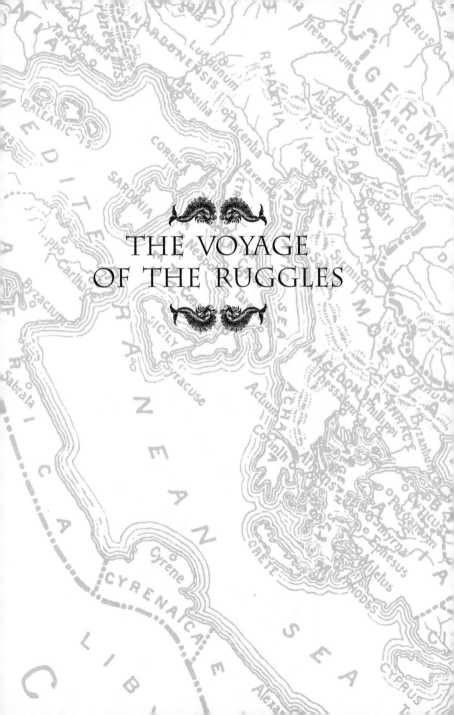

THE VOYAGE
OF THE RUGGLES

She saw an island shining beneath the sun

CHAPTER NINE:
A HAT HAD WASHED UP ON THE BEACH

T HE NIGHT BEFORE, JENNY'S GODMOTHER, WHO WAS the Wise Woman of the Woods Nearby, woke to see Pawlikins the cat looking into her face. "Yes," she told Pawlikins. "Jenny is very wet, I know." Then she sat up. "But where is she?" the Wise Woman added.

She crept down the ladder and sat in a wicker chair before the cold fireplace, slouched in thought and pulling at her pipe. The smoke drifted in strange, weaving shapes. Suddenly Jenny's Godmother sat up and threw a handful of sticks on the grate. They burst into flame at once. "I entirely agree," she told Pawlikins, "that *you* should never get so wet."

Then the Wise Woman stared hard into the fire, until she saw the flames move like the waves in a tempest, and the crackling of the wood sounded like strikes of thunder. And then her sight left her parlour altogether, and visions of the Philosopher's storm came –

There was the wind and the waves and the wreck of the *Otter*, and Jenny saving the First Mate. There was Jenny and Sparky and the fallen mast. There was the mast carrying the bodies through the tempest, oblivious to the heaving waves, to the lightning splitting the purple air above the strange, green sea. There were Jenny and Sparky turned over in the storm, twisted and swallowed, and spat out again, until the storm was spent. And there was the mast coasting with the long swells that followed the storm, until dawn broke, and Jenny opened her eyes at last.

Then dawn came to the house of the Wise Woman, too, and she looked up from the fire. Young Tom stood inside the door to her stone hut, and Pawlikins looked at him with round, black eyes.

"I had a dream," Tom said, shivering from three kinds of dread. "I dreamt that Jenny and my dog were drowning."

Jenny's Godmother looked at Tom, having decided almost at once not to change him to a toad. "They are not drowned," she said, "but have come to the Temple of the Maid of Saltwaters, which is to be as close to drowned as you can without perishing."

"What can I do?" asked Tom.

Pawlikins and the Wise Woman exchanged glances. "Do you know the tales of the wee, knocking men who hammer in the old mines?" asked the Wise Woman.

Tom nodded. "My Dad told me," he said. "And Jenny says you tell the same tales."

Jenny's Godmother nodded. "And are you afraid of the knocking men?"

"They are kind to those who treat them fairly, my Dad says," said Tom. "But I am afraid of them."

The Voyage of the Ruggles

"Good," said the Wise Woman. "For you would shudder if you saw them, with their great pale eyes gleaming in the dark.

"And are you afraid of *me?*" the Wise Woman asked. Tom nodded. "Good again," she said. "Pawlikins will lead you to the mouth of the mine. You must climb down through the cold stone stairs, and down again, down until the air grows warm and you come to the mine's bottom where there is a great brass door, and you hear the knocking loud about you.

"Then cry aloud, 'Let me wait here in peace until the morning, and I will leave you a bowl of bread and milk.' And then cover your light, and wait in the dark, at the bottom of the mine. Wait by yourself in the dark until morning, alone at the bottom of the mines."

"How will I know morning, in the darkness at the bottom of the mine?" asked Tom.

"If you are brave enough to wait alone in the dark until morning, you will hear the wee knocking men cry in thin voices for their fee of bread and milk. Then you can uncover your light and climb again."

"And will I see Jenny and my dog?" Tom asked.

"That depends on their tact and courage, and not yours," the Wise Woman said.

"But how –?" Tom began.

Jenny's Godmother looked at him sharply. "Do you truly wish to know the awful secrets of my craft?" she asked.

Tom swallowed. "Only if I need to," he said.

129

The Voyage of the Ruggles

Then the Wise Woman of the Woods Nearby smiled and spoke more kindly. "I will pack you bread and milk for the wee knocking men," she said. "And better food for a young man as well."

As the Wise Woman saw, Jenny and Sparky had lived through the night, clinging to the mast even in their sleep. And when dawn broke, they were still borne by the sea, still lashed to the mast, and they were as wet as you can be without drowning; they were beaten and bruised by the storm, but alive. And when Jenny opened her eyes, she saw Sparky staring at her piteously.

"Alive," Jenny croaked. "Good boy. Alive." She moved some of the wet hair from her eyes and saw the morning sun before them, and she knew the Old Sea was bearing them East, through seas like burnished copper. Jenny wondered where they would come to, and if they would arrive before they perished.

And then she saw an island shining beneath the sun.

The mast carried them to the island as if they were being drawn on a line. They could hear gulls as they drew nearer, and they could smell last year's apples, but there was a mist over the land, and Jenny could make out little more than the dark edges of a rough coast.

And as they grew closer still, they could see rocks and

shoals, and if Jenny had had any strength left, she would have tried to manoeuvre clear, but the waves still carried them along, slower now.

At last the water carried the mast over a sandbar and into a small lagoon, and then they drifted gently into a low sea cave, and came to rest on a sandy shore within. Around them the cave had many pillars where the floor and ceiling met. The water was deep and clear and green, and it shone softly, making pale patterns of light and shadow that rippled slowly in the water. The air was damp and thick with brine; great crystals of salt had formed strange shapes on the cave walls.

Then Jenny untied them, and they crawled higher up the shadowed sand. There was a small recess in the nearby wall where fresh water spilled, and Jenny and Sparky drank.

Other openings disappeared into darkness. Properly, Jenny should have explored them to see what dangers or surprises they might contain, but then she had just survived a tempest. Sparky whimpered, but they only lay on the soft sand, in the cool shadows, and slept.

WHEN JENNY WOKE AGAIN, the cave was bright and warm, for the sun was strong and low in the West. She looked around the walls and pillars in astonishment, for she hardly remembered where she was, and then out to the lagoon, which shone like gold in the setting sun. And beyond the lagoon was the sea. Her blue glasses, her speaking-trumpet, and her case of Necessities for the Voyage had been lost to that sea. And her ship had been lost, and probably all of her crew.

Jenny sat by the green pool and pulled Sparky onto her lap. Her ship had been lost, and probably all of her crew.

She sobbed and sobbed then, and in the strange echoes of the cave, a hundred girls might have had their hearts broken. Jenny clutched Sparky and wept, and the tears rolled down her face and into the water below.

Jenny cried like that for a long time. She was alone, but at least Sparky was there, and he licked her face.

The sun was almost setting on the day after the storm when Jenny saw the strange, green water shine bright.

132

Suddenly, the Otter with a Golden Collar around his neck splashed onto the little beach.

"You have not done well, and you have wasted much time," he said. "More or less what I expected, really."

Sparky barked at him then, even though the Otter was a Chief Pet, and he was only a dog of no speech. But Jenny looked up, and wiped her face and nose.

"I have lost my ship, and all my crew to this Old Sea," she said, her voice rough and dry. "I have been humbled and brought low already, and so your estimate of my actions does not interest me."

The Otter looked away and adjusted his collar. "Well, to be fair –" he began, looking around as though he didn't want to be overhead, "and I don't like to be fair – but to consider your tender years; that you're not a proper, grizzled captain; and that you have only a dog, and not a talking otter for a pet – then to be fair, I suppose you might have done worse."

Jenny didn't know how she might have done worse, unless she had been given a second ship and crew, and had lost them as well, and she was about to say so, when the Otter said, *"Hush!* For She comes."

For a moment, Jenny thought of throwing something at the Otter, just to make him go away. But then she heard the echo of light footsteps, and then at the opening of a passage in the rear of the cave a strange, young woman stood in the water with her back to the darkness. She was clad in rags and green weeds that dripped with sea water, and her damp, black hair was so crusted with salt it might have been grey. From her looks, she might have survived a shipwreck, too, Jenny thought, or perhaps *not* survived a shipwreck.

133

But the green light seemed to spread from her, like ripples in a pond. Everything grew quiet, and even the soughing of the sea was low and hushed.

"Slow," the woman said, "slow, slow, despair and sorrow."

JENNY KNEW that she must look distressed herself. For she had lost her tricorne hat in the storm, and her hair was matted from the sea, and patches of salt had dried on her

The Voyage of the Ruggles

clothes. All this was proper for a shipwrecked sailor, but somehow the Maid of Saltwaters – for who else could it be? – managed to be waterlogged and salt encrusted after a much more dignified fashion, Jenny thought. She got to her feet, as Sparky did beside her.

The Otter swam over to the Maid in a moment, and curled obsequiously about her feet.

"Your grace will forgive me," Jenny said. "But my sorrow *has* been slow, and has grown for a night and day since I lost my ship for following the directions of your pet, the Otter." And you can see what despair had done to Jenny, that she would begin her conversation with the great-great-granddaughter of the King Beneath the Sea in such a way.

The Otter drew itself up onto its hind legs and looked at Jenny as though the business about being fair was over. "Your Grace," he said, "this obstinate child was clearly told to not antagonize the Philosopher, and yet spoke to him with a rude brusqueness and so caused her own misfortune, as well as the loss of a fine portrait of your Chief Pet and the ship named in his honour. Also, its dog barks at inopportune moments."

The Maid of Saltwaters gathered the Otter up in her arms and smiled slowly at him; and then looked at Jenny, who had her chin up, even though she was trembling; and then at Sparky, who did not bark, for he was a good dog, and knew he was in a sort of temple.

Sea water dripped from the Maid's hair, and even as she

smiled, she bent her head and tears fell from her sea-green eyes. "Such a burden for little Jenny Fisher-Girl," she said.

Jenny looked up at that, and if she still had her hat, she would have flung it against the ground in vexation. But the Maid of Saltwaters went on:

"My waters give sorrow," she told Jenny. "But still my great-great-grandfather, the King Beneath the Sea, has decreed it time that the Lost City be found, and many sorrows raised. I remember all the tears of all the ages past, of all the times the City was found, but never before has a child been chosen for this discovery. And it is strange and sad that the task has fallen to you."

"It is *not* sad," Jenny burst in. "And I am a fine captain, but was given a task that was too – that was almost too hard. But it *is* sad that my ship was lost, and my crew, even the tedious imp Gimlet, and especially the First Mate, who was becoming my friend."

135

Then Jenny wept once more, until the Maid of Saltwaters spoke again:

"My waters wash sorrow away as well as bring it," she said. "As my Otter brings both aid and trouble." She wiped her cheek, smearing the salt that had dried there with new tears. "Attend to my words," she said: "There are three passages in the back of my cave," she said. "On the left is the Passage of Sailor's Rest, which winds down and down again, and through the sea for years until it comes to the mansion of my great-great-grandfather, the mansion of the King Beneath the Sea. That is the way you do not want to go, unless you want your doom pronounced, the doom of a sailor."

Jenny shuddered. "But I want to find my doom for myself, and not be told what it is," she said, wiping her eyes.

"It comes to the same thing," said the Maid. "But on the right is the Passage of Safely Home, and if you follow that, you will find your way through the bowels of the earth, until you come to a great brass door, and beyond that waits the deeps of a tin mine."

"Why would I want to find a tin mine?" asked Jenny.

"Your friend Tom waits for you there," said the Maid.

"Tom is there?" exclaimed Jenny. And at that, Sparky did bark, and wagged his tail. "Why is Tom there?" Jenny said.

136

"He stands watch in the dark, alone amidst the knocking of the strange wee men, to take you through the dark night to your Godmother's hut, where warm welcome waits for little Jenny Fisher-Girl, and Tom's dog Sparky."

Jenny's tears fell. "But why do they wait?"

"Because it is the old and the young who feel absence most sharply," said the Maid. "And they saw the wreck of the *Otter* by dream and firelight, and so they wait and worry."

Sparky was sniffing now, and his ears were high. He whined softly. "Your struggles will be over, and you will be home again," the Maid said.

Jenny thought of seeing Tom again, and her

Godmother, and hot tea by the fire, and butter tarts. It was too much to bear. "Why do you tell me this?" she cried. "Why do you torment Sparky with the thought of his master?" Then she covered her face.

At last Jenny looked up again. "It would be most unsailorly to return in such a manner," she said. "Ola Olagovna would never have done so," she said. "Maxim Tortuca would never have done so," she said. She swallowed. "What is the middle passage?" she asked at last.

The Maid bowed her head. "That is the Passage of Trial Ongoing," she said. "Which will take you to a new ship and crew, where my Otter will explain that you are to be their captain."

Jenny stared at the dark opening. "But I want my old crew, who were lost in the tempest," she said at last. "For they were seafarers of great resource, if somewhat prone to complaint." Jenny stared at the Maid of Saltwaters until she felt her eyes sting.

"Don't be a lubber," the Otter told her at last. "Haven't you been listening to my mistress?"

"Jenny Fisher-Girl, your crew's not drowned, but only weeping," the Maid said, and Jenny felt her heart begin to lighten. "They've lost you," said the woman in green, "and are in sorrow's keeping. Find them, comfort them, and sunken city go seeking."

"What do you mean?" Jenny asked, and though she knew now she could never hold back tears in that place, she at least refused to sniffle.

The Voyage of the Ruggles

"After this," the Maid of Saltwaters said, and her face was streaming now, "I won't be able to help you again. Not for any libations of tears. Nor for all the sorrow you will find."

"I want my old crew," Jenny said again.

The Maid of Saltwaters looked at Jenny, considering. "Perhaps there was some strange and hidden hope when you were chosen," she said. Then she brushed her hands through her hair and cast salt into the waters of the pool, which glowed brighter as night came and darkness fell over the lagoon beyond.

"My Otter will conduct you," she told Jenny. "And may your saltwater not be all sorrow and woe."

For a moment, Jenny felt neither fear nor vanity.

"But what is this hope? Why was *I* chosen rather than some older, weathered captain?" she asked.

The Maid only shook her head.

"Not even the Powers themselves understand the ways of Fate," the Otter answered. "Much less their humble, though clever and well-adorned servants."

Then Jenny heard the woman in green laugh at the Otter. It sounded like sunshine after rain.

ON THE BEACH of the Isle of No Return, a strange wind was blowing from the Southeast; not a storm, but rough enough that waves rolled foaming onto the sand. There some of the sailors had gathered with the Cook and the

Carpenter for a conclave. But not the First Mate, for he was still too hurt to move, and not Gimlet, for he was gambolling, faun-like, with the Lady.

"Prisoners," said the Cook, glumly.

And, "Prisoners!" wailed the two sailors from amidships. "We've nearly drowned and been eaten so many times, and now we are prisoners!"

"We could build a boat," the Carpenter said, looking about at the trees on the island.

"How long before the Lady found that out?" asked the Cook. "And what would she do when she did?"

"Make us prisoners!" moaned one of the sailors from amidships. "But with less free time!" moaned the other.

Then for the first time, the Cook saw that the rolling waves had carried another piece of flotsam onto the beach – a hat. He picked it up. It was battered and faded, but it was a tricorne hat.

"Jenny's," he said.

"Jenny, our drowned captain!" moaned the sailors. "Jenny, who was never frightened! Jenny, Tom's friend! Poor, drowned Jenny!"

"Yes, Tom's friend Jenny, and poor Jenny, and Jenny who got us into this fix," the Cook said. Then he looked away, for he knew that it was his fault, too, that Gimlet had run away and annoyed the Philosopher. "It was always bad luck to have a little girl with a hat be our captain," declared the Cook, "orders from an Otter with a Golden Collar or not, and now, as the First Mate would say, the

139

bad luck has come to sad fruition."

And "fruition" was a word the First Mate would use, what with his weakness for fine language, but he was too loyal to have ever called Jenny the cause of their troubles. For while on the one hand, it was Jenny's adventure they had all been caught up in – and now they *were* caught – on the other, hard luck is what's to be expected on an Exploration, as they all knew.

"Poor, wee girlie," the Cook said, after a moment, still talking of Jenny. "She was in over her head, and here's her hat floated to prove it."

"But we shall never get away without her!" one of the sailors cried. "Doomed! Captive! Imprisoned! Hostage!" the sailors shouted variously.

"Never's a long time," said the Cook, who was only encouraging when everyone else had given in to despair. "And as I've said before, if no one gets out of a scrape, there's none would hear tell of how miserable it was, so it hardly counts. And at least things can't get worse."

The other sailors were quiet then, for it was true that in their voyage North with Tom they had been in spots as tight as this, and they had all come back, somehow, just when things seemed as though they couldn't get much worse.

Then the two sailors from amidships looked out to sea, and scunnered back in fear.

"Corsairs!" one of them cried.

"The black sails of Corsairs!" wailed the other.

The Voyage of the Ruggles

CHAPTER TEN:
NOT FLOTSAM,
BUT JETSAM

T OM HAD SPENT THE NIGHT CURLED UP AGAINST THE brass door, at the deep bottom of the mine. The knocking had resounded strangely, sometimes faint and quick, sometimes loud and slow, and Tom knew that somewhere around him were the wee, knocking men, the wee, knocking men with great, pale eyes, with picks and hammers. It reminded him of being in the cold dark North, where goblins and ice trolls lurked unseen; it reminded him of many unpleasant things, but he had no one to talk with about it.

But really, he wondered if the great brass door would ever open. If – somehow – Jenny and Sparky would come back. And then something whispered right by his ear:

"*Breakfast* was promised."

Tom jumped, of course, and then he got out the bowl and the bread and the milk, and then he crawled away to find the bottom of the ladder. He uncovered his light, then, just a bit, and he kept his eyes squinted tight, for he had no wish to see the knocking men and their great, pale eyes. And then he made his way to the surface, alone.

Tom wondered whether Jenny and Sparky hadn't

returned because they lacked courage and tact, or whether they had too much.

To the sailors on the beach of the Isle of No Return, the Corsair ship looked uncomfortably like the lost *Otter*, only all black, and larger and more stern and frightening, and the eyes on its prow were painted red, and squinting and bloodshot. And as it came coasting in to the landing, rough, uncouth sailors with knives between their teeth and pistols in their belts jumped out to run it up the beach.

"Like the Boogey Pirates," whispered one of the sailors from amidships – for when they had sailed with Tom, they had fought off attacks by the dread Boogey Pirates (twice).

"But better armed," said the Cook, who wished he had just one of the muskets from the *Otter*.

The Corsairs glared at the little band on the beach. *"Arr!"* one of them said, and the two sailors from amidships jumped back.

And then there was a tremendous barking, and Sparky jumped out from the Corsairs' galley, with Jenny after him. She was brandishing a cutlass.

The two sailors from amidships fainted with surprise, and Jenny smiled triumphantly at the rest of them – it was the largest smile she had ever made.

"Lead us to the Lady of the Isle of No Return," Jenny said, taking her hat back from the Cook. "For my crew of bloodthirsty Corsairs are expecting treasure, and we must

The Voyage of the Ruggles

have a parley, she and I."

The Cook looked away, for he didn't like to smile at Jenny after having blamed her for the shipwreck. But, "Aye aye!" he said. And, *"Arr!"* said the Corsair lieutenant after him.

Then the others began cheering and shouting questions at Jenny – "What happened?" "Are you really alive?" "How do you command this ship?" and, "What happened?" and so forth. But Jenny would only say it was a long story, which would have to wait.

PARLEYS ARE TEDIOUS TO RELATE, for there is so much in the way of formalities and fine points of law involved, but this is how it worked out in the end:

The Lady of the Isle of No Return agreed to adjust her rules and allow Jenny's crew to leave, as long as the Corsairs stayed in their place. And the Corsairs didn't mind staying, for they failed to understand that this rich island had captured them, rather than the other way around. And Jenny didn't mind leaving the Corsairs stuck there forever, for though they had sailed mighty hard under her command, they were after all still dim-witted, bloodthirsty, slaving, uncouth Corsair brigands. (The Corsairs took this as a compliment, and wandered off to search the island for loot.)

But the sticking point was this – the Lady didn't want to part with her Gimlet, who grew hairier each day, for he seemed happy enough. And besides, as he was a faun now, and not a boy, she claimed him to be salvaged flotsam from the shipwreck, rather than a rescued castaway like the other sailors.

Jenny scratched her head, for she didn't want it to come to fighting, especially over Gimlet, and especially because he seemed more wilful and annoying than ever now that he had started growing horns. Still, Jenny felt the boy was her problem, and someday, she thought, his brothers and Grandmother might miss him.

Then the Cook spoke up, unexpectedly. "Technically, ma'am," he told the Lady, "he's not flotsam from the wreckage, but *jetsam,* for in the last moments of the storm, I tossed him overboard in a barrel. And as there was a line attached for later retrieval, that makes the imp a *lagan.*" They all stared at him.

144

"Most jetsam is finders-keepers," explained the First Mate. "It's the Rule of the Briny Deep, as you well know, because it counts as thrown away. But a lagan is something tossed overboard for safekeeping. So if you find a lagan again, it's still yours."

"That's the Law of the Sea," the Cook insisted, although the smile on the face of the Lady of the Isle had become ever-so-slightly less friendly.

"What do *you* want to do, boy?" the First Mate asked from the couch where he lay, recovering.

"If I come can I be-ee captain?" Gimlet asked. "Ca-aptain?"

"No," Jenny and the Cook and the First Mate all said at once.

"Can I have a ha-at?" Gimlet asked.

Jenny looked at the others. "If your horns ever go away," she said.

"Quibble as you like," said the Lady, smiling as always still. "But the faun is my beloved pet, and I won't give him up for nothing." Then she looked at Sparky and smiled in a particularly awful way, but the poor dog began whining at once and crawled away backwards on his belly.

Jenny fingered her new cutlass, thinking that whereas she was small and had never fought in earnest, the Lady was great and terrible, and had uncertain powers. The last thing she wanted to do was fight over Gimlet. But she couldn't leave him here for the rest of his days. Not after she had rated him Ship's Boy.

Then the First Mate spoke again. "I'll stay in his place, my Lady, if you'll have me," he said. "For I am hurt almost beyond mending anyways, and always knew this would be my last voyage."

"No!" the Cook shouted. "You'll mend, and we'll sail on, and see the Navel of the World, and find the Lost City, and –"

"I'll never mend as we sail in that galley," the First Mate said, gently interrupting his friend. "For it's too jarring to the bones, as you well know. And this isn't a bad place for a sailor to end his days. Often enough you've said to me, 'A lush land with fruit on the trees and lovely attendants all about.' A sailor's dream. And sooner or later, the boy's family might miss him."

The Voyage of the Ruggles

"Gimlet!" the Cook said. "That gangrel lubber! I wish we'd never set eyes on him."

"Squid-breath!" Gimlet shouted at him. "Fi-id brain!"

"For the whole rest of the voyage we'll hear this," the Cook said to the others. "We're cursed indeed."

The Lady of the Isle of No Return stroked the First Mate's grizzled hair back from his forehead. "You would do as a pet," she said, thoughtfully. "For you are hairy too, and have a blue tiger tattooed on your furry chest."

Then Jenny burst out: "I can't allow it! No, Mate, you're not to stay behind, and that's an order."

The First Mate smiled sadly. "But I can't come, regardless, Captain Jenny," he said. "Not with my cracked pate and broken hip. And my old bones will take so long to heal."

"But who will help me and be my guide?" Jenny demanded. "Who will know to give me quiet counsel without impairing the dignity of my command?"

But the First Mate only looked at the Cook, who dashed tears from his eyes. "Curse your salty hide!" the Cook swore at him, and then he turned to Jenny. "I'll serve if you'll have me," he said at last. "Otherwise you're doomed for sure."

GOODBYES ARE SAD, and long to describe, and this parting had many: the Corsairs to Jenny (they gave her three cheers and a *yo-ho-ho!);* Jenny's crew to the food and the friendly attendants of the Lady of the Isle of No Return; and everyone's to the First Mate. He sat in luxury now, while the Lady made a strange and healing music by sliding her fingers around the rims of wineglasses until they hummed.

The Cook only said, "It's called the Isle of No Return. But here we are leaving anyway. So maybe I'll return to the Isle of No Return and see you again."

And Jenny's eyes were red, but she took off her hat to the First Mate, and he touched his rough hand to hers. "I'll be fine," he said. "For nothing more can happen to me now."

"But what will I do?" Jenny whispered, so no one else would hear.

"Be brave and spirited, which you're good at," said the First Mate. "And make friends, which comes less natural."

AND AFTER ALL THEIR TEARS and goodbyes and hoorays, Jenny's crew ran the Corsair ship out into the sea. The strange wind that had blown it there was gone, and they pulled at their oars, facing the Isle of No Return as they bore away, the only ship but one ever to have escaped.

The Corsairs' ship was larger but of the same kind as the *Otter*, having ten oars on either side rather than eight, and a larger, blacker sail, marked with a two skulls and shinbone. "That's a sail appropriate for either pirates or funerals," said the Cook (who was now first mate, though no one called him so), as he set to work organizing the sailors. "And as we don't have enough hands to manage all the oars, any real Corsairs we meet may be our funeral."

This gloomy thought seemed to give him satisfaction amidst the sorrow of leaving, and he busied himself otherwise by generally supervising. "Belay those luffing giblets!" he'd cry, or, "Boom-frap the beckets!" These orders hardly made more sense to the sailors than they do to you, but making them kept the Cook occupied, and not thinking of how they had left his friend behind.

As for Jenny, she'd grown stronger in the voyage, and now stood back in the stern and managed the steering oar by herself, while the hairy faun and Ship's Boy Gimlet sat ahead on the foredeck and beat the drum (when he remembered).

"And have you called this ship the *Nonesuch*?" the Cook asked, remembering Jenny's first idea for naming the *Otter*.

"No," said Jenny. "For this is no extraordinary ship, but only the conveyance of a small and dim-witted pirate band of little imagination. And it already had a name: the *Ruggles*."

"The *Rug-lugles!*" laughed Gimlet. "That's a stoo-oopid name!"

"It's a rough, rude, brigandish name, anyway," said the Cook. "But the ship handles well enough, and is full of weaponry." Which was true, for stowed about the galley were pistols, cutlasses, whips, clubs, brass knuckles, slingshots, and a sort of fireworks rocket which was used by

Corsairs to intimidate the easily awed. And of course, like all Corsair ships, the *Ruggles* had one cannon mounted in the bow, pointing forward.

And it was properly provisioned, too. For while the Corsairs might have been dim-witted, bloodthirsty, slaving, uncouth brigands, and so forth, at least they knew what sailors thought was decent eating. Which is to say, there was no fish jerky.

Then, as the island, and the First Mate, and all of the fine food and lovely attendants, faded in the distance, a faint, cold wind sprang up from the North, and the current, the waves, the wind, and the steady beat of the oars all bore the *Ruggles* at a fresh clip, South and East across the sea, fairly leaping as it met the waves. Sparky barked for pleasure to be underway again, and the sailors too were happy to be back at their work.

149

"Well, girlie," the Cook called. "Missy Jenny, I mean, captain-missy. Well, where are we headed? Where is your adventure leading us?"

"Just as before!" cried Jenny, enjoying the feel of the *Ruggles* answering to her helm too much to be bothered by the Cook's words. "Past the strait of Doom on the One Hand, or On the Other Hand, Doom, and so to the Navel of the World, which lies in the centre of the Old Sea, and there to take our bearings. And then East again to the Oracle of Babbylantium, and so, somehow, to the Lost City that sank beneath the waves."

"Well, that sounds easy enough," said the Cook, darkly.

The Voyage of the Ruggles

"No, in truth, there are many attendant dangers!" Jenny called, almost happily. "For all tales say the Lost City cannot be found without first evading the Island of Enticement, and then surviving the Clashing Rocks at the narrows of the Old Sea."

"The Clashing Rocks!" wailed the two sailors amidships. "Don't they crush ships?"

"Only if you're between them when they clash," Jenny pointed out.

"And how often is that?" the Cook demanded.

But this was something Jenny had looked up in her waterproof *Representative Encyclopædia*, which had survived the tempest tucked safe in the pocket of her peacoat.

"Every two and a half minutes," she said. "Less one second for each day after the new moon, plus or minus a seasonal adjustment which is – which is too complicated to explain."

At that the Carpenter's ears picked up, for he enjoyed a mathematical problem. But the Cook had spotted where the danger was. "Two and a half minutes," he said. "But is that time enough to pass between them?"

Jenny looked in the air as if she were calculating.

"How long do the rocks stretch?" asked the Carpenter.

"The length of two anchor cables," said Jenny. "Or about six hundred paces."

"Well then, at top speed, with all oars going hard, we might cross it in two and quarter minutes," the Carpenter said, right away. "Leaving us a margin of fifteen seconds

150

without being smushed into jelly. All things being equal, and before seasonal adjustments, of course."

"That's exactly right, Chips," said Jenny, as if she had already figured it out herself.

"Before seasonal adjustments," repeated the Cook.

But most of the crew were glad to see how calmly Jenny could speak of such things, though two of them did whisper: *"Smushed!* Smushed to *jelly!"*

By EVENING, the *Ruggles* had come to a long peninsula stretching South, and found a landing where they made camp.

After dinner, which the Cook no longer made, as he was now First Mate, but only gave orders for, the crew stretched out and relaxed while Sparky and Gimlet chased each other about the shore, barking and bleating respectively.

Then the sailors demanded to know how Jenny had come to be captain over the Corsairs, and sail to their rescue.

Jenny didn't know why, but she didn't want to share the story of the temple of the Maid of Saltwaters, of all the tears and temptation she had found there. But she did tell them about finding the Otter with a Golden Collar, and how he had led her to the crew of Corsairs, who had landed on that island to careen the *Ruggles* and clean its hull, and elect from among themselves a new leader, or *navarch,* as Corsairs called their pirate captains. For the old navarch had fallen over the side and drowned after being frightened by the sudden appearance of a flying squid.

"They were a dastardly lot," said Jenny, "but slow-witted and subject to intimidation. And on the one hand, Sparky frightened them –"

"Sparky!" cried the sailors in surprise.

"Yes, Sparky, for Tom's dog is a fine animal," said Jenny stoutly.

"And Captain Jenny did say the Corsairs were slow on the uptake," the Carpenter pointed out.

"Yes," said Jenny. "And on the other hand, the Otter represented the Law of the Sea, which is the only law Corsairs respect; and besides they lacked initiative, and were in need of a resourceful captain. And they much admired the idea of capturing the Isle of No Return, which seemed like an enterprise of much dash and spirit. Though of course, it's the Isle that's captured them."

"Still, they get to lie about and eat as much as they like," one of the sailors from amidships said. "Like pigs!" the other sailor said, enviously.

"It's lucky we have the friendship of the Otter, and of the Maid of Saltwaters, for we might find ourselves in other fixes yet," the Cook observed. And actually, he thought that with Jenny for captain, they were likely to find themselves in several fixes – as well as more than a few tight spots, numerous close calls, and one encounter too many with nearly certain death in the bargain.

The Voyage of the Ruggles

Jenny put more driftwood on the fire. The sparks rose up and floated South among the stars.

"We can't presume on their goodwill again," she said at last. "For escaping the Isle of No Return used up the favours due our Exploration. We must get to the Lost City on our own merits."

Then the crew were silent, sitting there under the stars, except for the barking and bleating.

THEY HAD ALL MADE THEIR BEDS on leaves laid out under the turning stars (for Jenny's tent had been lost in the tempest, of course), and Sparky and Gimlet were already asleep when one of the sailors from amidships suddenly sat up.

153

"But why do we have to find the Lost City?" he asked. And, "Why do we have to find it *now?*" added his friend.

"Because we were after being asked to, by the King Beneath the Sea and his minions," Jenny reminded them. "Which his reasons for choosing us – fair, cruel, capricious, or perhaps obscure even to himself – are not for us to enquire, no more than you'd argue with the Queen of the Hall of the Stars about which constellations should guard the North."

"True enough," admitted the Cook. "We are fated to go, as we've known from the start."

The Navel of the World rose from the sea

CHAPTER ELEVEN:
THE GROUND BENEATH THEM QUIVERED

For a week or more, the *Ruggles* kept south, always in sight of the great arm of land that ran down along the middle of the Old Sea. Sometimes the wind blew with them, sometimes against, but more often it was from the West, which could be some help, but some trouble too, for that meant there was always the danger it would drive them East, against the lee shore.

But here they saw the advantage of the shallow galleys of the Corsairs, for while they were fragile in high seas, along the coast they could ride over shoals and shallows that would have foundered a deeper ship like the old *Volantix*, sturdy though it was.

Sometimes they found farmers along the coast; decent enough, but rugged and wary, and warning of hard times and bad omens. And sometimes they interrupted strange ceremonies where people ran singing for miles among the mountains. And once, Sparky barked in the night, and to everyone's surprise a family of centaurs started away and out of sight.

But Gimlet grew hairier day by day, and his golden circlet was no longer in danger of slipping off, for it was tight around his horns.

"Gimlet!" shouted the Cook one day. "Are you growing a tail?"

"I like it!" called Gimlet. "No-oh one else ha-has one!"

"Sparky does," Jenny pointed out, but the boy didn't seem to care, and only began to chew at an old leather oar-lock.

So THEY SAILED SOUTH, as the spring passed and Midsummer drew near.

At last came a day when they made camp expecting to come to the end of the peninsula the next morning. For from the top of the mast, Gimlet reported he saw a gleam of sea stretching across the South. And as the sky grew dark, they could see a sort of shifting glow to the Southwest.

"It is only the Burning Mountain, the Lighthouse of the Ancients, and will not harm us," Jenny said, before the crew could become alarmed.

Their camp that evening was by the mouth of a stream, under tall cedars that crept near the shore. It was the sort of wood where fauns and wood nymphs (and wood-goblins) might be found, according to the *Representative Encyclopædia*.

But that night, Jenny and Sparky went off by themselves for a walk regardless, as they usually did. For Jenny felt lonely as Captain, especially since they had left the First Mate on the Isle of No Return. And even though Sparky was a dog of no speech, Jenny could at least talk to him freely, and he listened, which is generally the most a friend can do.

So they followed the course of the little stream farther back into the cedars, and stopped when they thought they were quite alone. They sat on a shadowed bank that overhung the trickling water, where they could just see the light of the watch-fire. But Jenny and Sparky were entirely hidden by the dark wood.

"I miss the First Mate," Jenny told Sparky, who sat with his head on her lap. "For he always gave me good advice, but never forgot the Otter picked me to be Captain." She swung her legs slowly, listening to the hush of the stream. "The Cook is an admirable sailor of vast experience," she told Tom's dog, "but he doesn't like me." Sparky looked up at Jenny then, for whether the dog understood her or not, she was Tom's friend, and so he liked her.

Jenny scratched behind his soft ears. "The Cook blames me for the First Mate not being here," she said, permitting herself to shed tears now that no one could see them. "But I need the First Mate most. The Cook blames me for the First Mate having almost died in the storm," she said, weeping harder. "But what was I to do, when it was the Philosopher who caused the tempest? And it was Gimlet's fault the Philosopher was roused, as much as yours or mine! And it was the Cook who drove Gimlet off to bother the goats!"

Jenny cried while Sparky licked at her face. "And it was the Otter who made me Captain, and the King Beneath the Sea who picked me," Jenny sobbed. "And I'm just a little Fisher-Girl."

So Jenny sat there holding Sparky under the whispering cedars. And if wood-goblins crept about, they must have been frightened by the sight of Sparky, although most people wouldn't be. And if wood nymphs were disturbed, they tiptoed away sympathetically, being used to weeping for their own sorrows. And if fauns peered at them through the trees, they caused no trouble out of respect for Gimlet, which was the first time that had ever happened.

158

But the next morning, when Jenny discussed the course ahead with the Cook and the other sailors, she was as firm and dry-eyed as any weathered captain, as resolute as an old admiral, and (she hoped) as undaunted as Maxim Tortuca.

"To the South of this peninsula is a great island," Jenny said. "You can see the clouds over it. And the smoking mountain in the Southwest is the Lighthouse of the Ancients, which we saw last night; it marks the passage between that island and this peninsula. It is the strait of Doom on the One Hand, or On the Other Hand, Doom, of which you've no doubt heard, and leads to the Navel of the World."

And of course all sailors knew about this terrible strait, and had morbidly contemplated it, even if they were whalers far off in the Northern sea, for it offered a pleasantly forlorn topic for reflection. Although it wasn't so pleasant when you were going to sail through it that morning.

"Indeed," said the Cook, who was expertly gloomy. "For if we sail on the left hand, monsters hurl rocks from the cliffs and reach to devour you with long, wormy arms. Which would be the end of us," he said, with a kind of murky relish. "Whereas, if we sail on the right hand, we meet the Great Drain of the Seas, the waters of which swirl mightily down to no one knows where, like when you pull the plug in a bathtub." Most of the sailors had never seen a bathtub, but they roughly understood what he meant. "Which if we were caught in it, would also be the end of us," the Cook finished.

"Doom or doom!" the sailors wailed.

159

The Cook nodded. "This would have been a good time to have the blessing of the Maid of Saltwaters," the Cook said, staring at Jenny.

"I'm after thinking it was a good time to have her blessing when she sent a wind, a ship, a crew of Corsairs, and your captain, who was me, to rescue you all from the Isle of No Return," Jenny said.

"Well, what's your choice, then?" the Cook asked. "Doom by boulders and devouring, or doom by swirling down the Great Drain?"

"Boulders!" called some of the sailors, and "No, swirling down the Great Drain!" called others. Only the Carpenter was silent, calculating the odds.

The Voyage of the Ruggles

Jenny stared into the bright-blue morning sky as if she were thinking, but really she was just happy that she had looked up this very matter in the *Representative Encyclopædia* during the night. It had described the situation much as the Cook had. But somehow, after her talk with Sparky, Jenny had seen the matter more clearly.

"I think we'll keep sailing South instead, and go *around* the great island, and so avoid the Strait and both its attendant Dooms altogether," she said.

The Cook stared at her, miffed. "There's probably a doom that way too, only we don't know it yet," he said, quietly.

160

AVOIDING THE STRAIT was more easily said than done, for the winds always tended West in the Old Sea, and wanted to blow them East into the passage. And the sea itself flowed East toward the Great Drain, and it pulled hard at them, too. But they couldn't sail too far to the West either, for there stood the Burning Mountain, where the sea was steaming and hot, and ready to melt the seams of the *Ruggles*.

But now they were glad they were in the *Ruggles*, which was bigger than the *Otter*, and had extra oars. With Jenny steering, and the Cook supervising, with Gimlet bleating and Sparky hiding in the captain's cabin, there were still eighteen sailors all rowing at once.

The oars rose and fell, and dug into the blue sea like the

The Voyage of the Ruggles

hooves of a draft horse; the sailors breathed together like one great beast; water snorted from handholds at the end of the *Ruggles'* long prow; and the keel of the ship ploughed the sea and left a furrow of white foam behind.

And when they had made the crossing and rounded the corner of the great island below the Peninsula, the sailors tossed the sweat from their hair and blew out their cheeks. They sounded like horses, too, Jenny thought.

THE ISLAND WAS GREAT, and from time to time as they sailed along its coast, they could see the figures of giants roaming about, so they never made camp, but only dropped their sleeping stone and slept on board. For the giants might have been friendly, but then again they might not, as the Cook pointed out, and where would that leave them?

"Do giants li-ike go-oats?" Gimlet asked. "Goats?"

The Cook nodded. "For dinner," he said. If Gimlet had still been a boy, he would have sung his goat-eating song again, but then he also wouldn't have worried so much about the giants. So Gimlet only put his head down and butted the Cook from behind. The Cook nearly fell overboard, but being a sailor of vast experience, he recovered his balance and began cursing magnificently instead.

So it went, and in a few days they had come South around the Island of Giants without any doom at all.

Now the sailors could rest, for the West wind carried

them easily. After two days on the open sea, they saw a cloud hanging below the morning sun. And when they got closer, they saw a small, high-cliffed island beneath the cloud.

"You've steered us to the Navel of the World," said the Carpenter.

Jenny only nodded, for she was too proud and excited to speak of what it meant to her. She had brought them this far, at least.

"To see the Navel of the World today, on Midsummer morning!" said the Carpenter.

"I never saw a more dangerous, ironbound coast," said the Cook.

But Jenny told him: "You've sailed North through the icy Eaves of the World, and crossed into the South Seas, and so circumnavigated the globe. Few sailors can say as much, but now we'll add, 'and took bearings from atop the Navel of the World.'"

"I wish the First Mate could have seen it too," was all the Cook said.

162

THE NAVEL OF THE WORLD rose from the sea in cliffs more straight and unexpected than an iceberg.

The waves broke across its Western edges, but when the crew of the *Ruggles* had pulled South around the cliffs, they found a sort of jetty cut from the living stone on the Eastern side of the island, and by it a tall staircase wound upwards. They made the ship fast there, in the shelter of the cliff. Then, with the morning sun against them, they began climbing up the stone steps. There were thousands of them.

Jenny went first, her battered hat on straight, for she was captain, and Sparky ran along beside her (although, after the first five hundred steps, he stopped running). Then the Cook stumped stolidly up after her, and then the rest of the crew. The Carpenter came last of all, for he had a practical mind, and took the time to bring both rope and waterskins.

The stairs wound up the East side of the cliff – hundreds and hundreds of steps, until even the sailors who were most used to skylarking about at the top of a tall ship's rigging found their heads beginning to spin. So they began creeping, all of them, leaning as they could against the cliff and never looking down, down to where the dark shape of the *Ruggles* grew tiny against the sea.

Only Gimlet didn't mind the height, for he was more goatish than ever. He ran up the steps four-footed and fearless, past all the others, past Jenny and the Cook. "Slo-ow old peg-eg-leg!" Gimlet called as he bounded ahead. "Bar-ar-arnacle back!"

"And if he becomes all goat, would it still be wrong to roast him for dinner?" asked the Cook.

So when Jenny took the last weary steps to the top, she saw a bald plain where eagles nested among the grass; she would have liked to savour the moment of arriving at last,

163

but Gimlet was already there, running to and fro, heedless of how near he came to the edge.

The others soon joined her, and then they all stood, a little clump of sailors atop the Navel of the World, panting and wiping sweat from their brows.

In the far North, they might have been high enough to touch the heavens, but here there were only wispy clouds that blew low over their heads – and all around of course, a fine view of the Old Sea, the endless blue sea.

"The Navel of the World," Jenny said, as she took off her hat for a moment, and gazed around the bleak plateau while the high wind tossed her hair. She felt slightly let down.

"May-aybe it's not the ri-ight one!" called Gimlet.

164

"Don't be stupid," said the Cook. "It's the centre of the Old Sea, all right. Though I thought there'd be more to it, myself." And it was odd; there was nothing: not a tower or a column, not a plinth or a cairn.

"You could build a fine fortress here," the Carpenter suggested.

"What does 'navel' mean?" asked one of the sailors from amidships.

"It's after being a belly button," Jenny said, still distracted.

"It's not that much to look at," said the other sailor from amidships.

"Neither's your belly button," said the Cook, sharp from disappointment.

The Voyage of the Ruggles

Jenny walked near the Eastern edge and looked out across the Sea.

"I'd build a railing there," the Carpenter said, "so people wouldn't risk falling overboard."

Jenny shook her head. "That would remove the challenge and romance of the place," she said. "For perhaps the Navel of the World is not so much something to see as a place to see from." Jenny pointed: "Look, there is the grey edge of a land where smoke dusts, which I guess is the great market of the ancients."

"*Babbylantium*, you mean," said the Cook.

Just then there was a gust of wind, and for a moment, Jenny staggered, leaning over on her tiptoes, staring down at the sea so far below. She grabbed onto her hat and stepped back, her head spinning.

165

"Yes, Babbylantium is one name for it of course," she said, for she had been reading up in the *Representative Encyclopædia*. "But it may also be named *Pestilentia*, or *Zuthblad*, for every hundred years a different empire takes their turn to conquer it, yet the Grand Bazaar at the heart of the city never changes. Wonders, diseases, and all manner of trade and strife may be found there."

The others stared at her.

"Tom's Dad says," Jenny added.

Then, as Jenny took bearings for Babbylantium, all the sailors began running about the plateau and looking out from the edges. They called out what they saw, for from that place they could gaze almost all the way around the

Old Sea. "There's the Island of Giants!" one called; and, "There's the Island of Fools where we almost met our doom!" cried another, and, "There's a shore of sand that shimmers in the sun!" called a third. But no matter how hard he looked, the Cook couldn't spy even the dimmest outline of the Isle of No Return.

All this time Sparky had been digging in the soft ground in the centre of the island, for the eagles circled high in the air, and there was nothing else to chase, and Gimlet was too busy gambolling about the edges of the cliff to play with him. Suddenly the dog began barking.

Jenny looked around for Sparky, but just then Gimlet slipped at the crumbling Western lip of the cliff. The boy gave one bleating cry and dropped over the edge.

166

"MAN OVERBOARD!" roared the Cook from habit, and all the sailors rushed to where Gimlet had been playing. Then Jenny got down and carefully crawled forward among the stones – for she was the smallest and lightest and least likely to have the edge crumble beneath her.

While the biggest and fattest sailor held her feet, Jenny lay on her belly and looked down onto the gently tossing sea. She felt her stomach drop away, and she couldn't help but imagine Gimlet falling and falling, almost forever before he struck the water. Then she saw what had happened. She motioned to be pulled back.

"My Godmother, the Wise Woman of the Woods

Nearby, says 'Fortune favours fools,'" Jenny said, once she was safely back on her feet.

"There's a ledge beneath, isn't there?" the Cook said. Jenny nodded. "The hairy, goatish lubber," said the Cook. "Of everyone in the crew, for the Ship's Boy to have such luck —"

"He sports about a little grassy shelf not farther down than the height of our mast," said Jenny. "Did someone think to bring a rope?"

The Carpenter had, of course, and naturally he and the other sailors were all more or less expert in knots and rigging. So in a few moments they had jury-rigged a sort of sling, and Jenny was being let slowly down the side of the cliff.

167

Of everything that happened during the Exploration, that was the one that Jenny remembered most in dreams. For now and then, all the rest of her life, she dreamt that she was being lowered over the cliff, and the rocks and seas were infinitely far below, and then she would swing and bump, and the rope would snap and she felt her heart in her mouth as she began to fall forever — and just then, of course, she always woke up with a gasp. You may have had a dream like it.

But in fact, the rope did not snap, for the rigging was expert, and soon enough Jenny was on the grassy ledge with two ravens and Gimlet. Gimlet was still capering about on all fours, with no care for danger.

"Fell!" he laughed, smiling idiotically. "Fell-ell-ell!"

The Voyage of the Ruggles

More goat than boy, now, Jenny thought to herself. But she fastened a rope snugly around him, and called for the sailors peering over the edge to begin hauling them up.

Going back up was slower, but not as scary, for Jenny could keep her eyes squeezed shut until she felt the sailors' rough hands pulling them to safety.

The first thing she did when they were back up safely was tie a long line around one of Gimlet's hooves, and after that she looked around for something to hitch it to. It was then that she finally paid attention to Sparky, who had been barking and digging in the soil all this while.

"LOOK!" cried one of the sailors from amidships. "It's part of a sundial!" And, "It's a big one of those things that stick up out of a sundial," cried the other.

And if the First Mate had been there, he would have called them numbskulls, and said a more proper term was *gnomon,* which is the part that stands in the middle of a sundial and makes a shadow when the Sun strikes it. But that was only one part of what it was, though the sailors didn't know that until they had all been helping Sparky dig for some time.

There in the middle of the plateau atop the Navel of the World, Sparky had found a great bronze disk, twenty feet across. The spike that the sailors from amidships should have called a gnomon seemed to be a decoration that had been buried by the slow creep of moss and grass. In any case, it was something to tie Gimlet to, before he wandered off again.

On the disk there were lines radiating out from the gnomon, and around the edges of the disk (although it took a great deal of cleaning and rubbing to see clearly), Explorers over the ages had scratched the wonders that lay in different directions.

"A sort of compass-clock," said the Cook. "Set here right smack in the Navel of the World." And so it was. Of course, much of the writing was so ancient that even Jenny and the literate sailors couldn't read it: strange runes, or writing made of hatch marks along the edge, or a sort of writing made of simple pictures. But by the end of a line that pointed Southeast (about where the Sun would have been at breakfast-time), Jenny read:

> *There lyies the Great Pearl Hoarde of the Oistres Lord*
> *— Tortuca*

Tortuca! It had been scratched by the great Explorer Maxim Tortuca!

"Look!" Jenny cried to the Cook. "That's the direction for the fabled Pearl Hoard of the Oyster Lord. It's a treasure which is every Explorer's dream. Maxim Tortuca wrote that, and Tom's dog found it, and we have read it!" Jenny couldn't believe her luck, and she hugged Sparky three times. "We could follow that line and become rich!" Jenny cried, wild with happiness. "What a good dog you are!"

The Voyage of the Ruggles

The sailors began to cheer. "Rich!" they cried. "The hoard of pearls!" they cried. "Hurray for Captain Jenny!" they cried.

So the sailors cheered, and they began to make plans for spending their share of the fortune, but Jenny only lay down on the bronze dial of the great compass and spread her arms and gazed up at the blue noon sky.

Nearby she could hear the excited sailors, and Gimlet and Sparky leaping about them. From far below came the sound of waves crashing against the Navel of the World, and around her in the sky she heard gulls circling. And as she lay high up at the world's centre, Jenny thought she could feel the whole face of the globe spinning around her, wheeling like the gulls, like the shadow of the gnomon moving over her so slowly; only she was still. She closed her eyes. Jenny was almost ready to sleep there, at the top of the world, when she felt a tiny quiver begin in the bronze disk beneath her.

Jenny opened her eyes and sat up. She looked over at the Cook. For all this time, while the others had been dancing and cheering, the Cook had been looking at the marks at the end of another line, a line that pointed Northeast. It was picture writing too, but the Cook thought he knew what it meant: a curve like an upside-down U, and three wavy lines crossing it.

"Missy Jenny," the Cook said amidst the hubbub, and Jenny looked at him fiercely, angry that he still wouldn't call her "captain." "Missy Jenny, captain," the Cook continued, as if he didn't care very much. "It sounds like a great treasure, if we could find it. But then again you might still want to go the way you say the Otter, and the flounders, and the Maid of Saltwaters, and the King Beneath the Sea, and all those sort of folk has told you to lead us, and if you does, then I think this is the line what points to it."

The other sailors went quiet, and Jenny came over at once, unhappy to have been reminded of her duty. From her hands and knees she looked at the signs scratched in the green brass.

"It's a hill, covered by water," the Cook explained carefully, while Jenny felt the metal below her quiver again.

Jenny nodded, "It must mean the Lost City that sank beneath the waves," she said, hoping to sound thoughtful and decisive. But really, as she sighted along the line in the disk, she was still burning with embarrassment. *This is a part of the Exploration I will not enjoy recounting to Tom,* she thought. *For the Cook thinks I am a dreaming, foolish child, and I have shown him right by so forgetting my duty.*

And Jenny might have continued reproving herself for some time, except that just then the shadow of the gnomon touched the mark for North, which meant noon, exactly.

"Here we are at the Navel of the World on Midsummer Day, and here it is just noon," said the Carpenter. "There's a kind of pleasant symmetry to that."

At that moment, everything went still. From deep, deep under the earth, they heard a sound like a crashing gong,

171

a great, deep gong, the gong of all the world. The teeth in their heads began to shake.

Then the ground beneath them shook, and Sparky began barking like mad. In the grey distance, just where the line pointed to the Lost City, a small spot of black cloud appeared. Jenny borrowed the Cook's spyglass, but still the cloud looked tiny. But a moment later, the cloud was larger. It was still far, far away, but now even without the spyglass, Jenny could see the cloud was spreading over the sky, and lightning sparked within it.

Jenny and the Cook looked at one another, and then Jenny stood up and faced the crew. Now she didn't sound at all like a little girl.

"It's beginning," Jenny said. "Now we see the flashes of the storm, and before long we will hear it, and then the wave will come, and then the wind and the cloud."

And for a moment, Jenny wondered again how the King Beneath the Sea had come to choose her to find the Lost City. "Not even the Powers themselves understand the ways of fate," the Otter had told her.

Then suddenly Jenny thought she knew how her Godmother felt when a rede came upon her.

"Now all things commence to move," Jenny told her crew; "Now the World may change."

IT HAD PROBABLY BEEN a hundred years since anyone else had stood atop the Navel of the World. And it might be a hundred years before anyone would stand there again.

But for now, the crew of the *Ruggles* raced down the thousands of stone steps that wound along the shaking cliff. They ran pulling Gimlet along after them, hoping to reach the jetty before the great wave that was rolling in from the East broke their ship, before the great wind that gusted from the East blew them off the cliff.

The Lost City that sank beneath the waves had begun to stir at last.

173

The Voyage of the Ruggles

CHAPTER TWELVE:
TORTUCA'S INGENIOUS, COMPACT, DOG-PRESERVING BARREL

B Y THE TIME THE SAILORS HAD MADE THEIR WAY DOWN
to the stone jetty at last, the rumble of thunder had
finally crossed the miles, and the sea had turned grey, and
was pitching about wildly. The Cook threw Gimlet into
the bobbing *Ruggles*, and then the rest of the crew followed.

Jenny cast off the hawser at once, and they began
pulling South, to get sea-room for the coming blast.

The mast was lowered, Sparky and Gimlet were made
fast to lines, and then Jenny steered the galley to meet the
waves head-on. They were coming quickly now, and the
Ruggles staggered as it rode over them. But beyond them all
there was a great wave coming, broad, rolling wide as the
sea and tall as a mast.

The Cook went to help Jenny brace the steering oar.
"Remember what we did at the Pillars of the Sea!" the
Cook told the crew.

"So far from where it started, and still it's so high!"
someone cried. Then they were plunging down into the
trough before the wave, and pulling hard. Gimlet

screamed, of course, a strange, hiccuping, goatish scream that accompanied them into the shadow of the wave.

Then it broke over them, and for a moment there was more sea than air around them. But the crew rowed on while Jenny and the Cook fought to keep the *Ruggles* from turning against the sea as the *Otter* had in the tempest, long ago. Then the wind came, and bolts of lightning split the dark cloud above, and then slashing rain, as the ship rode the following swells.

"Notice we do not panic, for having sailed through worse," Jenny yelled.

The Cook stared at her without replying. Jenny wished for the First Mate again, who would have said something back, even if she had spoken foolishly. But they *had* been through worse, for in ten minutes the wind and the rain had all swept West beyond them. Now the sky above was blue again, and now the Navel of the World loomed ahead once more, for they had been blown back the way they had come.

175

The Cook eyed the cliffs. "You marked our bearing?" he asked Jenny, for he had no desire to go stumping back up thousands of steps on his only one good leg.

"Easily enough," Jenny replied. "The West wind will rise again soon," she said. "Then we'll sail through the night, and make our course for Babbylantium."

Then Jenny told them about the skipping song she had heard at the Corner by the Sea. And if it wasn't the cheeriest of songs, still it seemed fitting for them to sing as they pulled at their oars:

The Voyage of the Ruggles

One wave, two waves, three waves rising
Big water, sea water, oceans tall!
Each wave's bigger, till it's surprising
Anyone's left to count at all!

BABBYLANTIUM! The great bazaar of the Old Sea! It stood where the first men and women had stopped to stare at salt water, and forever since Babbylantium had traded in all the wonders the East and West and North and South could contrive.

On the crowded streets cooks stood at braziers to sell you food of all kinds; in curtained stalls, fortune tellers waited to say, *"I have been expecting you,"* to whomever stepped inside; in a hundred markets you could buy the best and worst carpets, kilims, poisons, candles, lanterns, silks, books of ancient lore, teaspoons, bath sponges, swords, maps, sandals, hiking sticks, saddlebags, moustache wax, and advice the world had for sale.

Jenny and her crew smelled Babbylantium long before they saw it; before the dawn broke, the scent of a crowded city and a thousand breakfast fires reached them: fish and sweet coffee and cinnamon buns.

And with the first light of dawn, they reached the harbour, crowded with a thousand ships both great and small – little cockleshell boats, and tall, three-masted ships with elf names; red ships and gold ships, and ships no one had ever painted; hundreds of low, blue-sided galleys, and two

176

or three that matched the *Ruggles*: black ships of the Corsairs, rigged with black sails. Anywhere else the Corsairs meant terror and trouble, but there was a truce among all the ships in that harbour, for otherwise there would have been no harbour worth having at all.

The air was full of sailors' cries for the new day, and sailors' oaths for having to wake up no matter what they had drunk the night before; and from the markets nearby they heard the traders in their multitude begin to call the virtues of their wares. And beyond the harbour, beyond the crowded markets, they saw old buildings rise up: the temples of a thousand cults, the libraries of three empires, the palaces of queens and princes, of doges and sultans and kings.

"It's like Wan-daling, or Zunna-wundoor!" one of the sailors said, for those were the great market cities they had visited when they had sailed aboard the *Volantix* to other side of the world.

"You could say," said the Cook, "that this is our Wandaling, or Zunna-wundoor. For rivers from North and South and East all empty into the Old Sea, and roads meet here that travel longer paths still. And if you've ever wondered why tea and coffee arrive in boxes covered with such queer writing, it's because they pass through Babbylantium on the way to our home."

But for all that bustle — which would have been accounted normal at Babbylantium — there was more activity yet. There was a kind of disorder about the harbour. Wooden piers and wharfs were broken; there was a lighthouse at the entrance listing oddly to one side. There were ships that had been driven on shore, and broken hulks still drifting – and almost all the ships in harbour were in some kind of disarray, with torn sails or missing rigging, or broken masts. Even then, still under the bright eyes of dawn, crews everywhere were already working on repairs, with all the attendant cursing and hammering and heaving.

"The Great Wave struck here, too," the Carpenter said, tallying all the work yet to be done. "We were lucky to have seen its coming from the Navel of the World, to have met it forewarned at sea," the Carpenter said.

178

"We were lucky we knew it was coming at all," said Jenny. "For it must have caught these ships and this great harbour unprepared, and arrived like the stroke of doom."

"You see the advantage of always expecting the worst," the Cook said.

And so they were a sombre crew as they eased through the bobbing remains of disaster, and tied up, right under the nose of a two-decked Corsair galley. Then Jenny did something that raised her mightily in the crew's estimation, and made them feel that they were indeed worldly sailors who understood that the terror of Explorations was merely incidental to the glory of the undertaking.

"The *Ruggles* was full of loot the Corsairs had stolen before you ever came on board," Jenny said. "Which they left behind as insignificant compared to the prospect of the

Isle of No Return. So it's not theirs or mine or anyone's in particular. Let's each take a bag of coins and spend the day at leisure. For time is growing short, and soon we'll face the final leg of our Exploration."

Her crew cheered, but the Cook grew alarmed, for he knew what sailors were like in a strange port with coins in their purse. "But no one must wander about alone!" he cried. "And you must be ready to sail at sunrise!"

But the crew hardly paid him attention, for they were suddenly busy getting out the fanciest shirts and most elaborate bandannas the Corsairs had left behind, and retying the knots in one another's pigtails.

Jenny was more anxious to be onshore than any of them, but somehow she remembered to arrange for the Cook and the Carpenter and some of the other more steady sailors to take it in turns to stay aboard and look after the *Ruggles*. "A *baboon-watch*, is it?" said the Cook, for so sailors call this tedious duty. "Well, I'll take it first."

"A ba-ah-boon," laughed Gimlet. "You're a ba-ah-ah-boon!" And while the Cook was busy swatting the boy, Jenny and Sparky could wait no longer, but ran up the pier, and into the old city ahead of all the others.

When the Cook finished cursing at Gimlet and saw Jenny was gone, he would have run after her, but it was too late; Jenny was already lost in the babbling crowds. He stomped his peg leg in frustration, but it wasn't long before the rest of the crew had followed.

Left alone on the ship, the Cook looked hard at the

179

goat-boy. "We had a nanny goat aboard the *Volantix*," he told Gimlet. "She was brave, incapable of speech, and provided milk, and so enjoys a pleasant retirement. Whereas you're useless and annoying as boy and livestock both, and are fated to come to a bad end."

Then the Cook heard a loud laugh from the top deck of the black galley next to them. The Cook knew how small, how harmless the *Ruggles* must seem by comparison, but he looked up warily and ran his eyes along the big Corsair ship. It had two masts as well as two banks of oars, and rather than a snout at the end of its prow, it had a beak, a sharp iron ram meant for sinking other ships. And its eyes weren't bloodshot like those of the *Ruggles*, but red, plain and simple: blood-red. Worst of all, it had no bones painted on its black sails; instead it had a real skull, a large grinning skull, for a figurehead. It was a proper pirate ship, the Cook thought.

And a proper Corsair pirate stood at the railing of the big galley. He was the one who had laughed, and he was the Corsair leader, the Navarch, the Cook knew. Now the Navarch waved cheerily. "Have you hunted well?" he asked, which is accounted the proper greeting among Corsairs.

"Well enough," growled the Cook, who was painfully aware that the Corsair crew were not busy putting on shirts or fixing their hair, but were rather cleaning their guns and sharpening their knives. "And you?"

"We have hunted well," the Navarch said, smiling to

show several gold teeth. "But now we would like to vary our diet. Would you sell us your goat, perhaps?"

"He's not a goat," the Cook replied. "But a member of our crew."

The Corsair laughed. "So much the better," he said. "Perhaps we can discuss the matter again if we meet at sea." Which was a threat.

That roused the Cook's ire. "You've mistaken your prey," he said, dangerously. "For we've taken this ship from Corsairs already, and we've sailed against the Boogey Pirates and beaten them twice too. This is the crew of the famous *Volantix*, what sailed North through the Eaves of the World, and so circumnavigated the globe."

"Famous sailors," the Navarch said, straightening his pistol-sash. "We have many famous sailors too."

"Famous for what?" the Cook demanded.

"For being caught by us," the Corsair said, "and for being chained to the oars in the decks below."

The Cook spat into the sea, remembering how the Corsairs had been the great dread of his childhood. "Watch yourselves, then," he said.

"I am the Navarch of the *Terror*," said the Corsair, picking his teeth with an elaborate air of unconcern. "Others watch us."

"No need to put on airs," said the Cook. And then he remembered one of the First Mate's words. "No need for all this *fanfaronade*. I know *navarch's* just a fancy name for a low sort of pirate chief."

The Voyage of the Ruggles

"True enough," the Navarch said. "Only it sounds so much more sinister and frightening. Now tell me where is your captain, who led you around the world, and against the Boogey Pirates."

The Cook swallowed. "He is retired to write our memoirs," the Cook said. "And we are the chosen crew of – of Captain Jenny."

"Jenny," cried the Navarch, incredulously. "That girl we saw?"

The Cook flushed. "What of it?" he demanded.

But the Navarch only laughed. Laughed and laughed, until at last he smiled down at the Cook. *"Arr!"* he said, very gently.

The Cook didn't flinch, but once the Corsair had turned away, he put his hand on Gimlet's head. "Damn their hides," he muttered.

182

THE *Representative Encyclopædia* had several pages about Babbylantium, but it didn't begin to describe everything Jenny and Sparky saw. Jenny thought even the great *Universal Encyclopædia* couldn't contain all the marvels that were there. There were domes and towers and minarets, arches and waterfalls and ceremonial tunnels, sword swallowers and fire-eaters, snake charmers and dancing bears. There was a man whose sole employment was to support a giant curling moustache.

There were beggars huddled under every archway.

There were children busy doing unpleasant chores as slaves of the idle rich, and there were the rich lords and ladies themselves being carried above the mucky streets on palanquins. There were few dogs, but there were many ferrets led on silver chains, sly and quick to disappear when Sparky went over to investigate.

Jenny found that walking about a city with Sparky was a slow process, from the great variety of new smells, and from all the new places where he wanted to leave his mark.

And cities, she found, had their own streams and currents of moving people, and soon enough they found themselves swept along by the biggest stream, the stream of people heading towards the Grand Bazaar. And as the crowd carried them, they heard a confusion of tongues, as people argued darkly in many languages. Jenny only recognized one word in a dozen, but she heard some she knew more than once: *deluge* and *plague,* and *turmoil* and *portents,* and *doom.* Even the beggars in the streets called these things. But the tide of people swept on, for in Babbylantium, it seemed people went to the market even when they expected the worst.

183

The street that led into the Grand Bazaar led down a few steps, and then they were suddenly in shadow, for all the Bazaar was under one great roof. There were hanging globe-shaped lanterns here and there, and skylights, but overall the market was cool and gloomy. The Bazaar by itself was larger than any town Jenny had seen, and had its own cobbled lanes and alleys, dozens of them that stretched far into the patchy darkness.

"I have it in mind to buy a good journal here, to keep a record of my Exploration," Jenny said to Sparky. "Which I should have done since the beginning. And besides that, this is the great bazaar of the World, and who knows what useful things and convenient knick-knacks may be found?"

Sparky had no opinion on that, but he was preoccupied, for even among all the people, and the thousand new smells, he could tell there were cats nearby. Which was probably a good thing, since he smelled plenty of rats, too.

Though she wouldn't admit it, Jenny was unsure of how to find her way about. The *Representative Encyclopædia* said there was a whole street devoted to journals, and another alley where every shop sold pens, and it listed a dozen other specialties as well, but it offered no help in finding any of them in that shadowed indoor maze.

So Jenny only picked a lane at random, and then stuck her head in a little shop. Inside, there was nothing but carpets, elaborate, beautiful carpets, and a short pleasant man wearing a gold fez with a bright blue tassel.

He said something to Jenny in a language she didn't understand, and then he quickly changed to one she did, "You are a sailor from the North, from the Corner by the Sea?" Jenny shook her head.

"Farther than that? From across the channel even?" said the man in the fez, who knew more about geography than Jenny would have expected.

184

"Yes," said Jenny, and she began to tell him about the coast where she lived. Normally, Jenny talked more than other people, but here she had met her match, for without even interrupting her, the man in the fez made her some pleasant apple tea, and asked her several penetrating questions about the weather, markets, manufacturing, crops, foods, clothing, ships, and nautical customs of her home. And he also told her at some length about the difference between carpets, druggets, kilims, and rugs; a fund of information that left Jenny entirely overwhelmed.

"Your account is both fascinating, and comprehensive –" she said at last.

"Not at all, my young friend," said the man. "There are many other intriguing things, in particular about dyes and patterns, which are both fascinating and significant, and as you are my guest here, I am obliged to make sure you are not taken advantage of by some other more unscrupulous merchant. So I tell you to be cautious, and to pay attention in particular to the *density* of the weave in carpets, and more particularly kilims, which –"

"But I don't want a carpet," said Jenny at last.

"Oh, my friend," said the man in the fez, "I am not trying to cheat you; indeed my prices are excellent. Look, I will sell you just two fine pieces – at a discount – then you take them back to your ship, and so if you like how well they look in your cabin, you can come back and buy more – also at a discount. Now, tell me which patterns you like best –"

185

The Voyage of the Ruggles

"I only want to know where to find journals, to record the events of my Exploration," Jenny put in.

"I will show you," said her new friend, "but first I worry that you will have nothing in which to carry your journal, so it is my duty to provide my guest with a woven satchel. It was originally made as a saddlebag by a tribe of fearsome midget-camel riders who were confirmed – what is the word – *diarists,* and –"

"But –" said Jenny.

"No, no, you are my friend, I will sell it to you at a loss," said the man in the fez.

So Jenny did buy a bright woven satchel, which she didn't need, but for a moment she thought she did. And then her friend took her by the arm and pointed her towards the Alley of Journal-Makers, and gave her clear, but very intricate instructions. "And be careful," he warned her, quite sincerely. "Keep your hand on your purse, for there are thieves in the market who look for unwary visitors."

And five minutes after Jenny left the shop, she was lost again, and when she went into another stall to ask for help, there was a man in a blue fez with a gold tassel who called her his friend, and gave her some apple tea, and insisted on telling her about the different patterns Northern and Southern nomads used for their weaving, and why it might be more convenient to use a woven pony-quiver than saddlebags from a midget camel....

Jenny had never made friends so easily in her life, but

The Voyage of the Ruggles

eventually she stopped asking for help, merely in the interest of time, and she and Sparky only wandered at random, deeper and deeper into the dark bazaar, through low arches and around sharp corners, until they were completely lost.

AT LAST, in the darkest corner of the bazaar, just when Jenny was starting to wonder how she would ever find her way out, she stumbled into a little shop crammed full of convenient knick-knacks. She looked happily on pocket chronometers and heliographs, walking sticks that turned into chairs and chairs that turned into umbrellas. There were infallible tinderboxes, swords with pistols built into the blade, and pistols with swords that came out of the barrel. There were telescopes and sextants.

187

Best of all, there were waterproof writing cases, and Jenny began haggling over one of these with the old man who ran the shop (he wore a scarlet velvet *tarboosh* rather than a fez).

"Does a girl as young as you write?" asked the old man.

"A girl as young as me is an Explorer," Jenny replied, "and so has a professional obligation to record the events of my journey, just as Ola Olagovna and Maxim Tortuca did."

"Like Tortuca!" said the old man. "Did you know Tortuca was once a customer of mine, just before his last expedition? He bought the finest waterproof boots for his whole crew."

"Little good they did, as the entire expedition was

drowned," Jenny pointed out, though in fact she was impressed despite herself.

"This is true," the old man said, "but that was no fault of the boots, which were proof against walking in puddles, whereas the gallant Tortuca was swallowed in a typhoon.

"Here," he said, "permit me to show you what Tortuca gave me in trade." And he disappeared to rummage around behind some curtains. When he came back, he lifted a small barrel onto the counter.

"A barrel," said Jenny, disappointed. "Still, I suppose it must be valuable simply as a relic of such a great man."

"In no way," said the shopkeeper. "You are the first person in twenty-seven years to mention Tortuca's name. Rather, the barrel is valuable as a dog-preserver against all the hazards of the sea. For in the event of a storm or shipwreck, such an intrepid young woman might save herself, or drown, but what would become of her pet?"

"In our most recent shipwreck," she said, trying to sound as though it were a regular occurrence in her career, "I saved Sparky from our capsized galley myself."

The old shopkeeper didn't reply, but only opened the barrel to display its features: a glass porthole in the front; a ballast line to keep it right side up; a propeller screw that a dog could turn by working a sort of miniature treadmill; and air holes in the top covered by a cunning vent which would remain sealed while underwater.

"Mr. Tortuca named it 'Tortuca's Ingenious, Compact, Dog-Preserving Barrel,'" the old man said.

The Voyage of the Ruggles

Jenny looked it over and admired its watertight seams. Sparky practised going in and out, and pedalling its propeller with his feet. "If it was so ingenious, why did Tortuca trade it?" Jenny asked.

"Alas," said the old shopkeeper. "Mr. Tortuca's faithful dog Rover was aged, and so retired from his share of their Explorations to spend the rest of his days pleasantly as the Supervisor of Cats for the Moon-Palace of the Empress of Sands. Although, it is true that on the same day that Mr. Tortuca's luck at last ran out, Rover ran to the top of a turret and howled for six hours before expiring of grief. I believe it is still accounted one of the great tragic stories among dogs."

And Jenny couldn't help but think how nearly Sparky had drowned in the wreck of the *Otter*, and how much Tom would grieve if his dog were lost. "How much for Tortuca's Ingenious Compact Dog-Preserving Barrel?" she asked. And here you can see where Jenny made her mistake, for when haggling in the Grand Bazaar, it is never wise to act as though you want the thing you mean to buy.

The shopkeeper smiled. "Empty your purse," he said. "Perhaps that will be enough."

The Voyage of the Ruggles

"We have travelled far to seek your wisdom"

CHAPTER THIRTEEN

RUMOURS OF DESOLATION AND CALAMITY

I F JENNY MIGHT HAVE MADE A BETTER BARGAIN FOR Tortuca's barrel (though she did get both the writing case and the carting back to the *Ruggles* included in the price), most of her crew did no better.

For a sailor in port feels troubled by a purse full of money, as it will be worth nothing for all the while they're back at sea. So the crew of the *Ruggles* spent their coins on wild and foolish extravagances – on new silk breeches and golden earrings, on exotic bandannas and garish, striped jerseys, on ceremonial lunch boxes, and various charms and medallions to ward off fleas, drowning, scurvy, and other dangers of the sea.

Many of them bought fezzes in different colours, too, to replace the sailor's caps they had lost in the tempest; whereas some of them had decided on buying an embroidered tarboosh instead. And when they met again, having perhaps bought some wine as well, there were lengthy disputes over the fez-tarboosh controversy, disputes which were conducted with good manners, elegant logic, fine cases in point, and the occasional use of fisticuffs.

Which was all to be expected, but in their argument

and enthusiasm, one or two of the sailors made loud reference to the even better caps and hats they would buy with the fortunes they expected to find at the Lost City.

And as he looked down on the little galley from atop the *Terror,* the Corsair Navarch heard about those fortunes, and learned about the Lost City. He raised his eyebrows for a moment and then he smiled. For he liked a treasure hunt too.

JENNY AND SPARKY had spent their money now, but there was something more important to do.

"The time has come to find the Oracle," Jenny declared.

192

So once they found their way out of the Bazaar, Jenny and Sparky wound their way up the mazy streets, climbing the heights that made up the Northern wall of Babbylantium. Jenny felt she was truly an Explorer now, finding her way through this far city, finding strange palaces that sat high on the hill. Of course, these palaces – gilded in gold, or silver, or bronze – were watched by tall guards in magnificent uniforms, and Jenny and Sparky couldn't enter, but around them were terraced pleasure gardens, and waterfalls, and benches carved with the heads of fabulous beasts.

There were a dozen kinds of temple, too: round, square, spiky, and squat; with priests and priestesses that had long hair, blond hair, and no hair at all. One temple had no clergy of any kind, but only monkeys; dozens and dozens of monkeys leaping and climbing among the carved walls and statues, running over the mosaic images.

At last Jenny and Sparky came to a high plateau, that stretched North into the sea.

THEY HAD EMERGED from the busy haze of Babbylantium at last, and breathed cool sea air again, and for a while they sat on a high bench and looked over the deep blue sea. Not far to the North there was land again; to the West there was only blue water. But Jenny looked East, where there was a kind of haze on the horizon that marked the beginning of a chain of islands, an archipelago. The islands were supposed to lead to the narrows of the Old Sea, and the Clashing Rocks that guarded them, but of those, Jenny could see nothing, even with her borrowed spyglass.

193

By land, there was a little more to see: hazy caravans of dromedaries coming from the South, lines of elephants from the East, and in the North, dust where lines of horses and donkeys were moving.

So they looked about, enjoying the cool breeze atop the city, and the last of the little meal they had bought from a breakfast-monger. (Jenny gave half of the sausage to Sparky, but kept all of the fruit for herself.)

But then there was a final climb to a cliff overlooking the sea to the Northeast, and standing there was a beautiful temple of white marble shining in the midday sun. It was the place Jenny had come to Babbylantium to see, the place the *Representative Encyclopædia* had called "the finest and most unadorned building of all, the home of the Oracle of Babbylantium, where wisdom can be found, and a drink of water."

The simple path they followed led up to great stone stairs, stairs so large that Jenny could hardly climb them, and Sparky had to struggle to leap each one. And beyond the stairs a portico held up by enormous, fluted columns shadowed the temple within. The inside wall had columns too, and between them there were doors, and at one door Jenny paused and looked down at Sparky.

"We must be good, as Tom would expect of us," she whispered to the dog. "We must be more respectful than we were with the Philosopher. We must be quiet and deferential." And then Jenny swung open the door a crack and they went inside, into shadows and cool marble, and sharp echoes that lingered for a thousand years.

THERE WAS A DOUBLE ROW of marble columns again inside; a colonnade of pillars carved like trees and envined with gold.

The walls were carved too, although Jenny's eyes weren't used to the shadows yet, and she couldn't make out the design. To her right, a narrow gap was open to the midday sun, and from it a thin, bright shaft of light poured down the aisle between the pillars.

Suddenly there was a burst of cawing and black wings

flapping. Sparky barked twice, and a pair of crows flew down from the ceiling, their feathers brushing Jenny's face, and swept outside. Then Sparky stood close, pressing against her leg. She could hear his breath resounding in the marble hall, and maybe the beat of her own heart as well.

Jenny took off her hat and stepped into the sunlight. "I am Jenny, Otter-Chosen Captain of the *Ruggles*, and a Fisher-Girl, and this is Sparky, Tom's dog," she began. "We have travelled far to seek your wisdom —" she said, and then she began to trail off, for she didn't know if the Oracle was even listening. Now her eyes were dazzled by the light, but she heard very well: Sparky's breath and the beating of her heart, and the echoes of her voice still sounding, and the wind through the columns, and faint roll of the surf far below. The surf, she thought, and a trickle of water.

195

The water is pouring into a stone basin, Jenny thought, *and then dripping out and falling to the floor, where it runs down a channel into the city below and is lost in the sea.* And her thoughts followed the water, into the deeps of the sea, and carried through the current of the world, until it curled through the walls of the Lost City, and then rose into waves and spray on the waves, and was taken into the air and formed into clouds high in the sky, clouds that began to rain and.... *And I am lost in thought,* Jenny told herself. *I never knew what that meant before, but I am lost and don't know how to return. Is Sparky lost, too, or is he only in himself, standing beside me?*

But in fact, Sparky had heard the trickle of water him-

The Voyage of the Ruggles

self, and was wanting some to drink.

So Jenny remembered who she was again, and let go of the dog's collar, and watched him run off, the nails on his paws clicking against the floor. There was a stone font bubbling in the gloom at the Northern end of the colonnade, and Sparky lapped at the water that poured over the edge.

There had been no answer from the Oracle, whatever she might be. *"Hello –"* Jenny tried again, but her voice sounded small and insignificant even to her. After a while, she turned to the walls, peering through the dim light, trying to make out the strange pictures carved there.

On the broad North wall there were pictures of farmers and fishers working, she was sure. Beside them was a battle, with swords and horses, and people fighting and dying. Then people dying with no battle; a plague, perhaps, she thought. And then broken, writhing forms hidden by smoke and troubled clouds.

The afternoon had grown, and the sun no longer shone directly through the gap now, and clouds must have blown in, for the shadows darkened in the marble chamber.

"Sparky," Jenny whispered, and the echoes cut through the hall disturbingly. "Sparky," she said, more boldly. "These are like the rumours of desolation and calamity we have heard all throughout our Exploration."

But the last carving to the East showed a city of towers and bridges and turrets and shining beacons, a city emerging from the sea, with waves flowing away in every direction.

Then Jenny went and drank from the font herself and

The Voyage of the Ruggles

sat huddled with Sparky, trembling in the cool darkness.

"That is why the King Beneath the Sea has sent us. That is why he wants the Lost City found," she whispered. "Finding the Lost City will end the world's turmoil. It will preserve us all from desolation and calamity."

Then Jenny wondered again why it was she who had been chosen. She was quiet, but her words – *desolation and calamity* – continued to echo for a long time.

AND SO THEY SAT THERE, Jenny and Sparky, until evening came, and what light that entered the hall was red, the light of a troubled sunset.

"We have shown our faith by waiting all the day, but have found no Oracle," Jenny told Sparky at last. "Unless what we have seen is all we are meant to know." Then Jenny and Sparky went out of the Hall of the Oracle, and down the hills and into the crowded streets that led back to their ship.

They only stopped once, when a little, grimy, runny-nosed beggar-child, a girl, more or less, tugged on Jenny's jacket. At first, Jenny only put her hand on her purse and tried to walk on, for she had no money left anyway, but the girl tugged again. Jenny looked around the crowded street in vain for someone the grubby child might belong to.

"Your persistence is admirable," Jenny told her, "but as I have spent all my money, and am without funds, you must find another benefactor. I speak truly; this dog and I have ourselves been hungry since noon." But the child only stared at her.

Jenny realized this scrawny girl probably didn't speak her language, but she felt she had to say something. "Nor should you be outside now that night is coming," Jenny added. "But ought rather to return home to your mother or father. Or perhaps your godmother. Or whoever looks after you." But of course there didn't seem to be anyone like that around, and still the beggar-child wouldn't let go, but only stared up at her.

Then Jenny couldn't stand it any longer, and pulled out a handkerchief and wiped the urchin's nose herself. The child made a face, but then she smiled at Sparky, and stroked his soft ear. And at last Jenny found a forgotten copper halfpenny in the bottom of her pocket, and held it out. The girl took the coin in one grimy hand, and then got on her tiptoes as if she wanted to tell her a secret.

198

Jenny bent down.

"If the bell is not sounded on the stroke of twelve, the Lost City will sink again," the girl whispered.

Jenny stood up in surprise, but when she looked again, the beggar-child was already lost again in the crowded streets.

THE SHOPKEEPER had delivered Tortuca's Barrel to the *Ruggles* long before Jenny returned. Indeed, it was almost dark by the time Jenny and Sparky found the ship again, and the Cook was already dividing the crew into parties of Explorers to search for her, lost as he thought she was, somewhere in the mazes of Babbylantium. "Doubtless robbed, beaten, or slain by some cutpurse or ruffian as she wandered foolishly," he said.

So when Jenny did return, she was welcomed with harsh words. The Cook shouted, cursed, and lectured at her; he turned red in the face, and not only said her absence was "irresponsible and unbecoming rantipoling from a girl what has the gall to name herself Captain," but called her a "frivolous, birdbrained lubber," in the bargain. And the Cook finished with the largest condemnation he could imagine: "Why, Gimlet himself – boy *and* goat – has shown more common sense!"

And when the Cook was done at last, the crew held their breath, for while Jenny had never shown the capacity to curse like the Cook, her vocabulary was daunting nonetheless, and more important, she was captain, and jealous of her position. And of course, the Cook had called her a lubber, too, which was an insult to any sailor – and was certainly not true of Jenny.

"What will she do?" whispered one of the sailors from amidships. And, "What does *rantipoling* mean?" asked the other.

Jenny spoke quietly then. "'Rantipoling' is like fandang-ling, only after a wilder and more childish fashion," she said. "Which term the Cook used for I gave him reason to worry about his captain, which is a first mate's duty, after all."

The Voyage of the Ruggles

Then Jenny faced her crew. They were silent now, for they hadn't heard her speak this way before, and there was a new, grim set to her mouth.

"I was delayed by the need to consult the great Oracle of Babbylantium about the mysteries of our Exploration," Jenny said, "but I am fine, now, as you can see."

Now she didn't seem at all like a little girl; now Jenny seemed not merely grown-up, but old – as if her task had aged her, as if she was a prophet weary with the burden of her understanding.

"And you will all oblige me if you make ready to slip out of harbour at first light," Jenny said.

Only the Cook spoke, still flushed. "There'll be no slipping out easily, missy Jenny," he said, jerking his head toward the black ship that floated beside them. "For we've been marked by these Corsairs, damn their hides."

"They won't pursue us until we're beyond sight of Babbylantium," Jenny said. "It's the Law of the Sea, that even Corsairs – damn their hides – respect. And then let them catch us if they can."

"It'll be our doom to race that ship," the Cook said.

"It is our doom we'll be racing, a doom that was given us long ago by the Otter, and the flounders, and the King Beneath the Sea," Jenny said. "But first we'll be racing for the Clashing Rocks at the narrows of the Old Sea, and then the Lost City, and whatever comes after, and the Corsairs can follow us if they dare."

The Cook stared at her then, for he had just accused

Jenny of being childish, but for the way she spoke now, she might have lived through the passing of ages. He wondered what she had seen at the Oracle of Babbylantium.

"And Cook," Jenny said, "I'd be obliged if you and the Carpenter would sit down over the charts with me and share your wisdom in plotting this terrible course we must run."

The Cook nodded. "Aye aye," he said, and scratched his wooden leg thoughtfully.

SO THEY LEFT EARLY IN THE MORNING, before dawn had properly broken, before the hungry eyes of the *Terror* were open. They rowed North until the wind stretched their sails and began to hurry them East again. East beyond the truce of Babbylantium, and East deeper into the Old Sea, the Sea of Heroes, the Sea of Wonders Found and Forgotten, until even the great city's smoke was lost in the distance.

201

CHAPTER FOURTEEN:
TWENTY SAILORS,
A DOG, AND A GIRL

THE SHIP'S BOY WAS FOUR-FOOTED NOW — ALMOST completely goatified, in fact — so they kept him tied in a manger of straw at the bow of the ship, "Along with the other superfluous cargo," as the Cook put it. Gimlet was hardly more nuisance than a real goat, and he hardly spoke, for he had begun to forget he had ever been a boy, but only bleated as the Cook stood and addressed the crew:

"We're sailing Northeast," the Cook announced, "along a sort of arky-pelly," by which he meant the chain of islands in the sea. "There are perils along the way, marvels and monsters we haven't seen, and we aim for the Clashing Rocks, which are worse than any of them. But keep your backs to it, for if the Corsairs, damn their hides, find us, we won't have a chance to meet any of the proper ends of a sailor, but will only find a commonplace doom, as captives and slaves of those lubberly, swaggering pirates."

"So we'll escape a commonplace doom?" asked one of the sailors amidships. "That's something, at least," said the other. And the crew of the *Ruggles* began generally speculating on whether it would be more fitting to be crushed in the Clashing Rocks (the majority view) or just stranded without hope of rescue, as the First Mate was on the Isle of No Return (the opinion Gimlet seemed to share, as much as they could understand him). Which, Jenny reflected, showed that her crew had grown used to peril, if not actually brave according to the normal use of the word.

"You might be wondering what the first danger we'll come to will be," said the Carpenter, who generally had his eye on practical matters.

"And that would be the songs of the Island of Enticement, where we must take our bearings, according to the sort of rough charts we have," the Cook said.

The sailors seemed more cheerful at the sound of that. "How can songs be dangerous?" they asked. "What's wrong with enticement?" they wondered.

"Everything's dangerous here," the Cook said. "And has been since we left harbour in the *Otter*."

And, "These small islands are much alike," the Carpenter said, thoughtfully. "How will we know which is the Island of Enticement?"

"Sparky will tell us," Jenny said. And by now the crew was used to her knowing things that surprised them.

But Sparky himself kept silent that morning, aside from sniffing around Tortuca's dog barrel. He even took his lunch inside it, while the sailors ate theirs – a kind of lentil curry made under the Cook's instruction, from provisions found at Babbylantium.

The Voyage of the Ruggles

BUT IN THE MIDDLE OF THE AFTERNOON, in the heat of the day, the West wind began to slacken in the sails.

The air was heavy and damp, and even the tar in the seams of the *Ruggles* had grown soft and sticky. But without a good wind, the sailors had to row, shirtless now in the shimmering heat. Even Jenny was soaked in sweat as she worked the steering oar.

No one was speaking much, but it was one of those moments on a voyage when everyone remembered how much more comfortable they would have been if only they had never left home.

Suddenly, Sparky woke from his nap, and went to stand beside Jenny. His ears twitched. Then Gimlet bleated in some kind of goatish agitation.

204

Jenny had younger ears than any of her crew, of course, so she heard it next: a faint song, rising and falling like the fading West wind. Then she stood, searching the sea ahead with a spyglass. The Cook looked at her, and she nodded.

"Listen!" the Cook cried. "In a moment, you'll be hearing the Island of Enticement, and you might like those songs, but you wouldn't like the Island, which is hemmed round by reefs and shipwrecks both. That's a clue as to what'll happen if you don't fix your attention on the rowing."

"But –" began the sailors, and it was just then they heard the faint strains of the song, and a lovely tune it was, too.

Several of them stood and began looking for its source.

"It comes from a shining Island to the Northeast!" one of the sailors cried.

"It's a tune more lovely than a summer flower!" one of the sailors cried.

"It sounds like fresh bread and warm spring rain, all mixed together!" a third sailor cried.

"A pause from our toils!" "A kind word and a shady bed!" "Balm for our rough, cracked, and briny hands!" they shouted variously.

Jenny could see no singers through the spyglass; only an inviting shore, with shady olive groves and purple wild-flowers, lush even in the summer heat. But she could just make out the words carried across the sea to the *Ruggles*:

205

> *Leave your labours, cease your striving –*
> *Homeward heroes need no driving,*
> *Commanding Captain-Girl like Jenny*

And for a moment, Jenny herself thought it would feel well to lay aside the burden of her voyage and rest in the cool olive groves.... But then she recollected herself.

"Cook!" Jenny shouted. "It would be well to sing a song of our own. Some loud, rough, sailors' chanty, sung with gusto and much...loudness." And you can see that even Jenny was distracted by how her vocabulary deserted her.

The Cook looked wistfully at the approaching island, but he began to bellow:

The Voyage of the Ruggles

So twenty sailors, a dog, and girl
All went to see the Middle of the World
The girl was Captain, the dog was Mate
And varieties of fish was all they ate!

The other sailors stared at the Cook. The melody of the island grew stronger:

Leave your labours, cease your striving –

They heard, but then the Cook yelled, "Sing, you lubbers!" and the crew sang back his last verse:

The girl was Captain, the dog was Mate,
And varieties of fish was all they ate!

And so they fought with songs, and if you were judging, you would have said the sailors won purely in terms of volume, whereas the unseen maidens of the Island of Enticement did better in tunefulness, versification, and overall presentation.

Jenny noted that neither song really flattered her, and wondered besides when the sailors had all learned the chanty. But then, she reflected that probably every crew needed a way to complain about their captain when she wasn't around.

The sailors sang on:

The ship's boy was a kid, the kid was a boy
Though a goat can't talk, he can still annoy!
The girl was Captain, the dog was Mate,
And varieties of fish was all they ate!

But back came the simple, lovely tune from the island:

Treasures taken soon are spent while
Sailors seldom lament our isle –
Free of Jenny's ill-fated journey.

Then the sailors roared out their own rough verse as loud as they could:

Pull men, row hard!
Poor lads, sail far!

How did the maidens singing know her name? Jenny wondered – and then she was distracted by the lovely melody again. And between the rowing and the singing, the sailors had lost their breath, and while they paused, the maids' voices sang on, soft and sweet:

Sailor heroes sleep and rest
For fame is fair but ease is best –
Childish hopes make childish ends

Childish ends! Jenny thought – and now she saw that

The Voyage of the Ruggles

the *Ruggles* was indeed coming to its end, for without wind or rowing to provide steerage, the ship was drifting towards the broken waves that mark the start of a reef, a reef that still held the masts and keels and bits of drifting rigging from other ships that had wrecked there.

Jenny pulled hard at the steering oar and shouted at her crew. "Lubbers!" she yelled. She hadn't had her speaking-trumpet since the Philosopher's storm, of course, but you wouldn't have known, she roared so loudly, shouting with her captain's lungs. "Lubbers! To be so distracted by the singing of such closeted, unseaworthy, lubberly maids!"

"*Lovely* maids," corrected the Carpenter, though he had seen no more of them than the rest.

"And doubtless they'd be useful in a storm!" Jenny shouted indignantly. That set Sparky to howling too. "Ballast they'd be to any proper sailor; and think of the words the First Mate would have had: 'Griding, widow-making termagants,' he'd have called them. 'Stramullions!' he'd have called them. Whereas his words for such sailors as would have been distracted by their simpering song, well –"

And during Jenny's tirade, the music from the Island of Enticement was nearly drowned out, so that the Cook was able to recover his wits. "Well, those words are best left unspoken," the Cook finished. "Now row, you lubbers!"

So they did begin to row again, while Sparky howled on, and Jenny continued to berate them. And so the *Ruggles* was saved by its captain's clamour. For somehow, when the maids of the Island of Enticement tried to be louder than Jenny, the charm of their voices was quickly lost.

And as the *Ruggles* slipped past the island, the maid's enticing song became unpleasant and discordant with vexation, for such a thing had never happened before, and it was a long time before their music was sweet enough to lure another ship.

THE ISLAND OF ENTICEMENT was a marker for the voyage, and once safely past it, the *Ruggles* crossed to the south of the line of islands they followed – the arky-pelly as the Cook had called it. By evening, they had found a pleasant landing on a low island covered with long grass turning brown under the summer sun. Sparky and Gimlet took the chance to run about, while the sailors stretched out under a few scraggly oaks and enjoyed their ease.

They were a quiet crew that night, for the music from the Island of Enticement still filled their hearts. "If they had only had instruments, rather than singing unaccompanied, think how well they would have sounded," the Carpenter said, wistfully.

Jenny's voice was hoarse from having harangued the crew so long, but she couldn't help adding, "Think how quickly we would have been wrecked."

"But since we're doomed anyway, it wouldn't have been such a bad end," one of the sailors observed.

The Voyage of the Ruggles

209

"No," said Jenny. "There are greater dooms to face." Now her voice was rough and heavy like tumbled stone, and all the sailors looked at her, and did not interrupt.

Jenny told them what she and Sparky had seen carved in the walls at the Oracle of Babbylantium; about the plague and horror; about the death and ruin that might grow for an age unless the Lost City was found. "So you see what waits us all," she said. Then, with her voice cracked and raw, she told them one more thing – the words of the urchin who Jenny believed had been the Oracle herself: *"If the bell is not sounded on the stroke of twelve, the Lost City will sink again."*

"That's our commission, then," the Carpenter said. "That's why we must be the ones to find it."

Jenny nodded. "I think we must find it and strike the bell," she whispered. All her crew was quiet, thinking about the task they had been given.

It was the Cook who spoke first. "Well, no sign of the Corsairs," he said. "Yet."

JENNY WOKE IN THE COOL MORNING, before the bright eyes of dawn had opened. But the Cook was awake already, and standing by the ashes of the fire. "We'll make no smoke this morning," the Cook said. "They're near; I can feel it in my bones. And my peg leg is itching, which is always a queer sign. We'll be chained at their oarlocks by evening."

The Voyage of the Ruggles

"We'll have found the Clashing Rocks that guard the narrows of the sea before that," Jenny replied. "And might rather be wishing we were held in those chains." Then they woke the crew, and the Cook made sure each sailor had a handful of raisins and oats for breakfast.

Under the direction of the Cook and the Carpenter, they shifted the cannon from the bow of the *Ruggles* to the stern, so that it pointed backwards, not ahead. "For we'll be racing, rather than fighting, if we can," Jenny said.

Then they ran the *Ruggles* out, stepped the mast, and began to pull hard for the East; all in the cool morning; all before the mists of dawn had broken.

And it was well they had done so, for by the time the sun had burned the air clear and warm, the Cook – who had climbed the mast to better scan the Western sea, wooden leg or not – gave Jenny a nod.

"Black sails," he said. "Black sails of the Corsairs," he said. "It's the *Terror*, the two-decker galley of arrogant slavers what marked us at Babbylantium."

"The *Terror!*" cried the two sailors amidships, and they might have begun wailing then, and all the rest of the crew after them – just from habit – but Jenny checked them with a look.

"Save your breath for rowing," Jenny said. "For we're after being the prey of Corsairs. Damn their hides," she added.

The Clashing Rocks loomed ahead

CHAPTER FIFTEEN:
THEY SAILED TOWARDS HOPE AND DOOM

S AILORS IN THEIR RIGHT MINDS USUALLY TRIED TO avoid the Clashing Rocks that guard the Eastern end, the oldest end, of the Old Sea, but that day the *Ruggles* raced towards them, pursued all the while by the *Terror*.

Jenny's crew pulled their oars willingly, meaning to save their lives, whereas slaves pulled the oars of the *Terror*. But the Navarch was determined to take this prize – and perhaps find the treasures of the Lost City in the bargain. So when the *Terror* slowed, its crew was mightily encouraged by whips; but when the *Ruggles* saw the Corsairs gaining ground, they only had to remember what fate awaited them if they were caught – and their pride. For were they not the crew that had sailed through the Eaves of the World and so made a circumnavigation? And had they not triumphed in battle against the snow-goblins and the Boogey Pirates (twice)?

But for all that, the *Terror* was a larger ship, with two decks of oars, and a crew large enough to row them in shifts, whereas on the *Ruggles* there weren't even hands enough to work all twenty oars. By the early afternoon, Jenny's crew was exhausted, and the *Terror* was near enough that they could see not just its tall masts, but the body of the black ship as well.

"Hull-up, and gaining," the Cook told Jenny. "They'll begin their ranging shots soon."

Then there was a sharp sound, a great noise heard from a distance. "There!" cried the Cook. "That's the crack of their cannon!" Sparky howled, and Gimlet bleated, but there was no puff of smoke from the bow of the *Terror*.

"No," said Jenny, looking ahead to the East. From the North the land curved down, grey and stony, leaving only one narrow gap in the sea. "That's the Clash of the Rocks, which are far away, but may yet be our salvation."

And as the Clash repeated, every two-and-a-half minutes or so, just as the *Representative Encyclopædia* had predicted, it grew louder each time, and the crew of the *Ruggles* pulled harder with each crack. For now they did see the *Terror*'s bow-chaser smoke, and heard its sound, too. And so they sailed towards hope and doom, away from the Corsairs, and towards the Clashing Rocks, the rocks that met like teeth.

THE CORSAIRS' SHOTS were growing closer now; Jenny could feel their splash as they struck the sea, and the light wind carried the smell and smoke from their cannon. Jenny had shut Sparky up in his barrel, where he felt safer, and Gimlet had fallen quiet in his manger, quieter than he had ever been, boy or goat.

The Voyage of the Ruggles

"Those shots are meant to scare us only," the Cook told Jenny. "For to really harm ship or crew would only hurt our price in the market, if you follow me."

And Jenny did follow him; he meant that the Corsairs hoped to frighten her into surrendering the *Ruggles* and its crew whole, and sell them for slaves. "But since you had us shift our cannon aft, we can shoot them at leisure!" the Cook added, with a rare spark of pleasure. "For we isn't concerned with market prices, and doesn't need slaves, but does our own dishes, except for Gimlet, who now eats them."

"We'll double-shot the cannon," Jenny said, thinking hard. "But hold our fire."

The Cook looked at her in surprise. For Jenny meant to load the cannon with two balls at once. A double-shotted cannon would throw twice the weight – like hitting them with a whole Gimlet, if only Gimlet were made of iron, the Cook thought, before his mind returned to practicalities. But while a double-shot would hit the *Terror* hard, its range would be much reduced.

Jenny meant to let the Corsairs come very close, it seemed, within pistol range, even, and then fire one terrific blast. It was a dangerous plan, but the *Terror* wouldn't expect it.

"Aye aye," the Cook said, his old eyes bright with battle. And if he still didn't call Jenny "captain," at least he didn't say "missy."

215

The Voyage of the Ruggles

Now the sea narrowed, and the Clashing Rocks loomed ahead. The Clashing Rocks too would have been enough to make a name for any sailor who survived to tell the tale, but this wonder brought no excited talk about the *Ruggles*. For the Rocks were two high walls that stood in the sea like a corridor of jagged black teeth between the land to North and South.

When the rock walls snapped shut, the *Ruggles* shook with the sound, and it lurched in the rush of water that followed. And the *Ruggles* lurched again when the *Terror*'s bow-chaser fired and the sea leapt up where the shot struck hard by.

But still Jenny held their fire, not watching the Corsairs to their rear, but gauging the time and distance left to reach the Rocks instead. For when they clashed, a wave spread out, but as they drew apart, the sea rolled back in, and Jenny was calculating hard. It wouldn't be long now.

"Oars up and rest!" Jenny called. "Strike the pennant!" The sailors stared at her in confusion, for a ship only strikes its pennant when it changes owners. "Strike the pennant!" Jenny repeated. "And raise a white flag." Then all the sailors stared at the Cook.

"You don't mean to surrender?" the Cook cried.

"There's just time to obey my orders!" Jenny called.

"But you can't lure the Corsairs close with a white flag and then fire point-blank!" the Cook shouted. "It's against the Law of the Sea! We'll be cursed and luckless forever."

"Now at last you call us lucky and see something

216

worse!" Jenny cried in frustration. "Then for once, and beyond any other time, treat me as captain and do as I say! Doubt me and all is lost!

"Listen, all of you," Jenny went on – "We have shared mistakes and triumphs both, but after all the signs that have confirmed my command; after escape beyond hope from one island and evading Enticement on another; after signs from flounder and Otter and Maid of Saltwater – after all that, I beg you to follow me now – or let me leap into the sea and swim alone to the Lost City!"

The Cook looked at Jenny, wild and desperate, and for that moment he trusted her. "Do as you're ordered," he told the crew. And as their pennant came down, and the white flag rose, they heard the shouts of victory from the black *Terror*, and mocking laughter as the Corsairs coasted close to take their prize.

Now the black ship loomed behind them, and they all saw the grinning skull on its prow, and the grins on all its pirate crew.

"Captured by Corsairs!" the two sailors amidships moaned quietly. "If only we could have been smushed by rocks!"

Jenny held the steering oar tighter as she watched the Corsairs close, and her heart beat wildly. The standoff in the forest, so long ago, had been nothing to this.

"Never fear, little captain fisher-girl," the Navarch of the *Terror* called to her. "We only mean to eat the goat." He was almost in spitting distance now, Jenny thought, and when he smiled, she could count his gold teeth (two choppers, a grinder, and one very large dog-tooth). Now the Corsairs were putting out poles to push the *Ruggles* out of the way of the beak of their ram. "Your sailors will live to pull our oars," said the Navarch. "And even you could be sold – as the cheaper sort of scullery maid."

"And what will become of my ship?" Jenny asked, counting the seconds in her head. The Cook stood by the cannon, with one eye on Jenny, but twelve Corsairs had their muskets trained on him, in case he tried to fire, in defiance of the Law of the Sea.

"The *Ruggles*," the Navarch said thoughtfully. "'*The Littlest Pirate*' I called her when her old crew sailed. I imagine it will be wrecked and used as salvage, for any real Corsair would count a ship captured by a little girl as bad luck." Now the bow of the *Terror* bumped against the stern of the *Ruggles*.

"I did not do it alone, but was helped by the dog Sparky," Jenny pointed out, just to pass the time.

"Let us see this fearsome dog!" shouted the Corsairs.

"Sparky is indisposed, and hiding in his particular barrel," Jenny said. And then all the Corsairs roared with laughter, and let their guns off in the air for the pleasure of capturing such an easy prize.

But Jenny had timed her parley just right; for both ships had been drifting nearer the entrance to the passage of the Rocks all this while. So it was just then the Clashing Rocks snapped together with a deafening clash.

The Voyage of the Ruggles

Then, "Row!" bellowed Jenny; and "Row!" roared the Cook, louder yet, and the crew of the *Ruggles*, who were still at their oars, did row, and met the rush of water thrown from the Clashing Rocks head-on.

But the *Terror* couldn't act as quickly, for the Corsairs above deck had been intent on their prize, while the captives who pulled their oars below had to be whipped before they took an interest in their work. So the rush of water met the *Terror* unprepared, and the Corsair ship slewed and nearly capsized before it began to chase after the *Ruggles* once more.

THE *Ruggles* had two and a half minutes, more or less, to get through the passage and into the open sea. Two and a half minutes in the shadow of the Clashing Rocks, before the jaws snapped together again, and crushed anything between them; and Jenny counted the time under her breath. The crew of the *Ruggles* rowed hard, helped at first by the water rushing back into the channel as the Rocks pulled apart again. Jenny had counted to thirty before the current slowed and they moved by oars alone.

219

"They are frightened!" the Cook called. "The *Terror* doesn't dare to try the Rocks!" And it was true; the *Terror* had not followed them into that perilous seaway, but had backed oars until it was steady in the water. But Corsairs never let a prize escape freely, as a matter of policy, and in order to guard their reputation as dreadful pirates. As the

Cook watched, the Navarch of the *Terror* sighted carefully along the barrel of their bow-chaser and there was a *bang!* and the water erupted where the cannonball stuck just behind the stern of the *Ruggles*, making the galley rock wildly.

"He's got us ranged!" the Cook called to Jenny, but she was intent on the passage.

"I count one minute!" she cried. "Row for your lives!"

"They're in reach of our double-shot now," the Cook suggested.

"No!" Jenny ordered. "Distract them with small arms."

The Cook smiled then, for the sailors had loaded a dozen pistols and muskets in case it came to a battle – and as they had escaped fair and square by the Law of the Sea, they were free to fire on their enemies once again, just as the Corsairs were.

The Cook fired the guns one by one at the Corsairs, pistols first, and then muskets as the ships drew farther apart. Finally, and purely for his own satisfaction, he shot off the fireworks rocket they had found on the *Ruggles*. None of it was to real effect, however, beyond distracting the Corsairs who were reloading their cannon, for it's hard to be accurate with small guns or rockets in a bobbing boat.

"I count two minutes!" cried Jenny. "Row for your lives!" There was half a minute left, but still the dark corridor of rock stretched on ahead of them. And now the Corsairs had reloaded at last, pistols and muskets and their cannon too, and began to let fly.

Then there were dozens of Corsair guns firing in a great crackling roll. It was like the grand finish to a fireworks show, only with real bullets and musket balls flying about the *Ruggles*. The sailors ducked, but the Cook fell when a bullet struck his peg leg hard.

"Fifteen beats left!" Jenny cried, though she knew it was only a guess, but she could see the black rocks begin to tremble, and a sort of quiver ran through the water. And they were still too far from the open sea. Then the *Terror* fired its cannon again, and the ball sailed true, and broke the mast of the *Ruggles* in half. It crashed down onto the manger at the bow of the ship, rigging, spars and all. Gimlet screamed in goatish terror, and in the damage and confusion the pace of the rowing slowed even as the Rocks began to hum.

The open sea was only a few lengths away, but now all of them – even the Cook, who'd just got to his feet again – could see they wouldn't reach it in time. The Rocks would snap together while the *Ruggles* was still in the narrows. They would be crushed.

The two sailors amidships fainted.

THEN JENNY CRIED, "FIRE!" and the Cook let off the cannon at last.

No one ever saw where their shot struck, for just as the cannon fired the weight of the double-shot backwards, so it kicked the *Ruggles* ahead. That had been Jenny's last hope all along.

And so the *Ruggles* had just darted out of the narrows, East into the open sea, when the jaws of the Clashing Rocks clapped together at last.

222

THE VOYAGE
OF THE NONESUCH

CHAPTER SIXTEEN:
THE COVE OF DESPAIR

T HAT DAY, TOM AND HIS DAD HAD MADE EXCELLENT
progress in sorting the slips of the great *Encyclopædia*
(they had some discussion on whether barnacles should be
categorized among the adventurous seafaring fish, with
their need to be attached to ships in order to travel
counted as merely accidental, or be placed rather among
the steady and unimaginative sea rocks, only with a strange
likelihood of being carried away).

Then they made dinner and washed up, and then Tom
went through the harbour and climbed the headlands that
overlooked the sea, as he did every day. Tom took out
Jenny's prize expanding telescope and scanned the sea,
looking for any strange ship or sail that might hint his
friend and his dog were returned.

And as the afternoon grew warm, Tom lay on the grassy
hill and closed his eyes from sea-longing. There, under the
midday sun, by the rolling saltwater, Tom dreamed of Jenny
and Sparky, of Jenny and Sparky floating in the warm old sea.

AFTER THE *Ruggles* had shot through the Clashing Rocks,

there was one wild moment of celebration, even amidst the confusion of the broken mast and tangled rigging. When the two sailors from amidships got to their feet, not sure whether they had survived, they heard great applause, and all the sailors began to shout:

"Hooray for Captain Jenny, the great pilot of the world! Hooray for Captain Jenny, what outwitted the Corsairs and the Clashing Rocks! Hooray for the *Ruggles*, and the Otter who chose her, and the flounders who sent us along!" And they cheered the Cook too, and Sparky, who had left his barrel and ran about barking with delight; and in a moment of great charity, they even cheered the bleating Gimlet, who just now emerged from the canvas that had fallen over the manger.

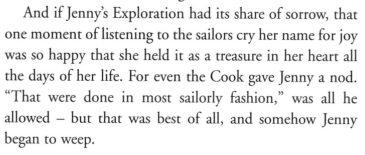

226

And if Jenny's Exploration had its share of sorrow, that one moment of listening to the sailors cry her name for joy was so happy that she held it as a treasure in her heart all the days of her life. For even the Cook gave Jenny a nod. "That were done in most sailorly fashion," was all he allowed – but that was best of all, and somehow Jenny began to weep.

THEY COASTED EASILY along the Southern coast of the oldest end of the Old Sea for the rest of that afternoon, and on into the evening. For after their giddy relief at not being crushed had passed, Jenny and the crew of the *Ruggles* were exhausted from making the trial of the

Clashing Rocks. And besides, their mast had been snapped in half by the last shot of the *Terror*, and until the Carpenter had time to properly repair it ("If we find a ten-foot pine and scarf the joint, it will serve well enough," he said, in his carpenter's lingo) their sail would be little help.

So by sunset they had anchored the *Ruggles* in a sheltered cove, and waded ashore where they started a driftwood fire, and generally began to stretch out and take their ease under the bright summer stars. For now, they thought, they had passed the Isle of Enticement, and made the passage of the Clashing Rocks, and escaped the terror of the Corsairs, and it was only clear sailing left to the Lost City, even if they still weren't sure where that was.

Sparky and Gimlet played in the browning grass among the scrubby trees, as was their habit, while the sailors enjoyed their lassitude. And after that, Tom's dog began digging in the ground, close to one lone gummy tree. He dug until nothing but his hindquarters could be seen sticking up, and then he began barking. And after he barked for a while, Jenny went over and found that Sparky had discovered an oilskin pouch.

Inside was a letter sealed with the mark of a golden collar. "It's from the Otter!" Jenny exclaimed.

And, "The Otter!" the sailors murmured. "That's a coincidence!" one of the sailors called. "Who's it for?" another asked. And, "What if it's a different otter?" asked a third.

"If it's a different otter, *that* would be a coincidence,"

The Voyage of the Nonesuch

the Cook said. "But I'm guessing it's from the Otter we know, and it's for us."

Of course, he was right, and the Otter had written in large, fancy characters that could be made out easily in the firelight. Jenny began to read aloud to her crew:

Greetings to Fisher-Girl Jenny and her Flounder-Chosen Crew, from Otter and Chief Pet to the Maid of Saltwaters, the Great-Great-Granddaughter of the King Beneath the Sea –

"Flounder-Chosen...that sounds well," said one of the sailors from amidships.

"It only means we was picked by fish, if you're proud of that," said the Cook, whose grumpiness wasn't sincere that night, but only habitual.

"Flounder-Chosen," the other sailor from amidships repeated, dreamily.

The other sailors were pleased too. "An heroic epithet!" they called. "A rare and noble title!" "It will look well on our tombstones," and so forth.

"Proper sailors don't have tombstones," the Cook said. "They dies at sea and are laid to rest in the bosom of the waves."

Jenny was about to tell the story of the last voyage of Maxim Tortuca then, but on reflection, she continued with the Otter's letter instead:

I am surprised that you have survived even this long, considering that you are not a proper grizzled Captain of Vast Experience. But I expect you have wasted a Great Deal of Time along the way. For the hands of the Clock of the World move on whether you are diligent or tardy, and the Lost City will rise again with the Third Great Wave, and a new age may begin.

So Fate decrees that plague and turmoil wait for everyone – sailors, fisher-girls, and Dogs Who Bark at Inopportune Moments regardless.

P.S. I have enclosed a map, which I have made rather cleverly.

"A map!" the sailors cried. "A map to the Lost City that sank beneath the waves, and the treasures therein!"

"Yes," said Jenny, unfolding the second sheet, which had also been sealed with the mark of the Otter with a Golden Collar, and tied with a knotted, blue silk ribbon besides. "A map," she said, and then fell silent.

The Cook looked over her shoulder. "That Otter is a rare funny animal," he said. For the island of the Lost City was indeed drawn in the centre of the map, but the rest of the sheet was blank.

"How will that help?" asked one of the sailors, and "But which way is the island from here?" asked another, and "Is the Otter really a friendly animal?" asked a third.

"Perhaps there are signs which we will only see by

The Voyage of the Nonesuch

daylight," said Jenny.

"How is that clever?" asked one of the sailors from amidships. "If it had been a map you could only read by starlight, that would have been clever," the other one added.

"You mistake the sense of it," said Jenny, still staring at the map. Then she folded it up slowly, and tucked it in her new satchel, trying not to show her disappointment. "The Otter means he was clever to include it, not that there was ingenuity in its construction."

"He would have been more clever to tell us which direction to sail," the Cook couldn't help saying.

"Speak well of the Otter!" said Jenny. "For he is a magical beast, and Chief Pet to the Maid of Saltwaters, who is patron of this voyage."

230

"All due respect to her Maidship," the Cook said. "But she might run a tighter ship, so to speak, if all her crew wasn't otters and flounders and suchlike."

"This third Great Wave –" the Carpenter said. "When is it due? Or more to the point, when is the *second* Wave due? For surely we've only seen the one so far –"

"Which nearly foundered us," the Cook pointed out.

"I am only captain of the ship," Jenny said, "and not an oracle. Let us see what the morning brings."

BUT THAT NIGHT, the wind began to rise in the middle watch, and if that hadn't been enough to wake any proper sailor, Sparky barked so madly that Jenny first thought he must have smelled Corsairs.

So all the sailors were awake, and had moved to the watch-fire, where they huddled close in a small circle under the moonless sky, for something was in the air, they knew: dangerous weather, or bad luck, or perhaps just Corsairs.

"I imagine it will be dangerous weather *and* bad luck, but with no Corsairs," the Cook said, "for I'm not one to look on the dark side, and besides we confounded those pirates at the Clashing Rocks."

Then they were quiet as the wind rose and began to rustle the olive grove about their camp. Only Sparky made a little noise as he shivered by Jenny, and the two sailors from amidships began to moan quietly. *"Dangerous weather!"* one whispered, more or less as an experiment, and *"Bad luck!"* the other whispered back.

231

At last the wind began to roar from the North, from across the Old Sea, and they saw inky clouds spill over the sky, covering the stars. "It's the second Great Wave!" cried Jenny.

"The Great Wave!" moaned the sailors from amidships. "Not the Great Wave!" and then they all felt the hair on their heads begin to rise.

Sparky howled once and raced for his barrel, and then a blinding flash of light split the sky.

The thunder came so loud it dwarfed the sound the Clashing Rocks had made; the thunder came so loud it made the roar of their cannon seem like a popgun; the thunder came so loud it stunned them into stones, made them deaf to the waves breaking against their cove. The sound of it rolled on like the end of the world, and before it faded, the lightning struck again and again.

So Jenny remembered the storm as a series of dazzling pictures: the circle of sailors, mouths gaping in the flash of lightning, and then the pitch-black of the storming night; over and over, while the rain and hail began to beat against them, noiselessly it seemed to their thunderstruck ears.

Then there was a strange pause before the Great Wave came like a towering black curtain and crashed down over the beach.

The Great Wave knocked them flat, swallowed them whole and turned them upside down. Then it spat them back on shore, and the storm passed over them at last.

As soon as her wits returned, Jenny began to crawl around the remains of their camp.

There were stars again, and the sailors were shaking themselves like wet dogs, surprised to be alive. The *Ruggles* had been ashore, where it had landed hard against a tree, and their camp looked like a shipwreck, but they were all alive, and Sparky came back to her, whining, from out of Maxim Tortuca's barrel. Even the goat Gimlet was dazzled but alive.

"There is not much time," Jenny said. "When the next wave comes, the Lost City will rise, and we must be there or it will be lost again."

The Voyage of the Nonesuch

232

But for now, the crew of the *Ruggles* gathered themselves in the dark aftermath of the storm, and fell asleep where they lay.

JENNY WOKE with the morning sun in her eyes.

Sparky was curled up beside her, and she patted him, and almost closed her eyes again. "There is a cozy pleasure simply in being alive," Jenny began to explain to Sparky, thinking this must be how Tom had felt when he had woken up warm in the Lodge in the cold North.

Then Jenny noticed that the Navarch of the Corsairs stood over her with a cocked pistol. He looked rather the worse for wear.

In fact, armed and bedraggled Corsairs surrounded the whole crew of the *Ruggles*. They had been captured without a struggle – captured in their sleep.

Jenny got to her feet, clutching her tricorne hat to her head so that she could take it off when she bowed. For all tales told how great captains and Explorers had been noble in defeat as well as victory.

"I congratulate you on your seamanship," she said to the Navarch of the *Terror*. "For you both made the passage of the Clashing Rocks and, I presume, met the Great Wave at sea, and yet survived."

"Many things can be done with a firm hand at the tiller," the Navarch said, gesturing back at the *Terror*, "and a strong arm at the whip."

The Voyage of the Nonesuch

233

And if the *Terror* had been a grim sight at Babbylantium, or during the race for the Clashing Rocks, it was awful to look at now, anchored at the end of the cove. Its sails hung tattered and torn like rags; broken oars stuck out at odd angles, and it listed to one side. And even the slaves at the oars seemed to sag in their chains, exhausted and bloody from the lashes that had driven them through the Rocks and on through the night and the storm.

"You'd never have got those poor wretches through the Clashing Rocks if we hadn't shown you the trick of it," growled the Cook.

"And you might not have made it through had you not been fleeing us," the Corsair pointed out.

"Your crew looks half-dead," Jenny said, picking up Sparky protectively. "What sense is there in driving them so hard when they must be alive to carry you home?"

The Navarch made a signal, and two Corsairs came close, bearing armloads of chains and manacles. "We knew we could find more strong backs here," he said. "For here is whole coast not yet sacked or looted by Corsairs, which is a great inspiration to us. And we had to have our revenge, of course. For to be beaten by a preening, loud, fisher-girl offends our sense of what is seemly for a Corsair."

Jenny looked around again at the Corsairs: four dozen weather-beaten, desperate, bloodthirsty, slaving, uncouth brigands pointing muskets and pistols at her crew. The Corsairs had extra pistols in their sashes, knives in their

234

teeth, and no pity in their eyes.

The two sailors from amidships moaned again, and suddenly the *Terror*'s first mate – what the Corsairs called a Whip-Hand, cracked a lash across their backs. "Silence!" he yelled. "You'll be the first ones in shackles – and the first to be used as shark bait." The rest of Jenny's crew gasped, and the two sailors began sobbing.

Jenny couldn't think of what to do, but she had to stop the whipping. She looked over at the Cook, but he just shook his head. She tried to think what Maxim Tortuca, or Ola Olagovna, would have done in such an extremity, but that wasn't much help either. So Jenny could only step forward and look around at her crew in what she hoped was an inspiriting way. "We'll meet our end with dignity, then," she told the Navarch. "Put the irons on me first."

235

But the Navarch of the *Terror* only laughed. "It's not worth our while to carry someone who could only be sold as the cheaper sort of scullery maid," he said, while his Whip-Hand began putting shackles – none too gently – on the sailors from amidships.

Jenny put her hands on her hips. "But I am Captain of this crew!" she shouted.

"But she's only a wee girl!" yelled the Cook, even louder. "You can't leave her as a castaway on a barren shore to starve and be eaten by wild animals!"

"Brave Captain Jenny who marooned the crew of the *Ruggles*?" said the Navarch. "I think that is the least she deserves."

Then the Navarch looked as though he had just remembered something. "But tell me how to find the Lost City," he told the Cook. "And I will grant your Jenny the privilege of being put in chains as well."

"That's your bargain?" demanded the Cook. "Not to release our ship or crew, but only enslave Jenny as well?"

"Generosity ill becomes a Corsair," said the Navarch. "Tell us about the Lost City."

The Cook thought for a moment, and then he began to spin an elaborate yarn, about a dangerous journey East along the coast: past coves guarded by giant eagles that devoured every third sailor they saw; beyond islands of one-eyed ogres who delighted in eating people; and so at last to a fabulous land where gold spilled in streams from the mountains. "Then you come to the Lost City," he finished. "If you're still alive."

The Navarch smiled patiently. "If we take this journey," he said, "I will cast one sailor into the sea for each cove we pass without finding these giant eagles, one-eyed ogres, or streams of gold."

"No!" Jenny cried. She looked at the Cook. "The Cook is merely trying to save me. We do not know where this Lost City is, though I was told to find it."

And then the Navarch stopped and stared at the bright satchel Jenny had bought at the Grand Bazaar, the satchel where she kept the letter the Otter had left for them. Jenny swallowed, and all her crew began looking away, pretending they were unconcerned. But the Navarch only smiled. "How much did you pay for that?" he asked.

Jenny told him, for she thought she had made a good bargain. But the Navarch only laughed. "So much for a saddlebag from a midget camel!" he said. "There are greater thieves than Corsairs in the Old Sea." Jenny shrugged as if the satchel didn't matter to her. Some of her crew began whistling idly, as if they didn't care either.

Then the Navarch reached into the satchel and took the letter from the Otter. The Navarch slowly sounded out the Otter's words. Then he unfolded the map, and stared at the drawing of the Lost City all alone in the middle of the sea.

It meant no more to him than it had to the crew of the *Ruggles*. "This is the kind of game that would be played by a foolish girl," he said, bitter from disappointment. "Lost Cities and talking Otters! Keep your map and study it in your lonely exile," he told Jenny. "There are real places and real treasure on this coast – for those who dare."

For once, Jenny kept silent, but the Cook stomped his peg leg. "I won't let you leave her alone to die!" he shouted. And then he began swearing loudly and profusely, using the most awful oaths from all the places he'd ever sailed, from the Puffin Islands to Zunna-wundoor. He didn't stop until the Navarch pointed a pistol at Jenny.

"I could shoot her, then," the Navarch said. And as the crew of the *Ruggles* gasped, he swung his pistol towards the Cook. "Or I could shoot you both."

And if the crew of the *Ruggles* moaned; if the Cook

237

couldn't think of any profanity adequate to the situation; if Sparky whimpered so that Jenny had to hug him close; if Jenny felt her knees shake – still, even when it looked like they were both to meet their end, still Jenny and the Cook both set their jaws firmly and stared at the Navarch: they looked their doom in the eye. Then the Corsair laughed, for he did at least admire courage.

"An old man with one leg," he told the Cook. "You're not worth taking either. Stay here, the two of you, then; stay and starve on olives, or be eaten by tigers, or try to cross the desert to the South with no fresh water – or you could pray, perhaps, that a giant balloon will land and bear you away to the Mountains of the Moon. But trouble me no more."

238

Then Jenny and the Cook had to watch as their crew was taken in a skiff to the *Terror*, and shackled beside the other galley slaves. The biggest, fattest sailor would have put up a struggle yet, but the Cook made a signal to the Carpenter, who restrained him. And if some of the others shook, and if some them wept, still they took this ruin of their hopes so bravely that Jenny and the Cook felt their hearts break with pride and sorrow.

At last, the Navarch and the few of the Corsairs left put a rope around Gimlet's neck. Jenny would have said something then, but the Cook put his hand over her mouth. Then the pirates dragged Gimlet into the *Ruggles*, and ran the *Ruggles* out into the water, and tied it behind the *Terror*. Then Jenny and Sparky and the Cook heard the

Corsairs' whips crack, and as the *Terror* began to leave the cove, pulling East, with the *Ruggles* towed behind, they heard the Corsairs sing:

> *Blood and gold is what a pirate craves*
> *Yo-ho-ho! and whipping fresh backs!*
> *And the* Terror *rules the Old Sea waves*
> *Yo-ho-ho! with lashes and cracks!*

And many other verses they heard too, foul and terrible, and all in time with real cracks of the Corsairs' whips, and the real screams of the slaves, their friends now among them. They stood and listened until the *Terror* was beyond hearing, stood and watched until it was hull-down, and only the masts still showed above the horizon, until it finally disappeared in the East. The East where troubles grew, where strife and turmoil rose like the sun.

239

At last, Jenny spoke. "Thank you for trying to save me," she said to the Cook. "But I was captain, and should have gone with my crew."

"Chips is a steady man, and will take command in our absence," the Cook said. "But you have still the Lost City to find. And the First Mate told me to look after you, back at the Isle of No Return."

"But Gimlet —" Jenny said. "They'll roast him when they get hungry, why didn't you let me try to save him too —"

The Voyage of the Nonesuch

And Jenny stopped suddenly, remembering how much the Cook had disliked Gimlet: more even than he disliked her, if that were possible.

"As long as they have Gimlet along, that's one member of our crew not in shackles," said the Cook. "And that might be handy, even if Gimlet's nearly forgot he was ever a real boy at all."

Jenny nodded, ashamed at what she had been thinking. "Now I have lost my hope of finding the Lost City before it is too late," she said at last. "Or perhaps Corsairs will find it instead as they roam this coast. For they have marooned us, and left us to die."

The Cook looked at Jenny, weighing her spirit. For he thought to encourage her, here at the end of all their hopes.

240

But it was then that she recovered herself, became Jenny proud and wordy once again. "For they think I am merely a helpless fisher-girl," she said, "discounting that I am also a spirited Explorer, hand-chosen by an emissary of the King Beneath the Sea; and they believe you are only an old man with one leg, whereas in fact you are a grizzled sailor of vast experience. And Sparky, he is faithful beyond words, even if he seems timid."

The Cook looked around at the flotsam on the beach: the wrecked mast and broken manger and tangled bits of rigging from the *Ruggles*, and the odd piece of driftwood. He made a kind of grin. "We'll build a boat, then," he said.

"And find where the Lost City sank beneath the waves,"

The Voyage of the Nonesuch

said Jenny. "Even if we are too late."

"And then take our vengeance on the Corsairs," said the Cook. "Damn their hides."

THE FIRST THING Jenny and the Cook did was follow Sparky to find pools of fresh water that had been left by the storm – so they wouldn't perish of thirst. And the second thing they did was collect olives and berries – so they wouldn't die of hunger. (The Cook boiled the berries into a kind of jam, and spread it over roasted olives.) And the third thing they did was set to work on a boat – so they wouldn't be lost from despair.

As they worked, Jenny tried to make conversation. "Although the Navarch spoke of it as impossible, in fact Maxim Tortuca did travel to the Mountains of the Moon," she said. "For it's little-known but true, that as well as being a great and intrepid sailor, Tortuca was also an expert balloonist."

"Did you ever wonder, missy, just for a moment," the Cook said, while he wiped the sweat from his eyes, "whether Tortuca wasn't so much a great Explorer as a tremendous spinner of yarns?"

Jenny stared at the Cook, shocked. "Tortuca!" she cried at last. "Why, anyone knows that he sailed the Seven Seas, roved the caverns at the Marrow of the World, and wrote majestic and authentic accounts of his travels, observations, and inventions that filled an entire hall at the Great

241

The Voyage of the Nonesuch

Library – before its untimely collapse."

"Maybe it couldn't hold up his reputation," said the Cook.

"How can you of all people doubt Tortuca!" cried Jenny. "Why, some of your adventures in the Northern circumnavigation of the *Volantix* were so fantastic that they can hardly be remembered, not to mention the more mundane matters of goblin battles, pirate attacks, ancient remains, and so forth."

"Ah," said the Cook. "That's where Tortuca has me beat, for I lack the patience to write 'em down."

Jenny kept working, lashing spars together, but she still fumed. "Who would believe *our* tale?" she asked.

The Cook laughed. "You write it down when we're home," he said. "And put 'A True Account' on the title page. That'll settle any doubts."

So Jenny and the Cook worked to stave off despair, but Sparky was untroubled, having simply been happy to see the Corsairs leave. And while they laboured in the hot sun, Sparky only dug himself a shallow pit and stretched his stomach out across the cool earth and slept the hopeful sleep of dogs.

When Jenny and the Cook were done working at last, what they had built was a raft, really, not a boat, although it did have one small mast and a scrap of sail. A small, crooked raft, just big enough for the two of them, and Sparky and his barrel – not big enough to have a name, even.

But there was daylight left, and rather than spend

242

another night in that place of lost hopes, they pushed the raft into the water and left the beach behind. Jenny gave the cove a name: "The Cove of Despair, I call it," said Jenny. "And may we never lay eyes on it again." But Sparky was already looking ahead, excited to be underway again.

"Which way now?" asked the Cook.

At first, Jenny only shook her head, for she had no idea. Then she remembered the map in her satchel. As it happened, there was nothing to be seen by daylight that they hadn't seen the night before; just the island in the middle of the sheet. But the Cook asked, "Why is there a knot in that ribbon?"

Then Jenny remembered something her Godmother, the Wise Woman of the Woods Nearby, once told her. "The right knot can keep any manner of things tied up," Jenny said, and pulled the silk knot open.

243

And as soon as the blue ribbon was loose, a new wind began to blow. A strong, steady wind that carried the little raft Northeast. And the wind blew on the rest of the day, and all the evening, and into the night.

"Perhaps the Otter made the map rather cleverly after all," the Cook said.

The Voyage of the Nonesuch

A great city was rising from the water

CHAPTER SEVENTEEN:
THE SUN ROSE OVER SHINING TOWERS OF BRASS

A FTER THE CORSAIRS SAILED OUT OF THE COVE of Despair, as Jenny was to name it, the two pirate ships began limping their way along the coast, the listing *Terror* towing the smaller, broken *Ruggles* behind.

For Jenny's crew, now shackled to their oars, the voyage was soon a nightmare of blisters and whips, and the terrible stench of a slaver's galley in the hot sun. For the Corsairs hardly gave them enough water to stay alive, and none, of course, for washing.

The two sailors who had served amidships weren't the only ones who whimpered from fear and dread, and it wasn't just the two sailors who screamed at the crack of the whip, and were whipped again for screaming.

But there were other slaves at the oars, too: the poor, filthy wretches who'd rowed the *Terror* in its long chase. And the Carpenter, always a steady old hand, marked that these experienced slaves hardly moaned when the whips came out, and so escaped half the lashing.

So he called out: "Flounder-chosen sailors from the Otter! Remember your pride and save your backs. For if these poor creatures can withstand the terror of the lash, so can we!"

And so even the two sailors who had been amidships restrained themselves after that, to a sort of mild whimper. But the Whip-Hand struck the Carpenter hard across the back. "No talking, either," the Corsair hissed.

So they rowed on, miserable and hopeless, but the Carpenter, like the Navarch of the *Terror* himself, noted that the galley was shipping water, and listing harder to port every hour. And now there was no rest for any of the slaves, for if they weren't needed for rowing, they were set to bailing, and if they were slow at either task, the whips came out.

BY THE EVENING, the *Terror* had come to a wide southern shore where the land climbed up high above the beach and groves of tall black pines stood in the shadow of a cliff.

Then there were hours of hard work yet, all with no food, for the *Ruggles* was run in, and then with a great set of winches and cables, and much sweat and hauling, the *Terror* itself was pulled ashore.

And while the Corsairs and their captives alike lay back on the sand, exhausted, the Navarch of the *Terror* came up to the Carpenter.

"Chips," the Navarch began, for he was trying to be friendly, "the other men call you Chips, from being a Carpenter, yes?" The Carpenter nodded.

"I will be your friend too, Chips," said the Navarch. "For I believe you are a steady old hand, and skilled with tools. And I will need my friend Chips to help us repair these ships, your little *Ruggles*, and my awful *Terror*."

The Carpenter's back was bloody and raw from the lashes of the Corsairs, but still he had some spirit left. "Promise you will let us sail away in the *Ruggles* and I will build your ship so it will be the pride of the Corsair fleet," he said. And as he spoke, his voice cracked with thirst.

The Navarch showed his gold teeth, for he admired spirit, to a point. "You ask too much, my friend," he said. "But help us and I will let your men drink water as they please and not trouble them with whips. And when the work is done, we shall feast on this goat you have given a golden crown. And we will let your men also have a very small portion."

247

The Carpenter was silent about the Corsair's plans for Gimlet, but he thought hard. At last he agreed, and then the Carpenter and the Navarch of the *Terror* toasted their bargain with fresh water from a stream. But the Carpenter hated it when a stranger called him "Chips."

AND WHAT HAD BECOME of Jenny and the Cook? The wind that had been tied up in the Otter's map had blown on, strong and steady, through the night and all the next day.

They spoke little to one another on that strange journey, for there was little work in such sailing. "We're being drawn to the end of our Exploration," Jenny said once.

The Voyage of the Nonesuch

"We're being drawn like a toy on a string," the Cook replied. "Away from the real world where we live and into some dream." And the Cook thought of the time when he and the First Mate and Tom and all the rest of the crew of the *Volantix* had dwelt in the lodge of Grandfather Frost, under the Eaves of the World; a memory that had almost been lost, but which came back now real as rain.

But Jenny thought of how her Exploration had begun like a dream, when the Otter had appeared out of the foam in the little cove where she tied up her boat. And Jenny remembered the Maid of Saltwaters' cave, which had been like the strange deep part of a dream where you are allowed to wake up, but she had chosen not to.

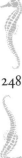

248

And Sparky only looked about and enjoyed the regular rise and fall of the little raft as the wind and waves bore it along, and what he made of dreams is hard to say, for he was a dog of no speech. But high above them were white tumbling hills of cloud in the blue sky, and Sparky thought of running on them, of bounding among their depths and folds.

Sparky thought he might find Tom, his master, there.

So they sailed on in the dreaming quiet of the oldest part of the Old Sea, the Sea of Heroes, the Sea of Wonders Found and Forgotten, lulled by the steady wind and waves, Jenny and the Cook and Tom's dog, Sparky. The waves rose around them, and then broke in white foam that fell like lace against the blue sea. For a while a little, grey bird with a cream breast

The Voyage of the Nonesuch

sat on the raft with them, resting in the middle of the sea, and then it flew away and they were alone again.

At last night came and the sea grew dark and then black, and the stars turned in the sky, and then in the light before morning they saw low clouds gathering far to the North.

Slowly the wind died as the day grew, and the waves calmed until the little raft rocked softly in the quiet beneath the gathering clouds. They saw dolphins rise from the sea all about them, leaping and racing away in all directions. Then the sea began to thrum, the longest, deepest note that has ever been heard.

I am about to wake up, Jenny thought. *The whole of the world is about to wake.*

And Jenny saw Sparky open his mouth as if to bark, and the Cook's mouth was moving, and Jenny meant to cry out too, but she heard nothing but the throbbing from far below – and then the little boat was rising.

249

Jenny pushed Sparky into his barrel and shut the lid, and she and the Cook looked at one another, wordlessly.

Then, right beside them, a tower rose up from the sea.

The raft nearly swamped, but a great city was rising from the water, a city built on a hill. Suddenly, Jenny and the Cook were steering their little boat down the rising streets of the strange city, racing the falling, rushing water, through arches and around corners and narrow lanes, until there was a final shiver and they were tossed from the raft and lay in a tumble on a wet, cobbled, quayside street – Jenny and the Cook, and Sparky in his barrel.

The Voyage of the Nonesuch

Away from them, away from the risen city, a great wave rolled in all directions, a towering wave, a great curl of dark green water that hid the noon sky, and they saw their raft rise and be swallowed and broken, while dark clouds and lightning swept after it.

Then they turned away from the sea and looked in wonder as the sun rose over shining towers of brass, over gleaming arches of marble, over the green brick roads that climbed the mountain-city; heard a thousand sounding chimes and clockworks begin peals of joy.

And Jenny cried out with delight as well. "The Lost City has been found again, after an age in the deepness of the sea!" she cried. "The Lost City which shines with hope and glory, for it is fresh as washday and tall as heaven!"

250

The Cook only scratched his peg leg for a moment, for he didn't know what to say. The city was a wonder, and it shone as though it were brand new, untouched by an age beneath the waves.

"Well done, girlie," he said at last. "But now I wish we had named that little raft what got us here after all."

Then Jenny let Sparky out of his barrel, and the dog began chasing up the strange new hills. And after the echoes of the chimes faded away, Sparky's cries and barks were all the noise there was. For the city was silent as a grave.

THE DAY BEFORE, the Carpenter had begun directing the repairs, as the Navarch had asked, for the Corsairs had few practical men among them, preferring to let slaves do their labour.

And while the Corsairs stood guard with their pistols and muskets and whips, the Carpenter made subtle gestures and small signs to let his shipmates know they should look busier than they really were, which sailors call "skating." Though of course, that wasn't the habit of Jenny's crew, the crew that had sailed through the Eaves of the World, and so circumnavigated the globe. In any case, they managed to bamboozle the Corsairs, and the other slaves were clever enough to skate along with them.

For the Carpenter was clever with calculations and constellations, and he had marked the phases of the moon and the times of the Great Waves. And he estimated that the third Great Wave would come sooner than anyone else expected, and he wanted his men rested for what came after.

251

Once the Whip-Hand peered at the slaves' work suspiciously, and demanded what they were about, but the Carpenter answered him without a pause in his pretended work: "The boom-scarfing requires a boffin-joint, which first requires us to bind wapping about the auger pin," which made more no more sense to the Corsair than it does to you, for in fact, it was only a jumble of the lingo of woodcraft; but it sounded well, and the Whip-Hand wasn't about to admit his ignorance to a galley slave.

So Jenny's crew, and the three-score wretches who were slaves with them, worked hard that day, but not as hard as the watching Corsairs thought, and drank their fill of fresh water. And if Gimlet knew he was meant to be roasted when the work was done, he gave no sign, but only watched placidly, nibbling grass, and bleating seldom.

By the evening, the *Terror* had been careened, and one of its sides had been slowly and carefully laid open, "The better to repair her damaged hull and innards," the Carpenter explained to the Navarch.

"Make sure the work is finished by tomorrow night," the Navarch told the Carpenter, while the Corsairs shackled the slaves together for the night. "For we mean to be busy on this new coast."

The steady old Carpenter remembered of the skipping song Jenny had taught them:

252

> *One wave, two waves, three waves rising*
> *Big water, sea water, oceans tall!*
> *Each wave's bigger, till it's surprising*
> *Anyone's left to count at all!*

And then he looked at the stars in the moonless sky carefully, calculating. But to the Navarch, he only said, "I hope you will be busy, too."

The Navarch laughed with pleasure. "You are smart, Chips," he said. "I will let you eat the goat's heart."

THE CARPENTER was awake at the first light, long before the sun rose. He passed the word to wake down the chain of slaves. There was a Corsair on watch of course, and when he saw the captives muttering, he snapped his whip menacingly.

But winds were already blowing, and in the East, high clouds glowed as they were first to catch the sunrise. The clouds were tall and troubled, and then the Corsair felt something too, and cried the alarm to rouse his companions. But he needn't have bothered: for just then the rim of the sun appeared.

Suddenly, lightning split the sky, cracking a tall cedar that stood on the cliff right in half. To the North, a shadow began to move over the sea. The Corsairs shouted, and cracked their whips, and threatened with their muskets, but there was nothing to be done, for the wave was coming, the third Great Wave. The Navarch ran to the top of the cliff and shook his fist at the sea and cursed in words that were foul, even for a sailor; but the wave rolled on regardless, a rising wall of grey, and their ships lay open and exposed.

If the first Great Wave had been a danger at sea, and the second had nearly wrecked the *Ruggles* where it lay at the Cove of Despair, this third Wave was greater than both together. It swept over the sailors, so they tumbled and nearly drowned. It gathered up the *Ruggles* and hurled it against the high land. And it crashed into the open side of the *Terror* and broke it completely, and washed half of it out to sea, just as the Carpenter had hoped.

So when the storm had passed, the Corsairs and their

slaves alike staggered to their feet to see the beach strewn with wreckage. The *Ruggles* might be mended, but the awful *Terror* had been smashed to pieces.

"And Captain Jenny and the Cook!" wailed the two sailors from the masts. "What will have become of them, marooned in that evil cove?"

Then the Navarch roared down from atop the cliff: "I was tricked! You knew, my friend!" he screamed at the Carpenter. "You knew!"

"I didn't know, but only hoped," the Carpenter said, reasonably. "The Waves come at significant moments in the heavens," he explained. "The first was at noon on the day of Midsummer. And the second at midnight on the night of the next new moon. And I knew that this morning, dawn would arrive at the very moment the Throne of the Queen of the Hall of the Stars was highest in the sky."

"I hold you and your stars and calculations responsible!" cried the Navarch. "Whip them all! Then whip my friend Chips a second time, for being so smart."

254

CHAPTER EIGHTEEN:
WE ARE COME TO THE HOUSES OF THE DEAD

Bᴜᴛ ᴏꜰ ᴄᴏᴜʀsᴇ, ᴛʜᴀᴛ ᴍᴏʀɴɪɴɢ, Jᴇɴɴʏ ᴀɴᴅ Sᴘᴀʀᴋʏ and the Cook were not still marooned in the Cove of Despair, but had been at the Lost City to see the wave leave, long before it ever reached the camp of the Corsairs.

At first they only wandered after Sparky, who was entranced by all the places to mark, all the strange things to smell. And the city itself had a particular smell that even Jenny and the Cook couldn't help noticing: it was briny with the sea, of course, but smoky, too, and cutting through it all was the tang of brass.

"Like a ship's chimney," the Cook said.

"But without the attendant grime," Jenny added. So they followed Sparky, more or less at random, though generally tending to wind upwards. For they were stunned with wonder themselves and had no other plan.

"I feel agog, and thrown on my beam ends," the Cook said.

"I am likewise blutterbunged and stupefied both," echoed Jenny. But she had at least the sense to tow Sparky's barrel along, for it had been fitted with a handle beneath the porthole in the front, and with small wheels hidden in its back end, under the propeller. "In case we find something that needs bearing away," she explained.

So they spent hours wandering haphazardly in the maze of the great turreted city, the city that had been lost beneath the waves, but shone now fresh-washed and gleaming in the sun.

"This is seven kinds of marvel," the Cook said, "But where's the people? Or do we walk among their spirits?"

"I don't know," said Jenny. "It's as dead quiet as the sacked town of Noan-mlee-gone-ger, which I saw with the First Mate."

Still, they had found shops full of silver pocket watches, chambers crowded with jewellery, towers with astrolabes, and in one huge vaulted hall, a *celestarium,* a great machine that mimicked the motions of the stars and planets set in the sky.

"Do you think the Queen of the Hall of the Stars would approve of this copy of her work?" asked the Cook.

"I think even She might wonder how it was made," Jenny said. "For surely the ones who built this city can only have been the Lords of the World."

"It's all bright-work," the Cook said of the copper and brass finish all around them. "And would require tedious amounts of polishing by a crack and fussy crew."

"It must have the virtue of shining without attention," Jenny pointed out, "for the brass having been under the waves this last age, and yet not covered with green verdigris, nor the oak become soft and rotten, nor the whole city otherwise sea-changed."

"True enough," said the Cook, as he stumped along beside Jenny. "And where's the crew to be doing the polishing anyway?"

They were stopped now by a courtyard fountain where the water pulsed in time with a huge whirligig contraption of brass gears and levers. "What if it was sacked, like Noanmlee-gone-ger?" Jenny asked.

"But that was merely the work of Corsairs, damn their hides," said the Cook. "Who could have harmed this great city? It's like a well-found ghost ship, with no one aboard."

"And if it had been the Corsairs, surely it would have been looted and broken," Jenny said. "Perhaps that is the reason we were chosen to find the Lost City first. For while I admit to hankering after the gems and treasures that lie in the halls and shops, I expect similar articles will be granted to us freely, as a reward, once we find the monarchs of this new realm."

257

"Indeed, I hope they are grateful, for we could fill that barrel of Sparky's with gadgets and gold and silver and precious stones, and no one would miss it," the Cook said wistfully.

Jenny looked at him Cook shrewdly. "Have you taken anything?" she asked.

"I only thought, since we was sure to be rewarded, to pick a few things out in advance," the Cook said. And he pulled out a fine chiming pocket watch, and then a small golden collar, which he handed to Jenny. "That might make that Otter less cocky," he said.

Jenny couldn't bring herself to chastise him, but fixed the golden collar around her neck. "I will mention this at once when we meet our hosts," she said. "And return it if they have unforeseen objections."

Then they stared at the clockwork fountain for a while. "This device is hardly chief of the wonders here," Jenny said. "But even so it would be counted as a great marvel even in Babbylantium. Not to speak of the rest of the known world."

"Is it a chain pump directed by a chronometer, or a timepiece governed by water?" the Cook wondered.

Just then a banging sound started from far below, a rude, clashing, coughing noise that shook the ground repeatedly, like some metal drumbeat.

"An irritating noise," Jenny said. "Although it has at least a solid regularity, which is not surprising, for this must be the great clockwork city of the world."

And then while they were admiring the great washes of water from the fountain, amidst the clamour they heard all the clocks of the Lost City make their noon fanfares – small and delicate from little silver timepieces, great and comically deep from huge brass and oak clock-organs – and then they all struck twelve, in a great discord.

The fountain shot high twelve times as well. "The middle of the day," Jenny said. "We have only till midnight to find the Great Bell, according the Otter's instruction."

Amidst the racket from the chimes and clocks and

gongs, there was no way to tell if any was the sound of the Great Bell, but Jenny and the Cook couldn't doubt that it was farther up, at the tower at the peak of the city, the tower that had almost capsized their raft.

EVENING WAS FALLING before the three Explorers found the great iron gate to the centre of the Lost City. They had climbed the winding streets and stairs for hours and hours, and even Sparky had begun to tire of new smells, and of exploring lifeless chambers, had become weary of the endless grating banging from far below.

But now at the gate, the tall doors swung open at Jenny's knock without a creak. Beyond was an avenue of tall houses with banners flying over every doorway. For a moment, Jenny expected to hear a trumpet sound, or at least some sign of welcome, but this avenue too was empty of life. But it led to the courtyard of the palace that stood at the pinnacle of the city.

259

The courtyard had three arches; and each was taller than the last. The first archway was of brass, and in the light of the low sun, it shone like fire. The second was made of silver, and it was taller yet, and gleamed like ice. And beyond that, the third archway stood, made of gold and taller than a schooner's mainmast, and it blazed like the setting sun.

And when they had passed this third archway, they found the heart of the Lost City at last.

The Voyage of the Nonesuch

THE GREAT TOWER that had nearly wrecked them stood in the centre, and on every side around it were halls that led into the chambers of the mountain.

"That tower looks to reach to the Roof of the World," the Cook said.

And, "Surely we will find the Great Bell at its top," said Jenny.

Around the tower, stairs wound up, and high above, they saw smoke pour out from the tower's top, and spread across the darkening sky.

The Cook scratched his wooden leg. "It could be the chimney of the great furnace of the world," he said. "But that explains the smell."

"Where is Sparky gone?" asked Jenny.

"Tom's dog –" the Cook began. And then they saw Sparky, and he was indeed disappearing into a shadowed hall, heading down into the depths of the mountain. "He's always wanting to be digging down," the Cook said.

Jenny left the barrel behind and ran after the little dog, calling his name, and the Cook hopped after them as quickly as he could.

"Wait missy Jenny, captain, wait; for we need a light. Wait!"

But in the shadowed halls, the odd clanging was louder than ever, and echoed oddly, and even if Jenny did hear the Cook, she wouldn't wait to find Tom's dog. Sparky was barking now, too, though the noise seemed to come from seven directions at once, and Jenny followed as best she could.

The Voyage of the Nonesuch

"Wait!" the Cook called again, but Jenny had gone down into the tunnels, and was lost in the dark.

IN THE TUNNELS, just as the dim evening light that crept in from the openings above was almost gone, the Lost City showed another marvel. For globes of crystal hung suspended from the ceilings, and they lit up now, in the seven colours of the rainbow.

But the strange new light didn't really help Jenny, for now Sparky had stopped his barking and the clanging was grown louder. There were doors that Jenny never entered, strange closed rooms with doors of bone and doors of iron, and there were chambers that seemed oddly cold as Jenny passed, and others where she shivered though they weren't cold at all. Jenny wandered for a long time, calling Tom's dog, as the Cook wandered, calling her, and neither of them had an idea of where to go, except that the tunnels that led down always seemed brighter and wider.

So they went in their confusion, chasing one another, deeper and deeper into the stone heart of the Lost City, the smoky sea-smell rising higher around them, and each of them was followed by dozens of strange, coloured shadows from the hanging lamps.

At last Jenny came to a vast underground hall, a vaulted and pillared chamber greater than any ship, greater than the temple of the Oracle. In that shadowed hall, deep below the surface, there were still a few inches of sea water,

261

The Voyage of the Nonesuch

and small white fish darted over the marble floor, among the pillars and platforms. And in one corner she saw Sparky crouched against a wall, wet and terrified with fear.

For on the platforms around them were crystal caskets, hundreds and hundreds of them; thousands of crystal caskets shining in the coloured lamplight, and lying in them the bodies of proud and handsome men and women, arranged in finery, in satins and silks, and even cloths woven of gold and silver. They had been laid out with gems on their fingers and precious stones at their brows. All of them still, and sealed in crystal.

Jenny picked up the shivering dog and held him close. "We are come to the Houses of the Dead," she whispered.

262

AND SO THE COOK found them in the end, huddling there together in the shadowed water. At first he quailed, for sailors are a superstitious lot, but then he stepped into the water and took Jenny's arm and pointed at a great clock set in the vaulted ceiling. "They sleep, missy," he said. "They merely sleep until midnight comes. You must strike the bell so it is safe for them to wake again; that's what the Otter wanted."

Jenny looked around at the sleeping Lords and Ladies, remembering the words of the Otter, and the Oracle, and the Maid of Saltwaters.

Just then the tunnels and the hall began to shake. The fanfare of the hour had begun, and the clocks in the Lost

City were about to strike eleven.

They had only an hour to find the Great Bell.

"Run!" shouted the Cook amidst the din of the striking hour. "Run, missy, up and up, and to the top of the tower. I can't keep up, so run, or the Lost City sinks, and takes these sleepers back to the bosom of the sea, and us with them!"

For a moment, Jenny only gaped, while the hour sounded and the echoes rolled through the hall. And then she nodded, and she and Sparky splashed out of the hall and began to race back through the tunnels. They ran past strange closed rooms, they raced through the odd, cold chambers. They didn't know the way, only that they had to take any passage that led up.

The Cook's voice came after them, mixing with the echoes of the hour. "Run!" the Cook called.

263

It wasn't easy to run up the winding stairs

CHAPTER NINETEEN:
THE NONESUCH

WHEN JENNY AND SPARKY EMERGED PANTING from the warm tunnels at last, and felt the cool night air against their faces, they saw the Lost City spread below them, lit in many colours. Crystal lanterns they hadn't noticed before shone everywhere, hung in every arch and doorway, set high as street lamps, and stretching on and on, down the twisting streets and towards the sea.

"The city is lit like a maypole!" Jenny exclaimed.

Sparky paid little attention to the city lights; he looked in the sky for any sign of the moon, which was dearer to his dog's heart, for he felt a howl coming over him. But the moon was still hidden, and so he only howled in a mournful kind of way, because it was gone.

Jenny stared at him, for Sparky was not regularly a howling dog, but then reflected that he must feel glad to be away from the tunnels, away from the caskets of the dead, or the sleeping. She looked up at the tower that rose from the heart of the Lost City, and the long stairway that wound about it. There wasn't much time.

Just then all the clocks in the city began to sound the half-hour. Only half an hour. Jenny and Sparky began to run up the winding stairs, up and around the tower at the heart of the Lost City, the tower that seemed to touch the Roof of the World.

IT WASN'T EASY to run up the winding stairs; sailors used to skylarking high in the rigging of a tall ship might not have minded the height, but even they didn't have to turn around and around as they climbed.

But Jenny and Sparky had to spin around as they climbed the tower. She kept her right hand on the smooth green stone of the tower wall for balance, but to her left the stairs were open to the sky, and to the thousand shining lanterns of the city below. Once or twice she made the mistake of looking down, and the network of shining lights dazzled her, seemed to twist and shift, and she felt as though she were falling already.

It was better if she looked up, up at the stars and constellations, which were the friend of any sailor. She looked for the moon too, but no moon shone; only the planet the Carpenter and her Godmother both called the Wizard Star, bright and green in the South, the planet that brought change. And that reminded her of the Wise Woman of the Woods Nearby, and of High Midnight Tea, and of Pawlikins the cat, who would never grow dizzy, no matter how high he climbed. But the Wizard and all the other stars were hazy with the smoke that drifted from the top of the tower.

The Voyage of the Nonesuch

Suddenly Jenny thought of what might happen if she didn't reach the top. She picked Sparky up. "Sparky," she said, "I know you are a dog of no speech, but a good dog, and a smart dog, and your master is my friend Tom. But your legs are too short for these stairs, and if the Bell is not rung in time...if the Bell is not rung in time, I think we will all be drowned."

Tom's dog looked up at her. "Find your barrel, boy," she said. She patted his head. "Get inside your barrel," she said. "Go on, Sparky, good dog – run!" And Sparky always wanted to be a good dog, so he turned around and began running down those high steps.

Jenny went on by herself, around and around. And if the spiral of the stairs grew smaller as she ascended, still Jenny moved in slower circles, for the stairs were made for the long legs of the Lords of the Lost City, not for a half-grown Fisher-Girl such as herself. Slower and slower she went, and as the spiral tightened, it became more dizzying, and the strange smell of smoke and brass and brine grew stronger. At last she could only go on by crawling. *I move on all fours now,* Jenny thought, *like Sparky, like an infant. Is this the manner of an Explorer?*

Now she wondered if there was any chance she could finish the climb, if it was even possible to reach the top before midnight struck. But then she remembered the nightmare climb Tom had made in the cold North, trying to reach the Roof of the World. *And Tom did not give up, no more than Maxim Tortuca would have,* she thought to herself. *For the crew of the* Volantix *depended on him. But my crew is already captured by Corsairs for the sake of this adventure, and all the troubles that brew in the world wait to see if the Otter's faith in me will be fulfilled.*

So she went on, on hands and knees, until she reached the landing at the top of the tower at last. She got to her feet then, and looked North, to see the lights of the city reflected in the calm Old Sea, with the tower's shape silhouetted like a bony, beckoning finger. It was like a long fang in the water, she thought, and somehow, she wanted to jump then, to fall down and down until she came to the end of all her cares and burdens.

For she was only a Fisher-Girl, she thought, and not a real Explorer or hero. And her adventure had amounted to this: the First Mate was lost on the Isle of No Return, and her crew were the slaves of Corsairs. And what would it matter if she perished here in any case? For she had no parents or brothers or sisters; only foolish dreams she'd found in books.

But books made her think of Tom's father, and that made her think of Tom, and that brought her thoughts to her prize expanding telescope, which she had once thought lost forever beneath the waves, but which Tom had brought back to her from the Eaves of the World; only now it was marked with a line of dolphins. And Tom used it to scan the sea and watch for her triumphant return.

And then Jenny was herself again, and turned and entered the chamber of the Great Bell on top of the tower,

The Voyage of the Nonesuch

just as the fanfare of the hour began to sound, the great chords rising from the Lost City below.

THAT SAME NIGHT, as the Wizard Star neared the centre of the sky, on the Corsair's beach the slaves and the sailors had finished their work at last.

They had made one small ship, an ugly, jury-rigged, makeshift galley, born from the broken *Ruggles* and the wreck of the *Terror*. This ship had only one mast, and that was scarfed together in two places, and the hull was cobbled together with planks from both ships; and its sail was stitched like quiltwork. Its oars were mismatched, and the whole was stuck tight with buckets of black pitch.

There wasn't a cannon aboard.

"Well," the Carpenter said to the Navarch, steady to the last, "it won't be the terror of the fleet, but it will take us home. What shall you name it?"

"Where shall we sail it?" asked the Corsair's Whip-Hand.

"Are we still slaves?" asked the two sailors who were painting the eyes on the prow. They were doing their best, but the boat was perhaps a little cross-eyed.

And, *"Shall I kill you all?"* demanded the Navarch. "For I have three-score slaves and four dozen pirates for this little boat, and all my luck has been ill since we left Babbylantium. Three chests of gold and jewels are all that are left, and now we're at the mercy of the cruel Old Sea, sailing in this clap-

269

The Voyage of the Nonesuch

trap rig, and at the mercy of our brother Corsairs, having no cannon to defend ourselves – and at the mercy of slaves and fools and cowards too, for so I deem you all."

Then Jenny's crew quailed, and all the other slaves cowered, and the Corsair crew tried to look fearsome, one and all, so that they would not be left behind. "Perhaps it's time for a Pirates' Council," the Corsair Whip-Hand said.

"I will take council," snarled his Navarch. "But not from my slaves, and not from my idiot crew."

"Well from who, then?" demanded the Carpenter. "For if your crew are idiots, then you're a bullying fool for sailing without knowing how to tend a boat."

And for a moment, the Navarch would have shot the Carpenter dead where he stood, only then he remembered Gimlet, and had a terrible thought.

"I shall sacrifice your goat with the golden crown," he said, taking hold of Gimlet's tether. "And then take council from the signs spelled out by its twisting guts."

One and all, Jenny's crew started forward, and even the Corsairs looked doubtful, but the Navarch levelled his pistol and they stood back. Then he began pulling Gimlet after him, up the path that led to the top of the cliff.

The two sailors who were painting the eyes began weeping, while the Corsairs mocked their captives for it. Even the other slaves said: "After all, he's only a goat."

Then they saw the Navarch set a bright torch on the cliff, and against its light, they saw his silhouette beside Gimlet's goatish form. The Corsair drew out a great blade, and then he turned to stare down at his long shadow wavering in the shifting sea. He had never seen himself look so tall.

THE BELL CHAMBER was open to the smoky constellations, to the light of the Wizard Star, and inside the chamber Jenny did find the Great Bell. It was wider than her outstretched arms, and Jenny wasn't surprised to see that it was really three bells, one inside the other: of brass, and silver, and gold.

The bells quivered, hummed a little, as the raucous fanfare for the hour went on, and their triple hum sounded loud in the chamber. Beside them hung a mallet, a bell-hammer, and Jenny picked it up. She needed to hold it in both hands for it was so heavy.

"I have reached the Great Bell in time," she said aloud. "I have fulfilled the Otter's Call, and justified the choice of the King Beneath the Sea and the Maid of Saltwaters; and think of how the Lords of the Lost City will reward me when they are awake."

It would have been better if someone had been there to hear her, but Jenny wasn't about to let such a moment pass without fine words.

The floor, and indeed the whole chamber shook as the clocks of the Lost City struck once, but Jenny did not wield the mallet yet.

"I shall savour the moment," she said. "For after this I

The Voyage of the Nonesuch

shall be changed forever by fame, riches, and renown."

The clocks struck a second time.

"I shall buy a ship, and a crew to sail it," she said. "And it shall be called the *Nonesuch* –" and the clocks struck a third time.

"– for it shall be paramount, and without peer, and simply tip-top in all respects," Jenny finished, as the clocks struck four. The triple Great Bell quivered along, making a noise almost too loud to bear. What sort of chord would it make when it was struck in time with all the rest?

And then Jenny thought of the Lords and Ladies of the Lost City, and how proud and noble they looked in their caskets, and while the clocks struck four, five, and six, she remembered the dolphins that had lived here in the Duke's dream, the dolphins she and the Cook had seen racing away before the Lost City rose. And she thought of the banging that had sounded, ever more clamorous since the Lost City had risen, and the smoke that issued still from grates all about the top of the tower. "The chimney of the great furnace of the world," the Cook had called it.

And while the clocks struck seven, and eight, and nine, Jenny remembered the Hall of the Oracle of Babbylantium, and how its pictures told the story of plague and death and trouble that grew until the salvation of the risen city.

Jenny raised the mallet, as the city, like one giant clock now, struck ten, and suddenly she thought of something. Her mind wandered in the Hall of the Oracle, but now it started from the East, where the sun rose, and saw the pic-

The Voyage of the Nonesuch

tures in a different order.

"Sparky!" she said aloud, though the dog was far below. "What if we read the pictures back to front?

"What if we misunderstood the beggar-girl?"

Then the Lost City sounded all together, struck for the eleventh time, and Jenny thought of the smoke and the proud look of the Lords of the Lost City as they slept beneath the hands of the great clock. *Pride goes before the waterfall,* were the words of her Godmother's rede, and now Jenny thought she understood them at last.

"But we shall be overwhelmed," she said, as though she were arguing with herself. Then Jenny let the mallet fall, and did not strike the Great Bell.

The thousand clocks of the Lost City struck twelve, all at once; the whole city, even the stones in the floor, quivered in a long discord that rose and grew louder and more jarring. It seemed like the tone would never end, but then lightning came out of the smoky sky to strike the tower.

For a moment, Jenny was deaf and blind, but as her sight came back, she saw a great wave gathering, a green dark wave as tall as the stars, a wave that came rolling over the Lost City. "Help me," Jenny whispered, and then she was gathered to the bosom of the sea.

273

IT WAS JUST THEN that the Navarch of the Corsairs was looking out across the sea at his torchlight shadow, and it was just then that Gimlet lowered his head and butted the

Navarch so that he fell screaming down the cliff, and landed dead among the other Corsairs.

"Woe to them all!" cried the Carpenter. *"Woe!"* And he swung his hammer at the Whip-Hand. Then the biggest, fattest sailor knocked another pirate down with his fist. And, *"Woe!"* cried all the rest of Jenny's crew, and, *"Woe!"* cried all the other wretched slaves, and they took their tools in hand and struck down the Corsairs.

"CAPTAIN JENNY," a gentle voice said, and at first Jenny thought she was still adrift in sleep, for hadn't that always been the dream of her heart?

"Captain Jenny, my wee girl, you float in the Sea of Heroes," the Cook said again, still more gently, and so Jenny came back to the waking world, and found that it was morning, and she was borne in the Cook's arms, and they floated in the warm, calm sea.

"The Sea of Wonders Found and Forgotten," Jenny said. "For now the city is lost again."

"Yes," said the Cook. "For they couldn't fool you, not Jenny Fisher-Girl, Jenny proud and wordy, they couldn't."

"I had the bell-hammer," Jenny said slowly.

"And so I was worried," the Cook said, "worried after the rooms I found as I tried to stumble after you. Rooms of whips and chains, and things I wouldn't tell to a young girl, even if she is a brave captain, for fear they'd trouble her heart. But I never saw such things, such monuments of skins and broken skulls, not in all my sailing days, not among Corsairs nor Boogey Pirates, nor even the Cannibal men of the bogs."

"The Lost City is the start of trouble, then," Jenny said, "and not the end."

"You're a smart girlie, Captain Jenny," the Cook said. "Which is doubtless why the Otter chose you. For anyone else would have been deluded by glory and rung the bell and lived like an Empress among those smug, cold sleepers."

"I almost did," said Jenny.

"Good," said the Cook. "That'll keep you humble."

They floated for a while in the calm empty sea, under the great blue sky, and then the Cook said, "Captain Jenny, are you all right to float on your own now? For although the wooden leg adds buoyancy, my sides was partly stove-in among the general destruction of the city."

275

Jenny slid away, and began to tread water on her own. "Cook, are you all right?" she said.

"For now," said the Cook, though it wasn't easy for him to speak. And so they stayed as the day wore on, and it was good the water was thick with salt, for it helped them float, rattled and shook up as they both were.

AND AFTER A WHILE, Jenny saw the Cook begin to cough as he floated in water.

"I always say it's a foolish sailor who learns to swim,"

The Voyage of the Nonesuch

the Cook said. "For my troubles would already be over if I hadn't."

"So would mine!" Jenny exclaimed.

"Ah, there's that," said the Cook. "And I promised the First Mate I'd look after you."

Then after a while he said, "Captain Jenny, I'm going to swim off aways now."

"No," said Jenny, "don't do that."

"I must," said the Cook. "For no matter how good a sailor is, if the end comes in the water, there's a sort of flailing and grabbing, and anyone near will get dragged under too."

"No!" cried Jenny. "No! Don't leave me. It's an order, and you're a good officer and won't leave me alone in the sea."

"You're my captain," said the Cook. "But you're a little Fisher-Girl, too, and it's how I must look after you." Then he pulled out the chiming watch he had found in the Lost City. "They made it waterproof, the devils," he said. "But I'll return it now, I guess." And he slowly swam several lengths away. "Omelettes fluff best if you beats the egg whites separately," he said. "Not many people know it."

"Don't tell me that," Jenny said. "Don't leave me alone," Jenny said. "Please."

"You'll do fine," the Cook said. "Captain Jenny, Fisher-Girl. Nor you won't give up, no more than that fellow Tortuca you're always on about did."

"Don't go!" cried Jenny. And the Cook shook his head.

The Voyage of the Nonesuch

"Look there, Captain Jenny," he said after a while, "the dolphins are coming back."

And Jenny did look, and saw a line of dolphins streaming through the water, and leaping and then diving down to where the Lost City had sunk beneath the waves once more.

But when she looked back up, the Cook had slipped into the water at last, and Jenny swam alone in the sea. Then she took off the golden collar he had given her, and let it follow him to rest in the bosom of the waves.

She was all alone in the vast sea, but Jenny wept only for the Cook, and her tears joined the salt water.

JENNY FLOATED ALONE that way for hours, till the darkness came and the slivery new moon rose. She was a good swimmer, Jenny, and buoyed up by the thick sea water, but at last even she began to tire, and once or twice her head slipped below the waves.

But what did it matter now, she thought? For she had lost her first command, the *Otter*, and then the First Mate, and then her second ship, the *Ruggles*, and her crew with it, and she had lost the Cook last of all. And Sparky, she had lost Tom's dog Sparky, too.

Another wave came and washed over her head just as she was breathing, and she took in water, and came up coughing. "Help me," she whispered. For suddenly she knew it would all be easier if only she stopped struggling.

The Voyage of the Nonesuch

Then Jenny heard a strange squeaking in the darkening sea. There was a shadow on the waves. The shadow was coming closer, but it was too dark to make out. And then when it was almost next to her, she saw Tortuca's Barrel, and through the porthole, she saw Sparky inside it, running the treadmill, working the little propeller.

Then Jenny grabbed the barrel, and clung to it, and thumped its side and called Sparky's name, over and over again, and heard his muffled barks.

AND SO THEY STILL FLOATED TOGETHER the next morning when Gimlet, who was nearly a boy again, spotted them from the top of the mast.

278

And when her crew had pulled them aboard and Jenny could speak at last, her voice was rough and cracked, but she asked, "What ship is this?"

Then the Carpenter replied, "It has no name, Captain Jenny, for it is only an ugly, makeshift thing, jury-rigged of old scraps and shipwreck salvage."

"But you painted eyes on its prow," Jenny whispered.

The Carpenter nodded. "For it is meant to take us home," he said.

Jenny smiled, and then she whispered: "It shall be named the *Nonesuch*, then. For this ship and crew are paramount, and without peer, and simply tip-top in all respects."

CHAPTER TWENTY:
THE TOWER AT SUNSET

J ENNY AND SPARKY SLEPT FOR A LONG TIME AS THE
crew of the *Nonesuch* pulled her through the calm old
sea. And sometimes Jenny woke up thinking of water
because she was thirsty; and when she drank, slept again.
And sometimes she woke up thinking of water because she
remembered the last Great Wave that had swallowed the
Lost City, and woke up gasping; but the kind faces of her
crew reassured her, and she slept again. And Sparky never
left her side.

But by the evening of the second day, she was sitting
up, wrapped in a blanket, and drinking coffee. Now they
were come to a Western shore, and sailed South along it,
the setting sun hanging low over the starboard bow. And
by now Jenny's crew had asked her what had happened
since they parted, and she them.

"I slew the Navarch!" Gimlet cried. "Even though I was a
goat, I remembered I was a boy and slew him before he read
my twisting guts! And then later I spotted you from atop the
mast. I think I should be promoted from Ship's Boy! I think
I should be an officer, or a lieutenant, or at least given a
position of standing like the Cook or Carpenter!"

Jenny smiled. "The Cook would say Ship's Boy was enough of a promotion from being Ship's Goat, considering you also gain the privilege of not being liable for use as dinner," she said. "But after such a happy ending, and your brave triumph, I shall rate you 'Seahand, Ordinary.'" Which was to say, he would be considered a proper member of the crew, though not actually skilled or useful like the other sailors, who were all rated Able Seahands.

"I am Seahand, Ordinary!" Gimlet shouted happily, bounding about and still slightly goatish. "What are the rights and privileges of a Seahand, Ordinary?"

"Like those of a Ship's Boy," the Carpenter said.

Jenny nodded. "For you shall still be called upon to perform all tedious and unskilled lubberly tasks," she said, "but will nonetheless be regarded with more respect."

"We were all lubbers once!" said one of the sailors amidships. "And boobies," said the other. "We were all boobies, too."

Then Gimlet climbed to the top of the mast. "My name is Gimlet of the *Nonesuch!* I was a goat, and now I am Ordinary!" he yelled proudly. "I am a lubber and a booby!"

"Captain Jenny," the biggest and fattest sailor said, shyly. "We found something adrift that you'll be missing."

"My tricorne hat!" Jenny exclaimed.

"It has become faded and lost its shape," the Carpenter said. "But I can block it for you."

Jenny put the hat on. "Do I look like a captain again?" she asked.

The Voyage of the Nonesuch

"A waterlogged captain," one of the sailors said. "A weather-beaten old salt," another sailor added. "Briny and grizzled!" a third one shouted, and then Jenny began to feel she was at home with her crew again.

"Chips, what happened to the Corsairs and the wretched slaves who were chained beside you?" Jenny asked.

"They fought beside us bravely to subdue the Corsairs," the Carpenter replied. "But they had no wish to ever go to sea again, after a period as galley slaves which varied from three months and two days in one case, to twenty years, seven months, and twelve days in another, giving a median length of service of –" but here he stopped, for he saw the calculations were too hard for most of his audience to follow. "So we gave them one chest of gold and one of jewels," he continued, "and let them chain up the Corsairs for once, whom they planned to lead overland, South across the hot hills to some slaving market."

"A horrible fate," Jenny said. "But no worse than they deserve."

"The world is a troubling place," the Carpenter said. "And what will count as good or evil isn't easy to calculate."

"No one has ever called me ordinary before!" Gimlet called triumphantly.

281

AND THEY RAN THE *Nonesuch* IN, and made camp that night, and did the same the next, but the sailors wondered what Jenny's plan for running the Clashing Rocks and making their way through the narrows would be. For the *Nonesuch*, as the Carpenter pointed out, wasn't the fast ship the *Ruggles* had been, and also lacked the cannon to help them through.

But Jenny had a strange, fey look in her eyes, and told them to be calm, and row for the dreadful passage without fear. And indeed, the Rocks didn't snap together, though they closed gently once the *Nonesuch* had passed. And the sailors saw the Otter with a Golden Collar appear from the water then, and Jenny bowed politely.

"You surprised us all, little Jenny Fisher-Girl," the little creature told her. "Captain Jenny," he added, with a bow.

"And was the surprise in our reaching the Lost City, or in my surviving its deluge?" asked Jenny.

"Either of those things would be unlikely for a little Fisher-Girl," said the Otter. "But in fact, no one has ever survived the deluge before, for no one has ever had the unfounded arrogance to choose not to strike the bell."

Jenny looked at him slowly. "Was I supposed to, after all?" she asked. "With all the horrors that would unfold? Are the Fortunes and Powers so cruel?"

"It would be more accurate to say the Fortunes and Powers had never considered another course," the Otter said. "For the chosen Explorers of all the ages before have rung the bell and preserved the City, purely from some heroic reflex. Of course, the results were horrible, just as you guessed, but then that is how every new age has been born."

"Then what will happen now?" Jenny asked. "How will

this age unfold? Will it be sorrow or joy?"

"No one knows," said the Otter. "Not the Powers themselves. Though the Maid of Saltwaters at least is not displeased, for now we begin a new age indeed.

"But it would be odd if we were to have either sorrow or joy without the other. And in both, the Maid has asked me to convey her blessing."

Then the little animal preened himself briefly. He spun around once in the water, and then disappeared beneath the waves, never to be seen again.

IT WAS WEEKS YET of steady rowing before they came to the Isle of No Return, and made a landing on the beach where the crew had washed up so long before. The First Mate met them at the shore, and he wept for joy to see them, and he wept for sorrow to hear of his friend the Cook.

"I have shed tears on the rock overlooking this beach every day of my exile," he said, "And looked over the waves overcome with sea-longing. But this is a greater grief than that."

"But it was a fine end to his career," Jenny said, "to have found the Lost City, and a brave and heroic one."

The First Mate nodded. "Why have you come again to this island?" he asked at last, "For there's no escaping again, not for you or me."

"Let me speak to the Lady of the Isle," Jenny said. And

283

so they all went the Lady's bower to have a parley. The Lady of the Isle was disappointed that Gimlet, who had once been her pet, no longer even had bumps on his head where his horns had been, but she still knew how to treat visitors, and welcomed and feasted them.

And so the crew of the *Nonesuch* told the story of their journey, and the Cook's brave end, and heard once more the music of the Lady's attendants. The Corsairs Jenny had left behind had grown corpulent from eating all the food they wanted, but they entertained too, performing several dances of a surprisingly intricate and delicate quality.

"We could do that too," one of the sailors from amidships whispered. "If we practised," added the other.

When the entertainment had gone on long enough, and the evening was well grown, Jenny rose up. "Lady, we thank you for your hospitality," she said. "But now we must leave."

The Lady rose up then. Tall she was, and robed in white, and all of the dancing Corsairs, and all of her other attendants, stopped and fell silent. "But you are my guests," she said. "And the rule is that you may not leave, not for your whole long lives."

Then Jenny drew herself up, and her eyes were fell and fey again, and the First Mate saw that she was no longer only a Fisher-Girl, but had become as stern and commanding as any weathered captain, as resolute as an old admiral – as undaunted as Maxim Tortuca.

"But now the World is changed, ma'am," Jenny said.

284

"And the rules are all stopped."

And after a moment, the Lady of the Isle of No Return bowed her head, and seemed tall no longer. She looked around the circle of columns, and the dome painted like the stars in the sky, and she saw the paint was peeling, and the white plaster was showing dingy and grey.

Gimlet came up to her then, and held out the circlet she had given him. "I don't need it, because I am Ordinary now," he said.

The Lady picked up the circlet. Now it was dull brass, not gold. "Play them out," she said to her attendants.

"A recessional-like," the First Mate said. "Why, thank you, for that's both fitting and proper."

And the music *was* fitting and proper as the sailors began to leave with Jenny and the First Mate. But on shore, as the crew boarded the *Nonesuch*, the Lady kissed her hand to the First Mate.

"Farewell," she said, sadly, and she seemed older now. "Farewell to you all. Remember me kindly."

285

THEN THE SAILING was easy enough, which was a good thing, in their jury-rigged ship, with its double-scarfed mast and its patchwork sails and its cobbled planking.

They sailed along the North coast of the Old Sea, and then down towards the Pillars, and so avoided the Island of Philosophy, where the *Otter* had been wrecked.

The Pillars were a terrible hazard too, of course, but

Jenny and the First Mate and the Carpenter between them worked out a plan to shelter behind the Northern Pillar until a wave rose high and fell back, and then dart out and ride the undertow through. Which they did, and counted themselves very clever sailors indeed, or very lucky ones.

And so in time they returned to the Corner by the Sea at last, and were welcomed heartily by the good Duke (or Deputy).

"I am glad to see you back!" he cried. "Although perhaps you are not as absurd as I once thought, for while the weather has been strange from the East, still the rumours of turmoil and strife subside. But you have one of my citizens aboard," he chided Jenny, "the boy Gimlet, and his Grandmother is worried."

"The boy Gimlet was left behind on an island!" Gimlet shouted from the manger, where he had been hiding. "And even if I were here, I am not a boy any more, but am Ordinary!"

"I am afraid you will never be so ordinary as we might hope," the good Deputy said. "But it is suppertime, and you are to go home at once."

The boy looked at the other sailors, looked at the battered *Nonesuch*, which had become his home. He looked at Sparky, who had played with him so often when he was a faun.

"I don't want to go," he said. "I want to make my career at sea and become a captain, and have my own hat."

And strangely enough, the sailors realized that they would miss him, too. Then Jenny put her own weather-beaten tricorne on Gimlet's head.

"It's time for us all to go home," she said, "but we did promise you a hat if your horns ever went away." And to the Duke, she said, "I commend him to your attention as a citizen of promise. For in the end, the boy was a both brave and valuable hand, if youthfully intemperate in speech. And he was equally essential in defeating the Corsairs and swabbing out the bilge."

Then Gimlet stood as tall and proud as he could, for that was the finest compliment he had ever received.

"A handsome recommendation," the Deputy said. "I will remember the boy when any daringly tedious tasks need to be performed."

287

THEN IT WAS THE LAST STRETCH HOME, home across the channel, home to their harbour. It wasn't easy work, but as the First Mate had predicted, after all they'd been through, they took it as lightly as a holiday – except for Sparky, who could not contain his excitement, but barked madly and ran about, for he knew he was coming back to his master after a long time.

And when the *Nonesuch* came into port at last on a warm fall day, there was much commotion, for Jenny lived in a harbour town where feats of mighty sailing were much admired, and no one could believe such a shabby craft had returned from such a voyage, especially not when it was cross-eyed.

And when Jenny had told Tom and his Dad all the story

The Voyage of the Nonesuch

of her voyage, Tom's Dad declared that she would have an entry herself, towards the beginning of his *Universal Encyclopædia,* according to his new scheme. "For you have been most adventurous," he said.

Jenny had not become rich, after all, or won much renown, but there had been one chest of gold left over from the Corsairs, which she divided among the crew. But she wasn't sure what to do with her portion.

THE EVENING JENNY RETURNED, she walked along the path through the Woods Nearby, and came at last to the stone hut where Godmother lived, and Pawlikins the Cat.

Another godmother might have fussed, but her Godmother only said: "You have done well, but you have come back almost too late for High Midnight Tea." Which made Jenny smile to hear.

But really, her Godmother thought, *She is like her friend Tom; she has seen much and is hardly a child anymore.*

And Jenny thought, *She is become old at last, unless I never saw it before from awe; she is bent and frail.*

Then, for the first time, Jenny made the High Midnight Tea herself, and told her Godmother everything that had befallen her, the joys and the sorrows both. She told how the Cook had become her friend and then was lost, told about the sinking of the Lost City that she had thought would bring her fortune and renown.

"So I understood the two redes that you gave me the

night the Otter with a Golden Collar came," Jenny said. "For I did need friends more than a sword: my crew, and the Carpenter and the First Mate, and Sparky and the Cook most of all. And it was when I gave up my proud dreams of fortune and renown that the water fell, and the Lost City sank beneath the waves once again."

"I am very proud of you, and the other Wise Women will be jealous and peeved by your success," her Godmother said.

Jenny thought she would be very happy not to meet any jealous or peeved Wise Women, for her Godmother was worrying enough, though she was kindly and calm.

"But at least it means we are safe from turmoil and strife," Jenny said at last. "And we can live calmly again."

Then her Godmother led her out to the Casting Stone. *She walks with a blackthorn cane, now,* Jenny thought, *and hobbles even so.* But her Godmother thought, *She has seen something beyond the cracks of the World, and the power of it hasn't yet left her eyes.* Then they threw the dregs of their cups onto the Casting Stone.

Now the night wind rose as Jenny's Godmother bent over the weathered stone; old leaves scattered along the forest floor; three owls perched on the roof of the hut hooted once each, in order of size; and Jenny shivered.

Then, "What do you read?" her Godmother asked.

Her Godmother had never asked such a thing! In any case, Jenny could make no sense of the wet marks.

"They seem disordered and confused," she said.

289

The Voyage of the Nonesuch

"Indeed, like the World itself," her Godmother said. "For you did a great thing, Captain Jenny, Fisher-Girl, and without the Lost City, turmoil and strife will lack a flag and standard, will have no palace or command. But trouble and disorder are part of the way of the World, and still they rise in the East and pass West, like the sun and the moon and the stars, and you will meet them again.

"For this is my rede: *'Trouble comes easily, but ease comes after trouble.'*"

"Does that mean that I have found a happy ending, or that my happy ending is yet to be found?" asked Jenny.

"There's no explaining a rede, as you well know," her Godmother said. "But any godmother would say this: You live in the World, and are due your share of finding and trouble, and ease and happiness, like everyone else who has ever been, including Tom's dog Sparky and my cat Pawlikins, your mother and father who were swept out to sea when you were little, and even the elves, who passed West a long age ago."

"Or, if you want," her Godmother went on, more gently now, more like an old woman again, "any god-mother would say: it is bedtime now, even for a Wise Woman on a full moon night, even for a brave Explorer-child like you."

So Jenny thought on her Godmother's words, and although she didn't take a whole captain's share of the

Corsair treasure, she still had enough to build a tower by her cottage.

And one evening, as the light shone soft and the waves grew gentle in her little cove, Tom and Sparky were visiting, and they found a bottle bobbing along the shore, and the message Jenny had put in it long ago.

"That was well done," Tom said, after he read it, "and most sailorly, as the First Mate would say."

Then they climbed the tower and looked out towards the setting sun.

"Your whole Exploration was well done," Tom said. "And my dad says you must write an account of it, just as Ola Olagovna did."

"I would not have survived unless you had loaned me Sparky," Jenny said. "Or given me the *Representative Encyclopædia*."

291

"Have we come to the end of our adventures?" Tom wondered. "For I journeyed North through the Eaves of the World, and you have found the Lost City. Not many can say as much as that." Still, Tom felt the sea-longing again.

Then Jenny had the fey light in her eyes one last time.

"We will have more adventures," she said. "But we must sail only West now, you and I together, and follow the sun, like the elves before us."

The Voyage of the Nonesuch

DUNCAN THORNTON is the author of the juvenile fantasy adventure *Kalifax*, which was a finalist for the Governor-General's Award for Children's Literature, the Mr. Christie Book Award program, and two Manitoba Book Awards. He has also written radio drama, theatrical drama, and several screenplays, in addition to his fiction and non-fiction prose.

Born at God's Lake Narrows in Manitoba, Duncan Thornton has Honours degrees in English and History. He is currently a new media instructor at Red River College in Winnipeg. His e-mail address is *thornton@kalifax.com*.

YVES NOBLET was born and raised in France and attended the Collège des Beaux-Arts in Bordeaux before emigrating to Canada in 1973. He received a Diploma in Visual Communications from the Alberta College of Art (Calgary) in 1977 and worked as a graphic designer and art director before founding Noblet Design Group, his current company, in 1996.

Yves has mastered the traditional and digital mediums with equal success, receiving a long list of awards for his designs and illustrations. He recently created covers for the Coteau books *The Blue Field*, *Buffalo Jump: A Woman's Travels,* and *Kalifax*. Yves and his wife Brigitte make their home in Regina with their four children.